THE SILENT VIOLINIST

THE
SILENT
VIOLINIST

GERTRUDE GIBBONS

Matador
9 Priory Business Park,
Wistow Road, Kibworth Beauchamp,
Leicestershire. LE8 0RX
Tel: 0116 279 2299
Email: books@troubador.co.uk
Web: www.troubador.co.uk/matador
Twitter: @matadorbooks

ISBN 978 180046 489 6

British Library Cataloguing in Publication Data.
A catalogue record for this book is available from the British Library.

Printed and bound in Great Britain by 4edge Limited
Typeset in 11pt Adobe Garamond Pro by Troubador Publishing Ltd, Leicester, UK

Matador is an imprint of Troubador Publishing Ltd

For Judith Farnham Carter

PREFACE

Written over a period of seven years, beginning at the age of thirteen and finishing at twenty, *The Silent Violinist* followed me as I grew up. It is not autobiographical, but in its fictitious form it is the closest I got to keeping a diary. I was fascinated by an idea suggested by a character in Eva Ibbotson's *The Morning Gift* as to whether one could live their life like a piece of music.

Listening for the first time to Tchaikovsky's Violin Concerto when I was eleven, I was convinced that upon the arrival of the second movement, someone in the orchestra had started to speak. But the sound of this voice did not interrupt or create discord with the music; it seemed to be a part of it, and complementary to it. My full attention was focused on uncovering what this voice was saying—perhaps there was a singer beside the violinist, I thought. Through the proximity of the sound, I felt as if this voice was reaching outwards, and I would be taken with it and become entirely enwrapped in it. I later discovered the softened voice-like tone emerging here was the result of a mute, placed on the bridge of the violin, to subtly dampen its sound, creating a lighter, broader and more haunting sound.

The lighting and landscape of this novel, while in my imagination a world dictated and guided by music, come from the paintings of the Pre-Raphaelite style and influence, in particular Sir Joseph Noel Paton's *A Dream of Latmos* and John William Waterhouse's *The Siren*. A sense of the atmosphere, as well as a visualisation of the lines on which people's lives might be 'composed', was inspired by the object of a Victorian cranberry-stained crystal glass, kindly given to me on a visit to the writer David Plante in London.

"People often complain that music is too ambiguous, that what they should think when they hear it is so unclear, whereas everyone understands words. With me, it is exactly the reverse; not only with regard to full sentences but also with individual words; these, too, seem to me so ambiguous, so vague, so easily misunderstood in comparison to genuine music, which fills the soul with a thousand things better than words."

Felix Mendelssohn

PROLOGUE

The applauding stopped and she waited with an irritated, recalcitrant expression, as the soloist continued to tune his E. She decided to make a physical assessment of him, realising that the coming two hours were to be tedious in the extreme.

There was not much to him: his curly hair was a vaguely interesting shade of burnt oak and his eyes a regular, dull grey. Ah! Why was she here? She addressed the situation. Two rows from the front; she could hardly go to sleep or read a book or even let her eyes wonder around the white-washed church to read the pompous-looking inscriptions in memory of 'Sir Someone of Somewhere who had left issue of Another Sir Someone of Somewhere in the Year of Our Lord etc., etc., etc.'

Her mind wandered off into a world of people on horseback, galloping through forests with messages of critical importance hidden within the folds of their hooded cloaks …

These pleasantly distracting thoughts were interrupted by long-haired, sweet-eyed Gabriel who was trying to catch her attention from the opposite pew. He found concerts boring too, she knew that, and she reluctantly admitted to herself that she would have felt better seated next to him, so they could amuse themselves in secret. But she felt superior and a little resentful, and made a point of ignoring him. And so, she remembered why she was here—her parents, his parents, her dictated life.

For as long as she could remember, Gabriel and the idea of a future husband had been synonymous. In fact, when she was very small, she had been completely convinced that 'husband' was simply another name for her playmate, and had given it no thought at all. Even as she grew to a more ponderous age, she had accepted it as one of the many things a girl must accept in this world. But now, being of 'twelve summers old' (as the people in her world of horseback might say), she had begun to feel exasperated at the prospect of becoming eternally attached to this person she had discovered to be highly irritating, however sweet he might be.

The marriage, of course, hadn't been arranged for her own personal benefit; it was, as most arranged marriages seemed to be, organised purely for financial convenience. Oh! Why had she learnt to read? If she had been like others of her age, half-heartedly picking up the occasional novel, she would easily have submitted to the life her parents had so *thoughtfully* set out for her. As it was, too many stories and fantasies flew about her head. She sighed. She had to be angry and bored at this concert, because she was angry and bored at the *reason for being* at the concert: bringing her and Gabriel to this concert was an attempt to get them closer, to give them something to talk about, since her antagonism towards him was becoming increasingly obvious, and their conversations now dwindled after about two minutes.

Finally, the tuning stopped, and there was a moment of silence before the soloist took a sharp intake of breath and played his first note. The girl swallowed, and sighed again. But then, despite herself, from seven notes in, she was captivated. His first chords drowned everything. There was no one else in the world. She could live. She could die. Nothing mattered—there was nothing but her, the performer, and the music. And somewhere in her own misted head she discovered her blindness, she realised how much she had shunned. But suddenly there was another voice: a voice quite different from that timid self-admittance at the back of her skull. She looked in vain for the source of this unnaturally soft voice which appeared to be mocking her from above.

It was too scary to look up into the heights and shadows of the carved wooden roof, so she forced her full attention on the person of the violinist. The mocking voice stopped. The violinist's right hand swung round to make a pizzicato chord, like a greeting just for her. There began the double stops which should not have been coming from a single violin, and her body seemed to somersault with some kind of joy never experienced before. Meanwhile, she tried desperately to suppress the laughter this somersaulting playfully encouraged. As she relaxed into this peculiar sensation, the voice came back. It was not mocking. It was beautiful. The voice stopped its continuous, incomprehensible murmuring and the girl was shocked to discover distinct words rising amongst it all. These words were becoming more frequent. The voice was clearer.

And yet, she could *understand* nothing. There was only one word she thought she had made out and that was her name, Edith, but surrounding it were so many other 'words' spoken by this most beautiful voice that this recognition was lost as soon as it had been found.

The audience were clapping, marvelling at the gift given by no human hand to one so young. His cheeks now held a red glow which lit up his eyes, and she was overwhelmed by his sudden attractiveness. Her own eyes were filled with water, triggered by the sublimity of the previous minutes. But the voice had been dispersed by the clapping, and though she felt slightly empty after its sudden departure, the disappointment was nothing compared to the discovery that she would not hear him again. He was a single, introductory act, used by the amateur orchestra to double the audience, since his age and talent drew curious people from everywhere.

The girl desperately wanted to speak to him. She had to sit through the concert (which really would have been as boring as anticipated had she not been so frustrated) knowing that this strange touching performer and his music might be disappearing out the back somewhere. Nothing could describe her exasperation during the third movement of the last piece. The interval had been short and impossible, and there had never been a slower piece than this last one, played just to torture her. She kept wondering how the violinist must speak, since he played so emotively.

4

Her hunger to hear his voice was something unbearable and quite irrational. Perhaps it was because to hear him speak would be to convince her that his beauty had not been imagined. It was such a disheartening idea, that everything she found beautiful came only from her imagination, and was not *really* beautiful.

At long last, a triumphant chord told the end of the concert. The orchestra bowed, followed by the lead violinist and the conductor, and then the conductor again, and *still* the clapping went on, with no sign of the first soloist.

She was one of the first to get up as the murmurings and arranging of coats began. A kind-looking clarinettist asked if she could be of any assistance to the girl approaching the bustle of performers.

"Where can I find the violinist … the one who performed first?"

"Ah, yes. Most young people are slightly *over*-impressed by him. One gets quite used to these young geniuses at my age. He had to leave to perform at St Margaret's; that's why he was the first performance … So—why is it *you* wish to find him?"

"I would like to ask him something."

The clarinettist laughed. "You wouldn't get very far with that! Didn't you know? Didn't you listen to the introduction? I thought that was another of his selling points: he's dumb, a mute. That's always the way in this world—something given, something lost." She said this last part casually, as though it were a saying, cruelly raising her intonation at the word 'lost'. The kind-looking clarinettist no longer appeared so kind-looking.

"But surely … Surely that's not possible …" the girl whispered to herself. There *must be a voice behind such music*.

The clarinettist would happily have explained how possible it was, had the girl's attention not been caught by a tall boy gesturing extravagantly for her to come. The girl was led out of the church in a state of high confusion. Everything Gabriel said to her was a blur. Her mind was filled with one simple, inconceivable thought that she somehow, and contradictorily, could not put into words.

"A painter paints pictures on canvas.
But musicians paint their pictures on silence."
Leopold Stokowski

I

It was dark, and all was silent. Edith's footsteps echoed loudly as she walked down the black country lane to the village. She knew she should not be in the middle of the lane; if a car did come whizzing round it would be the end. But the thrilling sense of freedom in this warm, wet stillness made it impossible not to feel a little reckless and mad.

She wondered why silence was ever considered scary. Fear of darkness she could understand in a way, because there were unavoidable associations with death. Silence, though, was altogether different. Even when she had first started learning the piano, with useless chubby fingers, she was adamant in the conviction that it was the instantaneous pockets of silence that made music what it was. Playing was not about the pressing of the keys, but the release of them. It was not the hammers forcing the vibrations out of the strings that created the music; it was the instant *before* the hammer hit the string, the preciously suspended pause, which passed the potentiality of the music to the audience.

But then, as much as she told herself that conversation was the same (and it *was*), as much as she convinced herself that silence was the most important ingredient of verbal interaction, she was painfully aware that the ratio of sound to silence in her house was unequally weighed to the latter. It was a rare occasion that she spoke to her parents or their friends, let alone had a *conversation* with them. When she was not having a lesson, she went and had chats with the servants. But they always seemed busy, so these discussions were unsatisfactorily short.

Well, the lack of sensitive understanding about her did not bother her while she had the village to go to. The village and villagers were her means of escape. It was her genuine belief that the working classes, the farmers and the carpenters, had a natural, innate openness and matter-of-fact way of being. They would tolerate no nonsense, but neither would they shut themselves off to different ideas. If she spoke to Mrs Baker about music, for example, she would listen attentively, despite being completely ignorant of the written note. In any case, if she was in desperate need of a technical discussion, or if she wanted help with her playing, the vicar's wife, Mrs Carey, was always happy to talk.

It was at Reverend Carey's house that she gave Mrs Baker's son piano lessons. Edward was the Bakers' eldest son, dark, tall and thin. He wanted to be a church organist. Edith loved the sense that she was shaping this boy's music. His fingers answered to her beck and call, his phrases imitated her voice. She knew that there would always be an echo of herself in his playing, just as there was always an echo of parents in one's speech. It made her happy. Well, there it was. Enough of the sentimentality, she told herself, as she sat daydreaming out the window.

"Was that right?" Edward asked her.

"Hmm? Yes, yes. Play E flat once again and try to keep a regular tempo on the descent. You hesitate on the shifts coming down."

She was in the window seat, her legs folded neatly beneath her on the comfortable red cushion. She looked out into the impenetrable blackness again. Would her parents ever listen to the village gossip, she wondered, and stop her coming here alone, in the dark. She knew it was not at all 'proper' that she should have such frequent and close involvement with the village people. The villagers, although they liked Edith a lot, spoke in loud whispers of her parents' negligence. After all, she certainly was not one of them. Nor could she ever become one. Several times, her involvement in village life had come too close to patronisation, and the villagers had had to pass her subtle, cold hints that she was not part of their world. To lower herself to their rank did nothing other than come across as patronising. It was, in fact, disrespectful not to take on that God-given responsibility of superiority.

"Good. A flat now."

But she was not part of 'her' world either. It was not her world, that world of her parents and their friends. And so she was trapped in this sort of limbo between the world she was supposed to be a part of, and the one she felt so much more comfortable with. Neither worlds would let her in, she was foreign to both. She knew full well that this would always be the way. There was no world in which she would not feel alien. Yet she dedicated her time to the learning of languages, the gateways to inclusion.

French, German, Italian. She was almost fluent in all of these, and had read several literary classics from each. When she was particularly bored, she liked to translate poetry between these three languages, trying not to think through this process in English. Poetry in French was the nicest. The syllables were so delicately dropped and delivered, rhymes and assonance so subtly suggested, that it was as though the mouth were not entirely in control of itself. Instead, it was as if crisp sea winds were passing gently through autumn leaves, never pausing to collect itself; the mouth ran away with the words before the mind comprehended them. Sensations, difficult emotions, however, were best captured in German. Often a word in this language saved a whole stanza of French or Italian equivalent. Then, as always, Italian was the most musical. Desire for lyricism was best satisfied if framed in Italian vowels. And it had to be said that Gabriel, her as yet unofficial fiancé, did in fact read Italian poetry as no one else. He almost made the worst beautiful.

"Perfect, well done. A flat, good. Right. Shall we start now with the A flat Fugue?"

"Of course."

"If you would try to play the whole thing through once, then we will go back over it."

He began to play.

"Wait! Sorry, I will not interrupt again, but try not to attack the keys so aggressively. It's a conversation between the hands, and should be done with a little more kindness."

He began again, crouching low over the keys to feel greater control over their delicacy.

He played with the mechanised air consistent with a certain technical uncertainty. He focused everything into placing his fingers on the right keys at the right time, such that there was not much room for any hint at emotional variation. Edith asked herself whether it was ever possible to teach a person to play with feeling; whether it was ever possible to teach anyone to feel, generally. Surely that was up to them. Then again, perhaps one could *show* someone the *way* to feeling? It was a duty, surely, to give the potentiality of rich emotion to anyone and everyone. But who was anyone to claim knowledge of what was truly valuable above and beyond another's idea of value? Some people—most people around her, in fact—seemed to live, dwell, only in the superficial. They seemed to like that narrow little path.

She shook herself again. God, she had superiority issues. And concentration ones. Edward finished playing and looked up at her.

"Yes, that was good. Much better. I think you know it well enough now to be a little more relaxed. Look, let me show you. It is Bach, I know, but freedom of expression is certainly allowed. Try to emphasise the different voices, the conversation. Low, high, loud, quiet. Accents. Subtleties. Here," she said pointing at the music, sitting beside him on the stool. "The fourth section. This should be markedly more confident than the beginning. The opening had the gradual introduction of the voices, so there you are right to be more shy, more expectant. Something like this. In comparison to this. Then here—follow it through, don't run," she lifted her fingers from the keys and turned to face him. "There is not much to it, but it makes a huge difference. Do you see?"

"Oh yes, yes. That's incredible," said Edward, eyes wide with a strange sort of excitement. "I don't think I can do that though."

"Don't be silly, of course you can."

When the lesson was over, and Edward had left, Edith went and found Mrs Carey. She was sitting by the fire in their small library, which was also her husband's study.

Mrs Carey looked up from her book, *Le Rouge et le Noir*, and smiled. "Hello Edith. Good lesson?"

"Yes, thank you," Edith hovered, waiting to be offered a seat.

"Do you have to get back in a hurry? Please take a seat," Mrs Carey was an observant woman.

Edith sat in the high-backed, green-grey armchair opposite the vicar's wife.

"Edward is very studious, isn't he? I can hear his progress—very quick progress. Of course that's also thanks to you, dear," Mrs Carey closed her book on her index finger.

"Is it the French?" Edith asked, motioning to the book.

"No, English translation. Not the best, I'd say. Have you read any Stendhal?"

"*La Chartreuse de Parme*, yes. I found it quite difficult to read."

"You read it in the French?"

"Yes, but it wasn't that. I don't know, maybe it's growing a little distant from our time? But I always find political intrigue hard to follow, so it could be that."

"I suppose you could say that. I certainly feel that with some of Eliot's novels. Not all though, it's interesting. Well, Tolstoy was very fond of *La Chartreuse*, but then he was closer in time and thought and all that. But of course Tolstoy isn't the One Authority. Perhaps you should try this one," said Mrs Carey shaking her book. "I think I prefer it; it seems quite ahead of its time."

Edith looked around her at all the books. Her library had lots more, but the books in hers were unread.

"Do you find it strange, all those books on the shelves, or is that just me?"

"How do you mean?"

"Well, whenever I'm in a library, I feel all those words— all those words that I can't see, but *are* there. And I'll never be able to read them all. No, that's not what I find strange. It's the idea of death, really. I'm sorry, I know I sound terribly young."

"No, no. Go on, I'm not sure I follow you."

"As in, well, I feel it a lot more with music, I think. With literature, it's more internal. But it's the same. Almost. Because, without the performer, the music is dead? The notes on the page don't move and, while they're on a shelf, are silent. It is only when the pianist, for example, reads the notes and plays them, that they are alive for the present. It is only through the performer that the thoughts of the composer come alive. And it is only when *we* turn a page, read a word, that the thoughts and voice of a writer is resurrected."

"You think so?"

"Yes, well, of course you could give a set of people the manuscript of Mendelssohn's Violin Concerto, and some of them might be able to hear it in their head as they read. In this way the thoughts, or voice, of Mendelssohn are given, placed directly, into thoughts of someone over a hundred years later. Then an orchestra can place those notes into the thoughts of a whole audience. They are injected into the air of our present, literally," she paused, confused. "I don't know, I just find it strange how that Violin Concerto would be silent, sort of dead, without borrowing a voice from the present. It relies on the people of the future. I suppose that is the case with everything though, I mean a painting is only alive when a person views it. But that is not with the same reliance, with the same necessary involvement …"

Edith broke off, slightly embarrassed. It was clear in her head, but she did not know how best to express it. The words, once sounded in the air, could not be taken back, and they seemed pathetic to her. She could not do much, however, but continue.

"As in, say a Medieval painter creates a painting," she tucked her hair behind her ear. "He is aware of the possibility of a future viewer—he is communicating to that future viewer."

Mrs Carey placed *Le Rouge et le Noir* on the round, wooden stool on her left. "Yes?"

"But it is all there—all at once," she sighed. "I mean all aspects of the work: all details, all the prompts that might provoke and mellow and grow into creative interpretation. They are all in front of one's face at once; a person walks into a museum five hundred years later and sees the medieval painting as a whole. In fact, no time is needed whatsoever for the entirety of the painting to appear. The only time taken is because of the viewer's mind—how long it takes their eyes to send messages to their brain."

"Aren't words like paintings too though? Letters are simply shapes after all. A word is placed before a viewer, taking no time to appear (unlike music I suppose). So, like a painting, the only time taken is the length it takes for the mind to process the meaning, and further meanings, of those shapes. It's the same no?"

"Yes, in a way, I suppose. But the viewer of a painting does not *partake* in its creation in the same way. Holding a novel, one is aware of the unread pages beneath one's fingers. All those words yet to enter one's head, become one's own thoughts, one's own internal voice. Reading or listening to a novel, one is always aware of *what is to come*. One cannot hold an unopened novel or poem and know it, uncover its secrets, without turning each page, reading every line." Her hair fell from behind her ear, and her cheeks were red. "While the Medieval painting is an image, or set of images *before you*, words *evoke* images *within* one's own thoughts. So rather than emotion coming from the images in front of you, it comes from the images evoked inside you—a delayed version of the same thing. People cry at paintings almost instantaneously; when did you ever hear of someone crying instantaneously at a word?"

Mrs Carey ignored this last idea. It would go on for too long. She found it amusing that the girl kept emphasising certain words so explicitly. "And music? You care more for music than literature, or painting?"

"I think music is a more *particular* world than painting or literature. Mendelssohn's Violin Concerto must, in the broadest sense, have performers to bring it to life. And performers are an interruption, a secondary interpreter, between the composer and the audience. Usually, with painting and literature, it is just you and the work, and there is no intermediator."

There was a knock at the door and Reverend Carey entered in his outdoor coat, flushed with the outdoors. He smiled to his wife, muttered some sort of apology and walked back out.

"And what of the *performer's* relationship with the music and composer?" Mrs Carey asked, continuing. "There is no mediator between *them* and the music in front of them. Surely, in that way, the performer is the same as the reader of a novel, or the viewer of the painting."

Edith paused a second. "Yes. But the performer is literally recreating the work for *others*. The performer *gives* the work to the audience. And anyway, often the audience would never be able to perform the piece of music for themselves. The viewer of a painting does not, generally, leave the museum and paint it for *others*?"

"But what about a blind person? They would not be able to read a novel, or see a painting, without hearing it, or hearing of it, from another's lips."

"They could touch it though, which they could not with music."

Mrs Carey laughed. "No, that's absurd. Following that logic, a blind person could just as easily touch a manuscript of music, or an instrument, as they could a novel or painting or sculpture."

"Alright. That is true."

"I'm sorry. I'm only teasing you. It's interesting. So how do you view yourself as a pianist?"

Edith began fidgeting; she could not grasp her own thoughts. "It is not the same! Music *is* different. The performer of music, or drama, is very different to the idea of describing a painting, or reading out a poem."

"Explain! Explain!" said Mrs Carey in a tone both quiet and excited.

"I don't know! Some things you can't explain! Surely you know what I mean, just go to a concert. Look at the soloist, look at the audience. I can't explain. But *it is different.*"

"I know, I do know what you mean. But you should learn to put it into words. After all, how many poets know how to explain what cannot be explained? They still try, and their attempts are sometimes very beautiful and inexplicable in themselves!"

"I wonder sometimes what it must be like for people who can't speak. How do they ever describe with any detail or accuracy how they feel? Being blind must be terrifying, but to me that is simply a different, scary and unknown world. In contrast, being unable to hear or speak seems like such a *half*-world to me. It must be like being enclosed in one's own bubble of thoughts, part of the outside world, but always alone?" Edith looked into the fireplace, hearing very clearly its loud, uneven crackling. She almost forgot that Mrs Carey was there listening to her.

"That was a little out-of-nowhere," Mrs Carey said.

"Hmm?" she looked back up at the vicar's wife. "Oh. No, it was the idea of reading out a novel, or describing a painting to a blind person—in relation to performing a piece of music. Singing is a strange one of course, because the singer is both reading out, describing a work in their own voice while literally using their own voice to do so. They kind of cross both worlds at once."

"Right. And you as a pianist? Where do you fit, so to speak? But then I think you should be heading home, your parents will definitely wonder where you are. My husband will give you a lift."

Edith nodded. "Well, if a musician's task had to be paralleled to the world of all these books, or to that of painting, I'd say a musician is like a critic, or a translator," she got up and they went in the hallway together to get her coat. "But they should be like a shadow, barely visible between the work and the audience. And this shadow should illuminate, not obscure the original work, subtly suggesting potential ideas." She put her coat on. "Forgive my idealism, it comes with my age I think, but I think they should be a time traveller, a transitory entity—passing, giving, the original work to others."

II

When Edith's tutor left on Saturday afternoon, her mother told her to return upstairs and get ready. By 'get ready', Lady Norton meant 'Gabriel's coming, look pretty'. Her family were archaic, to say the very least. Perhaps it came with the title. Gabriel's family were worse, but at least they sent Elizabeth to *school*. Even if it was one of *those* schools. Edith had to be content, now sixteen years old, that her schooling was easing off, and that next year the well-intentioned Mr Brook would take his leave. Her education was finished. It had to be admitted, however, that the villagers also seemed to live in the previous century. If not, they would never feel so upset, uneasy, that she, their superior, mixed with them.

Maybe it was she who was born in the wrong century. She remembered conversations she had attempted with her maid, Mari. But, Mari, people *are* people, she had said only three weeks ago. Surely we should talk to people we find *interesting*, and not talk to *boring* people simply because they are said to be *appropriate*. That doesn't make sense: to make 'friends' with people you don't like and exclude those you do!

Edith walked back upstairs with her hand trailing up the banister behind her. Mari was waiting in her room with a bowl of steaming water and a towel, so that she would not have to go to the bathroom, and could be helped 'get ready'. It was the first time Edith had felt annoyed at her maid, who stood there without a sound, or any sign of emotion. She remembered Mari's response to her argument that they were all the same in the end, all people. *We cannot be the same, Miss. If I may say that yes, we were all born, and will all die—that is the same. But we will not do so in the same way. We cannot be equal, we must not. It is right that you are at an advantage to me—you were born to deserve a better life, Miss.* It had angered Edith three weeks ago, and the memory of it emphasised the irrational anger she felt towards Mari now. No, she had replied, *you* have the advantage over *me*. You can choose the path you take; you can live and do what you like.

She shook her head without meaning to in a kind of disbelief. How could her maid be so inanimate? Mrs Baker's children were not like this. She took the towel and began washing her face, before sitting at her dressing table and watching in the mirror as Mari combed her dark red, softly waving hair. Her maid gave her the usual help choosing a dress and suitable jewellery, but no comfort. Any person with a modicum of motherly tendencies would have noticed the kindling fire of panic in the girl's wide brown eyes. It was that panic of indecision, knowing that once she was downstairs, there was no return. She felt her stomach in her throat, a wave of nausea, at the idea that this same role-playing, light chit-chat, and polite gesturing had been a never-ending cycle since before she could remember.

She gulped. It was such a dangerous feeling, the sense that she was on a cyclical track, entombed. This was not a rare occurrence, these times at which she became hot all over, excepting her hands which would be clammy with cold sweat. The danger lay in the sure knowledge that one of two things would follow: the heat would pass, her eyes would narrow to a natural size, and the sickly waves of nauseous adrenaline would cease; otherwise, though the heat would subside, the weight of some invisible and suffocating force would hover above her head, press upon her body. Invisible yet dark, oppressive, she could picture this force, and whatever she did, it would not evaporate. It had a life of its own. And so the danger was that she never knew which of these two things would happen, or if, in the second instance, she would ever again escape and breathe the cool air without hesitation, look up at the sky and see it as symbolic of freedom and flight, rather than a reminder of her own heavy, human inertia.

She had never spoken to anyone about this, she feared it. But, at the same time, she knew that since it only affected her, it did not really matter. Perhaps, in fact, it was only because she was self-centred, and spent too much time inside her own head. She also knew another two things which pointed to the cause and cure, but she feared sitting down to discuss such a diagnosis with herself and, as such, she had never connected and solved these two things. One was that she had never even felt the dark heaviness while she was in the village, or talking to her villager friends. (Was this the selfish reason for which she visited them so frequently?) It was as if she lived two lives, one at home and another at the village— that was how different she felt and behaved. And the second thing was that she was also safe when she listened to, or played, music. It even had the power to give temporary relief from her oppressive shadow during an 'attack'. No other art form worked. But music made her walk alone, cloud free.

Edith gulped again, staring into her own wide eyes in the mirror as she adjusted her earrings. She looked like a red squirrel running from a fire. Mari opened the windows to allow the care-free, early evening chirpings of the birds waft through the room. Mari should be given credit, despite Edith's misgivings towards her, for her observance. She did see, and feel, the tension, the panic, emanating from her mistress' every pore. She knew the cause of it too, unlike Edith in her muddled mind. But she was also aware that she, the maid, could not give Edith any comfort. Or at least not the comfort she needed.

"The birds are very excited, Mari," Edith said in a slightly shaky voice. The danger had passed. She could smell the delightful smell of evening dew on the freshly cut lawn below.

"They are. I think it will be a good day tomorrow—for the birds, that is. All those worms. Can you smell the rain?"

Edith inhaled. This was exactly Mari's intention. They inhaled together.

"Yes, there has been a very heavy dew. Does that mean rain?"

"Come now; let me have a look at you. Good, very nice," the maid put her hand on Edith's upper arm (which surely an inanimate being would not). "You should go; Lady Norton will be waiting."

Sure enough her mother was standing at the foot of the stairs, and the Loehills were already in the sitting room. Edith greeted her mother, deeply jealous of Mari as she passed behind her to get to the servants' quarters, and walked with her into the sitting room. She had smelt the arrogant masculinity of Lord Loehill even before hearing his rumbustious voice. Gabriel did not take after his father, she would give him that.

Shaking imaginary hair from her face, Edith envisaged herself as a proud actress about to step onto the platform of a half-empty auditorium. *Let it begin*, said a voice in her head. One which sounded a little like her own. *Let it begin—again.*

"That dress is wonderful, Edith. Very—most becoming. The shade is so—so *green*, so beautiful for your hair. I really must compliment you on your stylish taste once more," Gabriel said nervously as he sat beside her at dinner.

Edith looked across the table at Gabriel's sister and they exchanged a quick smile. Elizabeth was a pleasant girl with rosy cheeks and the same curly golden hair as her brother. A year younger than Edith and six years younger than her brother, they had become good companions and very much appreciated each other's company. They were fully aware of their parents' plans for their marital future and, for as long as Edith could remember, it was off mutual frustration stemming from this that their friendship lived. Otherwise, they did not have much in common; the younger got childishly excited over horses and hats, and could not for the life of her understand why the older girl grew animated over the slightest of things. Words, poetry? Music? Well, Elizabeth had grown to love Edith despite her perplexing nature, and Edith, with no school or siblings of her own, found light relief in the presence of her future sister-in-law.

"Thank you," Edith replied, adding, "It was Mari's choice." She immediately wished she hadn't, because it left Gabriel unfairly stumped and offended. "What have you been doing today?" she added quickly. Edith did not like to see him uncomfortable, however much the irritation she felt towards him continued to grow by the day.

"Oh nothing much; I wrote a letter to Blyth—he wants to come hunting sometime you know. He's keen on the idea of pigeon shooting while the farmers are sowing."

"Oh?"

"Well I'm not sure about it. He's a decent chap; he's certainly a good friend."

"Yes?"

"Anyway, I read a little after that. Some poetry." He lowered his voice, as he always did when he spoke of poetry in his father's hearing. For some reason, Lord Loehill was never pleased to hear that Gabriel read such unfruitful writing. He was of the firm belief that it only made for a sentimental, lazy young man, taking unseemly advantage of his wealth (of which there really was not much).

"What did you read?"

"Oh some Dante, Tennyson."

Alright, Edith thought, I suppose there might be something interesting in reading those two together. The overlaps were clear. But no, not with Gabriel. With Gabriel she could not help being critical. There was only boredom. Gosh, Dante, only because he had a name, so highly regarded, so surely established. Dante was satisfactory and some parts were good, even beautiful, but simply the fact he was so widely known and appreciated made her write it off as stuffy and dull. Like Shakespeare or Milton, it was very rare that she could read it without the shadow of tradition. She felt like she could only ever read this writing through the eyes and minds of others; it was never *hers*. At the same time, she was occasionally remorseful at the idea that she was missing out, never able to fully appreciate it because of this shadow. Then Tennyson, well, there had not been enough time since his death to make him too firmly established. But there was dust, and that dust *was* settling round almost all his work. (This was not the dust of neglect, but of tradition and stuffy minds.) Through no particular fault of his own he was, well, *Victorian*, dull. No, there was nothing to be said when it came to Gabriel's reading. It consisted of classics taken from his father's library. Books that had never been read (at least Gabriel *was reading them*) and were there for show. And he read them with nothing other than a wistful wandering imagination.

She sighed, returning to her monosyllabic acknowledgments. "Oh?"

"Yes, I enjoyed that. I thought the—well, I'm sorry, I can't for the life of me remember the titles, I'm never very good at titles. But beautiful, they were beautiful anyhow."

And again, Edith thought to herself sadly. And again, she thought, that confident assertion of beauty in art. Cannot remember, or *place*, exactly *what* was beautiful. But it was definitely beautiful. Yes, perhaps it was precisely the elusive nature of whatever it was that was *definitely beautiful* that made the *overall* beautiful. And so was born the art of *bluff*. How frequent was this conversation, and not only with Gabriel: "What did you think?" "Oh I liked it; I thought it was strangely beautiful." "Why was that?" "Well I can't remember precisely why or what I found beautiful. It was *complex*. In fact, I think it may have been the complexity and intangibility of this elusive beauty that made me like it so much. Yes, that was it." Had the writing in question even been read by the other? Because, other than a gradual development around the idea that everything was beautiful and complex, and beautiful because it was complex, and complex because it was beautiful, the writing itself was never referred to. It could have been anything. Quite a skill, really.

Gabriel was in fact, like Mari, not as insensitive as Edith condemned him to be. He noticed that she was depressed by their conversation and changed the subject to the first thing his scatty mind could find.

"I was thinking … if the Ancient Greeks were to walk among us, which one of them would you wish most to encounter?" The change in subject was not so very strange.

"Orpheus," she replied without thinking.

"Really? I suppose he is quite interesting. Why?"

"Oh I don't know. He just seems to appear everywhere, in everything. Music and mirrors. Music reminds me of him, and he makes me think of mirrors. Don't ask me why. Well, music is obvious. Yes, isn't it great, the relationship between the life of his music and the life of Pygmalion's statue?"

"The life of his music? What, his song in the underworld?"

"Yes, well. What about you? Who would you meet?"

"Me? Oh. I'm not sure. Icarus?"

"Icarus? He's a pretty minor character surely, why him?"

"His flight, of course. The poor boy, why would he do that to himself? But I can see myself in his position so well that it scares me a little."

"The falling part or the not-listening-to-the-father part?"

"Alright," he said keeping his voice just loud enough for her to hear. "There's no need to be cheeky." His agitation had swiftly returned as he looked nervously to check if his father had heard their conversation.

Edith giggled, but kept her voice equally low. "We're talking about Icarus not you. If you're so sensitive, that's your concern."

"Yes, but you know how big *my* fall would be if I didn't do as my father said."

"Said about what?"

"You know what."

"I don't think I do."

Gabriel gave a big sigh and raised his eyebrows. "Us—me, you. Everything. Can we change the subject?"

"How about English legend? How does that compare to Orpheus and Icarus?"

His face relaxed and he smiled slightly. "Like King Arthur?"

She nodded.

"I'm not especially fond of stories of him—they are a little nightmarish."

"And Icarus isn't?"

"Alright. A different sort of nightmare; and not to one I can so easily relate."

Edith looked at Gabriel quizzically. Her face suddenly lit up.

"Yes?" he asked a little uncomfortable.

"I was just thinking."

"What?"

"The nightmare. And Arthur's sword."

"What of his sword?"

"Well, how incredible would it be if Orpheus had left such a symbol?"

"Symbol? What do you mean?"

"The sword, Gabriel. The sword!"

He raised his eyebrows again, waiting for her to go on.

"The sword proved to the people that Arthur was the rightful king. If he hadn't pulled the sword from the stone, no one would ever have believed he should be king—he would never have become king. It seems so symbolic of the fact that everyone wants proof—*solid* proof to lay their hands on. It's all very well to *tell* someone that you should be king, or that a particular man should be king, but it's another thing to have something *prove* that they should be king. It's an idea used everywhere. You know—like in Christianity: the people needed Christ as physical proof of God. Then Thomas needed to see physical wounds, inflicted by solid objects, to believe in the resurrection. Yes … it starts to get quite complicated if one goes into the Eucharist and sacramental wine."

"But the sword isn't in every version of the story?"

She sighed. "That's not the point. All of it is Arthurian *legend* anyway."

"So what about Orpheus then?"

"Just the thought that there could be proof of art. No—that's not right. I mean the art itself generally is physical in some way or other. But its evocations aren't. Imagine if there was a physical symbol of art's *feeling*."

"But it's as you said. The object of art itself is the proof of its feeling! Why would you have an object to prove the power of the object?" His eyebrows had now lowered to a frown.

"True," she sighed again. "I don't know. It's only an idea. It made me excited."

"No, no, I didn't mean to ruin your excitement. I'm just not sure I understand you. So. Arthur's sword. I see that the sword was proof for the unsure eyes around him. I understand where you're coming from about people's constant need to be satisfied by solid evidence. What about Orpheus though? What do you mean about him leaving a symbol? A lyre?"

"Yes, that was it—Orpheus. Sorry, I remember now what I was thinking. Rather than a symbol of art's feeling, I mean a symbol so powerful that it could, if seen or touched—"

"What are you two talking so intently about?" Edith's mother interrupted with a knowing smile.

"They always did get along so well," said Gabriel's mother.

Gabriel looked down and Edith briefly raised an eyebrow.

"Hunting," she said.

"Hunting?" asked Lord Loehill with a short laugh. "That's not what you should be discussing with Edith, Gabriel."

"No, poetry and the moon, that's more the thing," Mr Norton took his turn.

"Subtlety was never your forte, David," said the red-cheeked Lord Loehill.

Always reminded, with Victorian-like strictness, of manners and proper etiquette by these same people, Gabriel and Edith flinched at their tipsy crudity. They waited silently for the parents to become reabsorbed in merry conversation.

"So do you essentially want a piece of art to symbolise all art? A metaphor for metaphor?"

"Oh no, you see I wouldn't want art to be merged like that, absorbed into one *object*. No, that would not do, though I suppose an ultimate metaphor is a good idea," she took a sip of red wine from her crystal glass as Gabriel glowed inwardly at her appreciation of his comment. "We couldn't meet Orpheus, so what if he had left a physical object that literally symbolised all he represented. Imagine if there was a sculpture or something, and this sculpture, if held, could evoke Orpheus' voice in any person's mind. It would send them mad of course. But it is such a beautiful idea, because—do you never get annoyed at the deafness of the audience in a concert, or the blindness of people wandering through a gallery. They never look at the work; they see the name and title and if unfamiliar, move on until they come to a recognised name. *Then* they decide to judge the work. They see and hear, but never look or listen. Do you ever have that?"

"I don't think of it too often, but yet, I suppose I occasionally get irritated at a certain arrogant ignorance. I suppose most people get irritated by it."

"You would hope. But how many people are well and truly excited by a work? Actually genuinely moved? Of course, I have not met that many people anyway, but it seems very rare for people not to think there is something wrong with you if you seem emotionally attached to a piece of art."

"Yes, I think I understand: if you express emotional excitement over a piece of art, people look at you in amusement. But I still don't understand how a physical symbol of Orpheus would be any different to any work of art that might be said to evoke Orpheus. Arthur's sword simply proved he was king. What would Orpheus' sword do?"

"Orpheus' sword would open the eyes and ears of even the most irritatingly stubborn of the lot. They would see the sun and feel its warmth right to their core; they would hear the excited morning birds and laugh joyfully at this excitement."

"Oh! I see." Gabriel nodded happily. "I'm sure this is what we were speaking about a few months ago, when we talked about music? This was what I was trying to say."

Oh no, thought Edith. This is the reason one should never criticise. Indeed, one should simply not think. Or at least not speak. If she really did sound as wistful as Gabriel—how embarrassing! His adolescent exclamations of 'O me, O my, O woe, O life. O! O! O!' It was pretty pathetic. And when, last autumn, she had tried to talk to him about music, about music and its relationship to other sounds and forms, he had gone into some sort of sentimental dialogue about life being made of music; some sort of airy idea that the birds, bees and flowers were our friends, united in the purity of natural sound. Something, he said, some deep part of every person, animal and tree, was connected by tiny threads of vibrations that were only felt during thorough concentration. In fact, he went on, the whole world's problems would be solved if only people listened to this inner music that held all life together in its airy-fairy way. He was so sincere. The stars practically sang to him.

Edith had cruelly and superiorly laughed aloud at Gabriel's quiet, sincere expression in the orchard. She had put a daisy in his golden hair. The thing was she knew he did not even care for music. Not really. Not actually. He was never interested in going to concerts, let alone playing an instrument. Although, unobserved by him, she did listen carefully as he sang beside her in Church: he sang beautifully in the congregation, but she knew he would never dare sing alone. Often, when Gabriel went into his bursts of romanticism and feeling, his voice seemed to her so irritating that she was tempted to ask him to sing it instead. Yes, if he only spoke as he sang, she might have been able to listen with greater tolerance.

What a hypocrite she was! She would laugh and sneer at Gabriel's airy adolescent romanticism, and there she was talking of the sun's warmth and morning birdsong! But she did not mean it in the way he did. Surely not? The line was so thin between airy depth and airy triviality.

"Oh yes, no. I didn't quite mean it like that. Well. I suppose it's not something I can very easily explain. It's just a sense. I think I've thought about it before, but when you asked about Ancient Greeks and we got onto Arthur, it prompted the idea again. I'm sorry."

"What have you to be sorry about? I think *I* understand you anyway. Orpheus could even charm the animals—as a half-god he is already represented in a mortal form. So why should his mortal form not also be represented by another physical symbol, like Arthur's sword? Yes, like Arthur, it would be a symbol proving his rightful position; the proof of his position alone as musical charmer, poet, lover and son of the sun, would demand that people look and listen."

"Erm yes … I suppose that is more or less—" Edith was interrupted by the arrival of dessert. Staring at her pear tart, she wondered once again why she did not, *could* not, understand Gabriel.

After dinner, she wanted to go on a little solitary walk, but the Loehills did not appear inclined to leave. The heat of arrogant conversation was getting to her, and she felt the need to breathe. Seeing and comprehending this urge, Gabriel offered to take her outside, and she agreed, asking Elizabeth to come too.

The darkness was like a thick blanket spread evenly across the garden. They walked in silence, each attempting to make out the familiar shapes of hedges through the blackness. At the edge of the garden, or this section of the garden, Edith stopped, respectfully still, and they absorbed the mysterious atmosphere around them. They took several breaths of the cool evening air, before Elizabeth said:

"Do you think there's anyone else here?"

"What? In the garden, now?" asked Gabriel.

"Yes, doesn't it feel like we're not quite alone?"

"It's good you should say that, Elizabeth, because I've felt that here several times lately."

"Have you asked anyone? Is that why you brought us here?" Gabriel asked Edith.

"No, I haven't really thought about it much. It hasn't felt threatening. I've called out several times, but there's been no response. It's probably just a new creature who's found a home in the hedge there."

"But it's not as if there's even any rustling. No, you know, I think I've been reading too many ghost novels," said Elizabeth.

Edith laughed. "It's alright. I don't mind if someone's decided to live here."

Gabriel looked at the dark hedge intently. "Are you serious? I don't know why you haven't brought this up before."

"It's only been a few days."

"Well, it's cold. Let's start walking."

III

The Reverend Darthur was tending his roses, as he did every Saturday afternoon. It was a thoughtless and soothing task that allowed him to ponder over the week's appointments and plan the sermon for the following morning. He never liked writing anything down, as he always stumbled over his words and forgot his train of thought if he relied on notes. Instead, he preferred to look over the readings for the next day while he sipped dandelion tea. Then, he would go outside to contemplate its relevance to this day, age and particular congregation, as he gardened.

This Saturday, his contemplation was interrupted. It would be wrong to say he was irritated, because this week's gospel reading was Jesus' resurrection of Lazarus which Reverend Darthur always found rather difficult to discuss. But he was not especially pleased at the distraction either, since he had just found a link between Mary's cleaning of Jesus' feet with her hair and Mary's discovery of The Resurrection. He was, as usual, struggling with the best way to phrase it for benefit to his congregation, and he knew if he did not have the full picture in his mind, conclusion and all, the thoughts would vanish. So, no, it was not without a little irritation that he called out.

"Yes, Mrs Rosamond?" It was not rare that he forgot to start with a word of greeting. This was a bad habit, and could cause offense, but he could not seem to help it.

He waited to hear the church warden's familiar response, followed by a discourse on the persistence of cold weather and the rest of life's woes, before eventually asking about a village announcement or the like. She always came round on a Saturday afternoon; her timing to coincide with his contemplative period in the garden always perfect. This time, she seemed to have come from the opposite direction to the village, no doubt conveniently calling by on the way back from taking her dog (what was his name—Tupsy? Mupsy?) for a walk in the woods. The vicarage was, after all, placed on the outer edge of the village, and its garden bordered the woods. He could hear her (or Mupsy's?) persistent rustling amongst the trees.

"Hello! Do you want a hand Mrs Rosamond?"

When, however, he looked up, anticipating the form of his church warden, he watched as a young boy stepped out from the trees' shadows into the dappled light which patterned the garden. For a moment, the priest was quite stunned, overwhelmed, by the sight. It seemed in that instant that he was experiencing a vision, and all the sunlight was focused on it, the soft afternoon rays bowing to this figure who seemed to exude his own pure light. The light was playful about him too; there was that same balance of merriment and respect that was to be found in the reflections of moonlight upon a lake.

He shook himself violently, resembling a wet Mupsy, to wake himself from this reverie. As he looked briefly away, he half expected the vision to disappear, and Mrs Rosamond to indeed step onto his lawn. But no, when he looked up, the boy was still there; this apparition would neither vanish nor refigure itself as the church warden.

Sort yourself out, James, he told himself. Just because you haven't seen the boy before, and he is certainly not Mrs Rosamond, does not mean you have to be quite so stunned. He is most probably new to one of the neighbouring villages and got a little lost exploring. Yes, so pull yourself together. What's so astounding?

But there was a stillness emanating from this glowing figure, a sphere of silence about him, which was not exactly peaceful. In his sensitivity, the priest could feel it, and it disturbed him that such glowing stillness could be so uncomfortable.

Stuttering, he called out. "Hello?"

The boy looked unblinkingly at him with large, deep eyes like a strange woodland creature.

"Are you alright?" Reverend Darthur gently called out again.

This time the boy blinked, but still did not speak. There was an encouraging twitch of his mouth, though, which evoked such an unfamiliarly strong paternal feeling in the priest that he did not know quite what to do with himself. He stepped right up to the boy and put his hand on his shoulder.

The boy, who must have been at least twelve, though

small, looked up at the priest searchingly. The unnatural sadness in his eyes made the priest gulp audibly.

"Would you like to come inside and have a cup of dandelion tea?" the priest asked, not completely aware of what he was saying.

He felt no resistance as he led him into the vicarage, though still no word came from the boy's lips. He had not even got a nod. It was not a case of foreign language, or some lack of intelligence; he could see the comprehension in those wide eyes.

The vicarage was a four-windowed cottage resembling the lid of a tourist biscuit tin. Each of the windows were framed and divided by thin white frames, and dark pink roses grew up and around the little turquoise back door. To the right of the cottage, as one came out of the woods and stepped into the back garden, stood a round-tower medieval church and kindly-kept graveyard.

Reverend Darthur led the boy through the rose-framed turquoise door to a seat in the living room at the front of the cottage. He did not look curiously around the room, as the priest was accustomed to guests doing, but straight out of the window which looked onto a wheat field. Having gazed for couple of minutes, no longer glowing but still sphered in silence, the boy looked up at the observing and confused priest. Caught in the act of staring, the priest mumbled something about going to make the tea.

As he prepared a tray with tea and his own homemade ginger biscuits, he furrowed his eyebrows, giving himself this one last chance to be perplexed. Never before had he felt embarrassed in front of a child less than a quarter his age.

But that was all; he refused to dwell on the irregularities and agreed with himself that he would simply take everything as it came.

"Have you tried dandelion tea?" he asked the boy in a casual tone. Here for the first time, he observed a flash of humour in the boy's eyes and a quiver of the lips, as though they contemplated a smile. He shook his head.

"Ah, you haven't. Well, it's very nice, I think. Of course, some people don't agree. Here." He handed the boy the tea and a couple of biscuits. "I made these myself; I hope they aren't too hard."

The priest sat in his own chair, well placed opposite the boy at a sensible distance. He took a sip of his tea and the boy mirrored him. He took another sip, watching the boy over the cup's rim. The boy did the same. Was there mischief in his eyes? Timidity?

"Tell me what you think?" Reverend Darthur said, taking a bite from his biscuit. The boy, as expected, also took a bite. He looked at the biscuit intently as he carefully chewed his mouthful and swallowed. He glanced back at the priest and nodded.

"You like it? The biscuit or the tea?"

The boy nodded.

"Both?"

The boy nodded.

"Good, I'm glad." A kind-hearted man, Reverend Darthur suppressed his urge to prompt a 'thank you' from the mouth of this strange, unmannered boy. He recognised a fellow sensitive being, and realised it could not be intentional that this child was quite so rude.

They sat in silence for another few minutes, the boy mirroring the priest's sips and bites. This happened until the priest made the thoughtful decision to look at his mantelpiece. Then, when he looked back at the boy's hands, he saw that an empty cup and saucer had been placed on the little side table, and the boy was gently brushing crumbs from his mouth. The priest smiled in spite of himself: he could tell a hungry boy when he saw one.

"So where do you come from?" he thought it would be sensible to find out about the child before he asked him to dinner.

The boy let his hands drop elegantly to his lap in a strangely hopeless manner. Holding himself unnaturally still for a moment, he began to shake his head slowly, his eyes falling in the same way as his hands.

"What is it? What's wrong?"

The boy continued to shake his head sorrowfully.

"I'm terribly sorry, my dear chap, but you're going to have to speak, or I'll never be able to help you."

The boy looked up with wide, wet eyes so full of desperation that the priest's heart gave a lurch as it never had before, travelling right to the top of his throat and back downwards to the pit of his stomach. The surge was so violent that his knees literally shook and the hair on the back of his neck stood on end. As imaginative as he was, he had never considered such things happened quite so exactly and dramatically in life off the page of a book.

Though no tears fell, the child's eyelashes had clustered in dark, moist clumps. And this time, it was the priest's turn to act the mirror, his own eyes gathering tears. The sadness was not that which he had observed in the garden as unnatural and uncomfortable; this was a form of all-knowing, all-seeing despair. The boy could not speak; he was mute. But that was not the end of it. He was consumed by his own silence, a silence that had evidently been imposed on him. (By what? By *whom*?) This was the pervasive sphere about the child that the priest had felt so strongly. This poor, sorrowful and desperate boy inhabited a separate, impenetrable world in which he alone spoke the language. Or else, more tragically, he inhabited the same world as everybody else, as the only one who *did not* speak the language.

The priest got over himself through another audible gulp.

"Do you not know sign language? I'm not very good myself, but I've met several people …" he had indeed met at least two people in his life that had been mute, but what was the use—

The boy shook his head.

"Oh. Well. That can be resolved quite easily. Where do you come from?"

And suddenly the boy was at the priest's feet, kneeling. Beautiful, deep grey eyes looked up at him, imploring. The tears fell now, soaking his soft, marble-like cheeks. How was it that he could cry so perfectly, without the usual stains or disarray?

So shaken was the priest that he remained absolutely still, watching the kneeling figure before him. The boy's eyes fell to the floor and his head dropped loosely onto his chest. Finally the priest moved, reacting to the normal instinct of a sympathetic human being, by placing his hand firmly on the child's shoulder. He went further and slid off his seat onto the floor beside the boy.

"Look at me child. Look at me. Everything is going to be alright. You might not feel it now, but soon you will."

The child did not look at him. He was trying hard to suppress his shaking such that with every few breaths his whole body gave a violent shudder.

"You can stay here with me as long as you like, if you *would* like that. There is no problem."

Over the following few weeks, an extensive search was carried out by prominent members of the village into the boy's history. The boy himself could give them no information by sign or written word. Towards the end of the third week, the boy's journey by foot had been traced back to what they thought was the origin—a port some hundred and eighty miles away. No record could be found of his birth or home, however, and it was only by hearsay that the boy was said to have perhaps lived with a mother and brother. They, inevitably, could not be uncovered. And so it was settled that the boy would live with the priest for as long as no one came to claim him.

The priest took the boy's education into his own hands, and delighted in spending every spare minute of every day caring for him. The boy did not know his age, so his date of birth was temporarily settled as twelve years ago on the day he arrived at the vicarage. He did not appear to have had any form of education whatsoever, but quickly learnt to read and write with a beautiful creative flair. He certainly had a gift for languages, because after taking a month to be fluent in written English, another three months and French and German were equally assured. The priest taught him Greek and Latin too, but there his knowledge of languages stopped, and he had to find other teachers to give him lessons in Spanish, Italian, Sanskrit and Hebrew.

That first Christmas, having got so many books for the boy already, James Darthur was at a loss for gift ideas. He always got everyone and anyone books. Occasionally food. But that was boring: once consumed, its potential for pleasure was short, whereas a book could be pleasurable both during and after consumption. Thinking this through for the umpteenth time the last Sunday before Christmas, the priest was sorting his decorations box in the attic when his gaze landed upon his old violin.

Of course, a violin would be the perfect gift! It would be a form of recreation for the boy, a break from reading. This could be especially good since, despite his skill and continual encouragement, the child was incredibly reluctant to write, meaning that practically *all* his time was taken up by the one occupation of reading.

He took it to his room and cleaned it up. It did not need any serious attention; it had kept itself in wonderful condition. And on Christmas day it was ready and waiting to be played.

When the boy had unwrapped the violin in the priest's candlelit living room, he stared at it for a long time. His face did not show any particular emotion, and for a moment Reverend Darthur thought he might have made a mistake and that the boy was upset. But no. A small grin gradually appeared on the boy's face, first in his eyes, then a small spasm at the corners of his lips. He stroked the violin's sides as one might imagine a squirrel would its long-lost nut tree.

"Have you played before?" the priest wondered whether the boy's affection towards the instrument was the result of forgotten longing.

The boy shook his head.

"Oh. Shall I show you how to hold it?"

He nodded, excitedly passing the violin to the priest.

"Like this. Here, let me place it on you. And then the bow like this, don't grip it."

The priest half expected the boy to be one of those legendary prodigies whose first stroke 'sounded as a gong from heaven'. But, somewhat comfortingly, it sounded more like a strangled cat.

At this sound, the boy threw back his head, laughing silently. The priest was delighted, hardly knowing whether to laugh or cry at the boy's silent pleasure.

Such strangled cat noises filled the vicarage for the better part of two weeks, and then notes began to be distinguishable in a form vaguely acceptable to the human ear. The priest gave him a couple of lessons, but mostly the boy liked to play to himself at any random time of day. He always went up to Reverend Darthur before though, to make sure it was not a problem for him to play. The priest did not mind at all, however jarring it had been at first or might occasionally be. He simply delighted in the boy's delight. Also, since three or four weeks after Christmas, he had dreamt every night of the most beautiful, soft and sonorous playing. In the dream he would get out of his bed and go downstairs to find the boy, barefoot and in pyjamas, playing his violin through the open window. The room would be unrealistically empty, coloured only in the deep navy and shadowy silver of the clear night sky. Sometimes, there would be a squirrel or two and a bird on the windowsill, listening attentively. The sight would evoke a certain inexplicable sense of nostalgia, so strangely familiar and soothing was this image. The boy's figure and dark shadow, thrown across the silver shaft of light on the floor, seemed timeless; it was eerie and mysterious and sacred, not entirely part of any particular realm of being.

Every morning, the priest woke unsure whether this had been a dream after all, as sometimes happens with dreams. In any case, it instilled in him a hope, a niggling belief that, if not a reality at present, it would become one. This, aside from the boy's own explicit happiness, was the main cause of the priest's constant smile.

Two years later, the priest hardly noticing the difference in the boy's playing it had seemed so gradual, Mrs Rosamond came wandering through the garden with Mupsy just as the boy was playing. It was a Saturday just like the one on which the boy arrived, and Reverend Darthur was, of course, tending his roses. Strange how some things never change.

The notes were floating out the back door and seemed to hover over the roses, just as the sunlight. Mrs Rosamond was moved. She felt that it was a scene oddly frozen in time; an instant that would pleasantly haunt this space for years to come. She approached the priest who greeted her as usual and asked her in for a cup of tea. Once seated with her dandelion tea and ginger biscuit, she told him that the boy should perform for the congregation sometime, nothing too serious, that it would give the boy something to be proud of.

It was at this first casual church performance that the priest saw his dream had, in some form, been a reality. At first he did not know if this was a kind of self-fulfilling prophecy, that he had projected beauty on the smoothness of the boy's simple playing. Nevertheless, he had the presence of mind to look around at the faces of his congregation, and almost all of them were hypnotised in emotive awe. Perhaps it was not so usual for a child to learn to play so beautifully in two years. Come to think of it, some performers seemed to spend their whole life in search of such beauty.

The notes had a little life of their own, and they teased and played with the church's air. The priest could almost imagine a cheeky angelic laugh amongst them.

"I don't know what to say. Your son is a gift and I'm touched," said a member of his congregation to him as they left. And it struck him then how much the boy did not belong to him. He felt the imminence of his departure, a departure without return. Perhaps Reverend Darthur was too wrapped up in the mysteries of the word and world, such that he placed a dramatic dimension on all aspects of his life. Either way, he could not help the fact of the feeling.

When the boy began making journeys into the woods, to be seen playing to circles of woodland creatures, the priest did not think to ponder over it. It vaguely passed his mind that there must be a reason for all those paintings of animals listening to music, and so there was nothing too odd about such a sight in the flesh. It was something about people who questioned all the time, and were always open to the possibility of doubt; these people were so permanently in a state of reflection that if faced with the strangest of things, its strangeness bore no effect upon their perception of it. James Darthur was one such open-minded man, questioning absolutely everything to its utmost potential. He was a great adherent of Saint Augustine and perpetually reminded himself of the existence of the signified behind the signifier, meaning behind metaphor. And everything was inevitably metaphor.

Nevertheless, when the boy turned sixteen, another two years after the first of his concerts to the local and neighbouring congregations, and the priest watched as his adopted son disappeared into the trees with his little packed bag and violin, Reverend Darthur could not help going through a period of distress such that he had never before experienced.

For the first time in his life, he feared the sphere of doubt which seemed to consume him, to eat right into him. He had no idea how he could have let a child leave his care with no sense of a plan. And yet, at the same time, he had never been so involuntarily sure.

IV

A s they were walking back to the house, Gabriel told Elizabeth to run ahead.

She looked at him a little nervously and half-laughingly said, "You're sure the ghost man from the hedge won't eat me?"

Gabriel laughed, "How should I know? Don't let him catch you."

"What about you? Where are you going?" Elizabeth asked her brother.

"We'll come inside in a minute; I just need to talk with Edith alone."

Elizabeth laughed, nodded, and ran back to the house.

"Are you sure you're not worried about the 'ghost hedge man' Edith?" he asked, clearly distracted. He was delaying the question he really wanted to ask for as long as possible. "It came a little out of the blue."

"Oh no I'm sorry, I'm a little curious that's all. It was only nice to know that I'm not imagining things. I really don't think it matters; it's hardly crossed my mind."

"Right, right. Good. I just wanted to check."

Edith watched him for a moment as he repeatedly mouthed 'right.'

"Well?" she asked.

"Well …" he was struggling. "Well … I … I wanted to ask what you thought about marriage."

"Marriage in general or our marriage?"

"Well—our marriage."

"What about it in particular?"

"Are you, firstly, happy about it?"

"I never think about it," Edith lied. "It's just what's always been."

"Really? I must admit I find it troubling—I feel too much out of my own control, like a pawn. Everyone has motives, but our motives are the only ones that don't seem to count for anything. Your parents were always satisfied at the prospect of our marriage purely on the basis of prominence in society; my parents have always felt the need for money, and the imminence of ruin. They desperately need the Norfolk estate which would solve their problems for the foreseeable future.

"I don't know if you knew how much they wanted, still want, you to marry as soon as I turn twenty-one, if not before. Recently I have heard them talking about it frequently—I get the feeling things must be getting rather more desperate. I don't know anything for sure, because although my father has ensured I have some competency with estate management, he never ever speaks to me of *his* financial concerns. Anyhow, I'm pretty sure another of his shares has gone."

"You're twenty-one this summer aren't you?" Edith said as though unfazed.

"Yes," he looked down at this face he had grown to know and love more than his own sister. He felt a wave of nervousness from below his ribs though to the tips of his ears. Did he really love her or had he simply told himself to? Was this surge of emotion imagined, invented?

"Gosh," he said, sighing. "Blame that damn cousin of mine. He's dictated all our lives."

"It's understandable, in a way, that he did not want another bachelor running the estate. After all, correct me if I'm wrong, but wasn't he your great, great uncle's second wife's cousin? That's pretty far from being a straight line of inheritance."

"Yes, that's right. He knew my parents would not let the opportunity pass. There is, of course, also a strong sense of family pride. And the house will remain empty until I marry, and if I don't, it will be sold after my death, which would mean it would never regain the family name."

"Might I ask how it kept the family name by going through a woman? The 'second wife' woman?"

"Inter-marriage. They were cousins of the same name before marriage."

"So for such a distant connection to be the most valid, how many generations have been bachelors?"

"That great, great uncle was the last married owner."

Edith nodded. "This is why it is understandable to have the marriage condition part of the will. Or at least understandable in someone of a certain mind-set. But that still doesn't mean that I have to be your wife, you could have anyone."

Gabriel was taken aback.

"I'm sorry Gabriel, that sounded harsher than I intended. It's just I don't quite understand why you should be forced to marry me. There are so many girls who would happily marry you and help you with the estate."

Gabriel put his head to one side, his eyebrows furrowed. Edith continued.

"I mean, surely it would have been easier to have someone exactly your age, or even older? Then you would never have had to wait at all."

"But—well, alright. That is true. It would have made more sense legally to have someone of my age. However, my father owed yours. I don't know why or how, but there it is," he left a dramatic pause before adding, "and anyway, aside from that, *I* love *you*."

It was cruel, she knew, but Edith could not help releasing a loud chuckle. Perhaps it was to ease the tense atmosphere, and she was nervous, in any case she could not prevent it.

"How can you say so, in all sincerity, when I'm sure you've never so much as met another girl? Not to be unkind but I think that perhaps you have read too many sentimental novels: such a phrase as 'I love you' is repeated so many times that it becomes empty of meaning. In any case, we have both been brought up to think of our getting married as inevitable, unquestionable. It is wishful thinking to project love on the good friendship we have somehow managed to maintain despite our situation."

"Please! Don't mock me!" he seemed to wince, and added quietly, "I find our situation very difficult, believe me. And of course, how could I ever know whether I would have loved you if I had not been told to? Though, I never have been told to *love* you, only take you as my wife. Well, I'll tell you the truth: I don't care if I love you *because* we have been forced together—I still love you, the end result is the same. And I'm sorry but you are cruel not to take me seriously."

He stood for a moment watching her before flicking the hair from his long-lashed, dark blue eyes. "Alright, I will not push anything upon you now; I only wanted you to know the truth about it all. And I do mean all that I say, I know my own emotions."

The girl's eyes were wet with angry tears and she blamed Gabriel for them, knowing he was right to call her cruel.

"I'm sorry Gabriel." She did not say anything more.

Gabriel left her to wander the garden alone. He did not return indoors immediately, however, because as he approached the house he heard talking. The sound of his father speaking to his future father-in-law through the open library window was very loud, and he could tell from the tone that the latter was in shock. He guessed that he had not been the only one to reveal the prospective wedding date that night.

"Sixteen!" he heard Edith's father exclaim. "In a month's time she will still be sixteen: a child! It's what housemaids are expected to do—peasants! That really is low!" His exclamations were short, each word hit with staccato spit.

"My dear fellow, it really isn't that tragic; it wasn't so long ago that at sixteen a girl could have married, borne children and been widowed."

"And my dear fellow back to you, this is the twentieth century, didn't you know? I like to think we're civilised now.

How long ago is '*not long ago*'? 1700s? Seventeenth century? 1450!? I cannot believe you could possibly think that I would allow my daughter …! What would the villagers say? I agreed to a young marriage, yes, but sixteen!? My dear chap that is asking too much—why must Gabriel take the estate as soon as he's twenty-one? I don't think a couple more years really makes much difference—either to the empty house or you."

"But don't you see? It's for the best. My son is very young too. Well. I can now say quite openly that London House is on the verge of ruin: its walls are literally crumbling, and our housekeeper has not had her wages for the past three months, not to mention Harry and Cook. You of all people should understand this: your situation is, I believe, almost worse than ours at the moment?"

Edith's father swallowed. He spoke more quietly.

"Let me sleep on it. I will talk to you tomorrow once I have discussed it with Helena."

"Of course. And please remember, David, that I am doing this for your benefit, in addition to my own—as a friend. I have not forgotten what you did for me in the—"

At this moment George the butler came walking into the library without knocking.

"Oh! Sir, I'm very sorry, I didn't realise anyone was here. I'm just doing the lights."

This confused Gabriel, since the men's voices were so very loud. Either George was going prematurely deaf or he was fed up and wanted to go to bed himself.

"Don't worry George, we are finished in here. Thank you," said Edith's father as he and Lord Loehill simultaneously drained their glasses of the last drops of whiskey.

Gabriel hurried round to the door in case he should be spotted as George shut the window. He stepped into the hall from the front door at the same time that his father stepped out from the library.

"Hello, Gabriel. Nice walk?"

"Oh yes, very nice."

"And Edith?"

"She wanted to stay outside a while longer—it is a beautiful night."

"Ah yes, indeed, of course. Alright. Well, we had better be leaving, Gabriel, I did not realise how late it was. Would you mind telling your mother we must be off?"

He waited for his son to be out of hearing before turning to Mr Norton as he too stepped into the hall. "I wait patiently for your decision. Good night, David."

Edith dreamed a very strange and different dream that night. She had, for several nights in a row, dreamt of swimming in deep, dark water. It had been a struggle; her arms and legs ceaselessly shredding water but getting nowhere. She had woken each time, three in the morning, soaked in sweat and lying by the window, several yards from her bed. Most disturbingly, on several occasions, mud-stains at the bottom of her nightdress told her she had been beyond her room in sleep. This was, incidentally, how she had first noticed the shadowlike figure in the grounds, the 'presence' she had mentioned to Gabriel and Elizabeth. She had not told them that she had seen the 'ghost hedge man' standing, staring at the distant trees beyond the hedge. His figure was almost completely obscured by the darkness of the hedge and garden shadows: he was a dark shadow amongst them all. Each time, however, that she had woken by the window she had looked out to see his pensive profile, and found it hugely comforting. Without this peculiar, eerie figure, perhaps she would not so easily have got back into bed and fallen calmly asleep.

Thinking the dream over in the mornings, she had decided it must be a subconscious reaction to her impending marriage. Though she told herself this was ridiculous, she could detach herself from her situation enough to realise she must be troubled, having those sporadic claustrophobic panic attacks even while she was awake. As the ever-present idea of her marriage became nearer and nearer a reality, it was not unlikely that her emotional tension might seek release when she was asleep.

Then this night, for the first time, it was a pleasant swim. Her arms cut gently through the water and the rest of her body glided smoothly behind. There was absolutely no light. She wanted, apparently needed, to swim right to the bottom of this water, anticipating the powerful sensation of its rush as the pressure would push her back up. The water was neither too cold nor hot. It was so comfortable that, as she made her way further and further from the surface of the water, she felt herself relax. Her panic of drowning in the previous dreams had been so childish and unreasonable. She realised that now, within this dream. It was, in fact, a nice idea to slowly drift; to slowly drift without ever reaching the bottom. Leaving all responsibility. Forgetting, giving up everything. A little like her walks down the middle of dark country lanes.

Well, surely she should have drowned by now, she thought. Then, as sometimes happens in dreams, she knew that she would nevertheless, at some point, wake and trundle through her boring day.

She looked upwards as she drifted further and further downward, continuing to move her arms in a lazy motion to prevent being returned prematurely to the surface. She could see the white globe of the moon, standing out extra bright in what had, only an instant ago, been pure blackness. And then suddenly, in the midst of her calm reverie, she felt her hands interrupted in their movement. Something brushed past and was gone. She waited for it to brush past again; it was not a displeasing sensation. She searched for it, still idle. Her fingers found something and she tried to keep a hold of it. Then to her shock, the thing she held grabbed hold of her.

At that moment, the water became icy cold. Her lungs felt full of water, her eyes stung and she knew, simply knew, that she was somehow not asleep. The dream was no longer a dream, it was no longer pleasant. She felt the rush of water as she was forced back up, hurting her ears. Not as anticipated. Everything was chaotic and confused. Her head broke through the surface, free of the water, and she was choking. The girl felt herself being pulled powerfully towards shallower water and soon her feet were upon soft, slippery ground, wet mud pushing through the gaps between her toes.

The same something still had hold of both her hands, but she had no strength to shake it off, or even look to see what it was. Her whole body seemed made of water. It poured from everywhere. The coughing would not stop, even as her chest seemed ready to burst and she collapsed on her knees, her mouth only just above the water.

It must have been a god who held her hands, not a clinging weed, fish or eel. For it brought her back onto her feet and took her, without any of her own effort, to dry ground. And, when it let her go, she felt an overwhelming sense of loss. She was now very much aware of the dreadful sound of her own wheezing after each unhealthy cough filled her body with raw pain.

What might have been an age later—there was no concept of time—the girl again felt the touch of the god. (Was this because she had spoken about gods with Gabriel at dinner? Perhaps she was still asleep after all.) From her position as a collapsed heap on the ground, she was taken to a wide and welcoming tree, upon which she gladly leant her whole weight. The hands of the god were now on her shoulders, their weight the perfect pressure upon her damaged lungs. The right hand slid gently down her left shoulder, fingers fanning out upon her back. She could feel the weight of each finger. Then, one by one, the fingers were lifted, releasing her lungs from their force, while the left hand still lay upon her right shoulder.

At this moment, she was suddenly conscious of the stillness not only around her, but within her own body too. It had stopped. No more coughing, no more pain. Everything was silent and still and for a second—a brief, incredible second—she forgot everything. She was in a small and wonderful sphere of perfection within which there was an echoing promise that free unconsciousness would never entirely leave her. It was a kind promise of her own strength and will. The escalation of this sense was so great that she had to suppress it; to stop it before it could bloom into culmination. The prospect was too scary.

Then once again she could see outside her bubble. And this was a big blow, because it was now that she actively realised she should have been in bed. She *had* been in bed, asleep, and yet, somehow, here she was, having woken in deep water. She let out a sound that was something between a gasp and a scream, but it was cut short at the sight of the god, hand still upon her shoulder. For he was a god, certainly. And happily she could see him properly now. He possessed such beauty that she was quite in awe. His perfectly shaped face was framed by dark, curly brown hair with glowing lighter streaks. Long black lashes were reflected in his pool-like eyes, resembling the branches of majestic oaks above a still lake, golden sun shining upon it. Shadows dancing. And along with his most wonderful hair, soft even though supposedly soaking, these ornate shadows crossed both his eyes and his delicately pronounced cheek bones.

She was sure she would be able to look at him for a very long while before she was ever tired. And anyone looking at his eyes, even for an age, could not grow bored, because, in every instant of that age, a new discovery would be made. It seemed each eye was a window, or a mirror, to the whole world. The lake reflected the world; the shadows protected it, held it, and told its story. The girl, however, was not allowed an age to watch this young god: these few brief moments were all she got to look and absorb because, through no other fault than that of her own physical human capacity, her mind shut down and all was blank.

V

As might perhaps be expected under such strange preceding circumstances, it came as no surprise to Edith to wake the next morning in her own bed with a dry, mud-stained nightdress. She could only think how delightful it was that the god who had saved her from 'sleep-drowning' should care for her so much, to the point of returning her safely home. She did not want to question the impossibility of it; she only wanted the memory of it to bring her, like now, a pleasant wave of warmth, which might only be compared to dark Belgium chocolate. She hummed merrily to herself as she changed her nightdress and carefully hid the dirty one to wash later. It was fortunate no one had uncovered her unconscious night-time activities; she did not want to imagine the consequences of such a discovery.

It was a few days later, on their way back from a visit to some old family acquaintances, that Edith was to have her first proper encounter with the god. They were about two miles from their house, driving silently along the road that ran through the woods.

The car swerved. "What was that?" asked Lady Norton, adjusting her peacock feather hat which had slanted to a ridiculous angle.

"Don't worry my dear. It was some kind of wild animal—another fox, no doubt." The car swerved again. "Again!? What the devil is going on? Charles?"

"Sorry, sir, it seems—"

But before Charles could get any further, to explain that it was a tramp who had caused the first swerve, and that there seemed to be a strange following of animals trailing behind, Edith's memory had clicked.

"Stop! Stop the car!" she shouted. "Now!" She jumped from the car before it came to a sudden halt.

"Wait Edith! Where are you going!?" Lady Norton called after her daughter who was disappearing into the tall pines. "Come back! Edith?" But her daughter did not turn back.

In the shadowy light of the heavily clouded day, the girl could not be entirely sure she was right. Like Charles, however, she had seen that it was a person, and not an animal, who had crossed their path. This person had turned their gaze onto the car for the briefest of seconds, and yet it had been long enough to enable a realisation that the eyes were beautifully familiar. Still Edith was confused as to why she had felt, and acted upon, such a sudden and irrational impulse. She pushed her way through the prickly undergrowth, trying to make sense of her own stupidity. She knew that the eyes, if she was indeed right, belonged to the god from her sleep-drown. But this recognition was hazy, like a half-forgotten dream when the dreamer, as morning breaks, grasps onto any tiny recollection in an attempt to recreate the full picture.

As she was re-picturing the eyes, she suddenly remembered some hands, beautiful hands moving, fleeting. The image was so vivid she felt she had seen them somewhere other than the sleep-drowning occasion. She had seen them in a church, she was sure—a church filled with music. Yes, she was certain of that; she could recall the peaceful atmosphere of reverence. Oh! It was so frustrating to know it was there, but not be able to reach it!

Ahead of her something rustled. She stopped and held her breath, everything instantaneously forgotten. She was in a small clearing filled with daffodils and a scattering of snowdrops. Among the pines under the dark grey sky, the bright yellow flowers seemed to emit their own sunlight, cheerful and glowing at the girl to the point she needed to blink several times to readjust to their light.

Into these golden petals, without dulling their glow, the boy stepped from out of the trees. The girl's heart beat unnaturally fast at the sight of the god, the god who had carried her from the shadowy lake. Never in her life had she been so dumb-struck. She could not even begin to think what to say or do. The only experience to which one might draw comparison would be to that of a baby before they had learnt to speak, surrounded by nameless, indistinguishable things.

He did not move amongst the daffodils, just stood in stillness, surrounded by a protective sphere of otherworldly silence. He seemed a bit like a deer, observing. She stood still observing him too. At the time, it did not seem at all awkward that she and this strange figure were standing like woodland creatures, or statues, watching each other.

Eventually, habit got the better of her; the moment passed, her tongue was untied and she spoke.

"Hello," she said.

He immediately smiled at her. A beautiful smile, it made her smile.

"Hello?"

He stepped forward, still amongst the daffodils. His gaze shifted to the ground behind her feet and, following it, she saw the woodland animals who had been trailing the god figure. There were squirrels, sparrows, blackbirds and hedgehogs, all seated in a semi-circle behind her. At his gaze they stepped forward to form a line standing each side of the girl. He held out his hand for her to step forward, out of the animal line and into the golden glare.

She instinctively offered him her hand in response and he gently took it. He did not shake it but held it there, looking at it softly. He was still smiling, though the curve of his mouth was more subtle now. When he raised his eyes again and allowed them to rest a moment on her face, the girl's sensations were in such turmoil she felt tears swell in her eyes. At last, a thread of thought emerged in her mind as she wondered what on earth she was doing here, with this unnatural being. She must be dreaming of course. Of course. Who was this who seemed to literally glow, who gave her this time, who had such soft but penetrating eyes?

He (if earthly designations could be assigned to a god) seemed to have grown straight from a fictitious ideal. The sort of figure only pointed at, impossible to capture in entirety, by art and literature. His complete silence convinced her shadowy thoughts all the more that he inhabited some small unconscious sphere within her own head.

She thought she should still introduce herself, whether she was introducing herself to her own imagination or not.

"Hello," she almost whispered. "I'm Edith. I think we've already met?"

He nodded, and then his eye moved to something behind her again. This time it was not at the animals seated in their observing, worshipping line. He blinked once hastily in his deer-like manner, and then again slow and lazily. She turned and saw Gabriel making his way through the trees. The boy let go of her hand, looking at her again and bowing his head a little, before silently walking back into the trees. The little woodland creatures followed him, but not before giving the girl what she was sure was a meaningful glance. She turned back towards Gabriel who was just then entering the small clearing, thinking to herself angrily how often he skilfully managed to appear at exactly the wrong moment.

"Edith?"

"Yes Gabriel."

"Are you alright?"

"How long have I been gone that they managed to get home *and* call you to find me?"

"Well—it's been a couple of hours since your parents got back. I volunteered to come and look for you with Charles, so they wouldn't have to send out a search party. For some reason they thought you were attempting to run away?"

"Two hours?" the girl looked at Gabriel in instant confusion. "Are you sure? Two hours?"

"Yes, certain," replied Gabriel looking at his watch. "It's just coming up to half past six, and they got back exactly as your hallway clock struck half past four. So."

"Two hours … and … where's Charles?"

"Somewhere behind me I think. Look, Edith, are you sure you're alright? You seem rather bewildered. Did you think you'd been gone longer?"

"No, no. I'm sure I've been standing here for a couple of minutes—five at most. I … I must have blacked out or something."

"Yes—perhaps your mother is right, perhaps you should see a doctor."

"What? What do you mean? My mother wants me to see a doctor?"

"Well, yes. The wrong kind of doctor. I don't think there's anything wrong with your head; I think you've come down with something."

"With my head?"

"She was quite hysterical I'm afraid, Edith. It was not a good thing for you to run inexplicably from a moving car. Why on *earth* did you do it?"

She looked at him blinkingly before suddenly bursting into tears.

"Oh. Oh dear. Edith, look, I'm sorry. I know what it's like to be over-tired. That's all it is you know, you need some rest. Come. Let me take your arm."

She let herself lean on him, quickly supressing her sobs. "No, I'm sorry, I was terribly shocked, that's all. I feel I've lost out on two strange hours."

"It's alright, I understand. I feel that way when I sleep

deeply during an early afternoon nap and wake up just before dinner. Even that has made me want to cry before, let alone finding myself in the middle of the forest and being told the time has vanished. Gosh. I'm glad I found you."

"In what way was my mother hysterical, Gabriel?"

"Oh—I don't think you need to worry about that now. She was saying something about this being the final act, that they would not be able to prevent gossip for much longer, despite her care. I don't know. It didn't make all that much sense."

"What's it got to do with a doctor?"

"Apparently this isn't the first sign of strange behaviour. It is, admittedly, odd for someone to run out of a car. I … I wouldn't say anything about your loss of time … Perhaps tell them you felt violently sick and then got lost."

"Lost?"

"Yes, if you were feeling faint, you could easily have become disorientated. Perhaps they'll call you a doctor who will simply diagnose tiredness. You—you haven't been having strange thoughts have you?"

"Strange thoughts? No? What do you mean?"

"Oh I don't know, anything out of the ordinary I suppose. How about that ghost hedge man? How are you feeling about that?"

"What? Oh gosh that was nothing, nothing at all. It really doesn't worry me in the slightest."

"I asked a gardener on your behalf, whether he'd seen a tramp or the like. He said he had noticed signs of unusual disruption in the part of the hedge in question. So, at least you know it isn't just you. That should be of some comfort?

Also, he's put up some wire so that the garden is safe from further intruders—you don't need to worry about it you see."

She looked at Gabriel, unable, even in her disorientation, to disguise her irritation at his meddling. His gallant attempts to help her. He was looking ahead, however, and did not notice.

"Oh I wasn't worried, but—but thank you. That's very kind of you to investigate and sort it out."

"You do know, Edith, that you can tell me anything? Anything at all?"

"Yes, thank you Gabriel. You've told me so before."

"I just want you to feel you can trust me, that's all. You did when we were little I'm sure."

"Nothing's changed Gabriel." She spoke the truth, because she never *had* fully trusted him, however cruel that made her feel. It was not exactly that she *did not* trust him, but that she knew he was unable to keep his mouth shut. If, when they were five years old, she had told him a little secret about the fairies, he could not help but burst forth the information to anyone or thing within the next few hours. Perhaps this was just something about little boys. Nevertheless, she had never quite got over it.

"Alright—well, here's Charles. Hallo! Charles, hallo there! I've found her."

What, Edith wondered, did Gabriel and Charles mean when they said 'her'? Of course, they were referring to her. But what unwritten, or unarticulated, facets were being attributed to this word? What secondary thoughts were attached to this word, that passed unsaid through the air as one spoke, and the other heard, this word 'her' as it related to her person? She shivered. Something about it made her shiver.

"Ah thank goodness," she could hear Charles say as he made his way through bracken. "Are you alright Miss Edith?"

"Yes thank you, I'm fine."

"She's a little shaken, that's all, Charles. Let's get her back as quickly as possible."

"Of course sir, the car is really not too far. I stopped it in the same place that Miss Edith got out," he looked at the girl questioningly, not wanting to prod for explanations too explicitly.

"Don't ask now, Charles. She got lost but managed to make her way back in the right direction. She probably would've got back onto the road without our help soon enough."

"I'm glad you found me, really. I'm so sorry for the trouble, Charles."

"Not at all, not at all. Let's just get you back."

In the car they sat in silence. Charles moved his head slightly to the left or right, mimicking the movement of the wheel, as was his habit. Edith sat looking straight ahead, trying very hard not to think at all. Gabriel spent the ten-minute journey trying to control his expression of concern as he looked alternately out the window and at Edith's pensive profile beside him.

When they drove up the drive and Gabriel took Edith to the front door, George, who was standing outside, let out a whistle of relief. The musicality of such an emission coming from so demur a butler made Edith smile, such that she felt once again connected to the solidity of the real world. George hurriedly suppressed his instantaneously raised eyebrows, shocked as he himself was to have momentarily lost his self-control. Were butlers meant to express such relief, musically?

"Christ Edith!" exclaimed Mr Norton when she entered hall. She had interrupted his pacing. "You had your mother worried half to death. What on earth happened?"

"I … I'm awfully sorry, father …" Edith had always considered herself articulate, but here she was lost for words. She could not think of any plausible combination of words to present a rational explanation for her completely irrational behaviour.

"I beg your pardon Mr Norton—I think Edith is rather shocked. I'm sure she'll be able to explain everything after a rest. It looks to me as though she might have caught something."

"Well! Alright, make an appearance to your mother and then go to your room. We'll speak later," David Norton wrung his hands, and then stepped over to the servants' corridor. "Mari! Mari, take Edith to Lady Norton and then to bed."

Lady Helena Norton was taking the opportunity, in this sudden catastrophe, to lounge on her green velvet chaise-lounge. She had Ana applying cool flannels to her forehead and the bored garden boy James rhythmically fanning her. Shaken though Edith still felt, the absurd sight, reminiscent of a scene from a Sheridan play, forced her second smile.

The appearance of her daughter only seemed to disappoint Lady Norton; the look of distaste which crossed her face when Edith stepped forward would not be something Edith would forget in a hurry. She knew it was not simply disappointment that the drama had come to an end (she could still play it out anyhow); it was a much fuller disappointment. It was as though she felt her daughter, in her subnormal waywardness, was purposely trying to reveal a fault in the mother; as though she was intentionally becoming the Family Disgrace.

She sighed a deep, laboured sigh, and turned her head wearily back towards the inside of the chaise-lounge, signalling that Edith could leave.

Mari, who had observed all this, said to Edith, "Your mother has been very worried about you. I think she hardly knows how to express her relief that you are back safe."

"Thank you Mari, I'm very tired."

"I'm sure you are. It was only a couple of hours, but the way we were presented with it has made us all relieved that you're back."

"Thank you Mari."

Gabriel had stayed with Mr Norton who had resumed his pacing.

"Why would she do this at such a time? What on earth made her do it?"

"I think she doesn't feel very well, Mr Norton."

"Just call me David now, will you?"

"David."

"Why would she do this?" he repeated. He paused in his pacing. "You do know your father's plans?"

"He wants our marriage to take place as soon as possible; as soon as I have turned twenty-one."

"Yes. Yes. Four or five months. Gabriel, I don't think your father will look too kindly on all of this."

"What do you mean? She was only gone a couple of hours. It is not all that uncommon people being taken ill."

"Taken ill? But in what sense?" he resumed his pacing. "I don't think you realise that this is not the first thing Edith has done out of the ordinary. I did not notice anything, but your mother has overheard the servants—this is not the first of odd things."

"What do you mean?" Gabriel repeated.

"I don't want to go into any details, Gabriel. I hardly know them myself. But I hardly think this bodes well for our family."

"If it affects your family, it'll affect mine too. We'll work something out. In any case, I'm sure there is absolutely nothing wrong with Edith that won't sort itself out in a few weeks."

"Ha! I envy your confidence. I'm afraid you'll be fine, yes Gabriel, you will be fine. Your parents can quite easily find you another wife to fulfil your relative's strange will."

"If they were going to find me another wife, I think they would have done so already."

"Yes, we had an agreement. But agreements only go so far … Gosh! Don't tell your father we had this conversation, I fear I've said too much."

"Don't worry, Mr Norton," (he could not get his head round picturing this figure as a David) he said. "I think you should call a doctor for Edith."

"A doctor? You really think so?"

"Yes, she ran out of the car because she felt very unwell. You should get your doctor."

"Pah!" he said under his breath as Gabriel went back towards the front door. "The amount that child costs me is obscene!"

VI

That night Edith could not sleep. She tried and tried to deal with the turmoil in her mind. It was as if she was picking at the strands of a tangled ball of string, but her hands were too tired to stay on the ball long enough to disentangle it. She did not even know what the actual knotted ball looked like; she did not even know what her problem was.

She looked out of her window. It was true what people said about the moon, that it appeared sorrowful, looking down on the world from which it was said to have been created.

None of it mattered in the eyes of the moon.

And the stars were so bright.

It was incredible; a concept, she thought, which could never quite be grasped, that the light from these stars had taken millions of years to reach her, standing here. And there had been so many before her who, too, had looked upon these stars. And, at some point, she would be part of the many before who had looked upon these suns.

Eventually, dawn came. The watery light shone through the window, forming elongated squares across her room. Before, she might have opened her eyes in astonishment at this wonder cast on her very floor. She might have put her hand in the path of one of these pale rays of light and felt the privilege of being part of this sun and world. She might have noted the similarity of the patterns with those made by the woodland trees or by the village church windows. But now the frames which cast the shadows, cutting up the sun's path, seemed to bear more comparison to the bars of a prison or strong wire cage.

Mari came and helped her dress, before walking with her downstairs to the breakfast room where her mother and father already sat. Edith looked around the room which, for the first time, seemed to her almost unbearably formal and unfamiliar. It was a relatively small room, in contrast to the other rooms of the house, and should have been cosier; but, like the dining room, its length was greater than its width, and the corridor-like effect of this suddenly made it feel cold and impersonal. She was shocked that she had never noticed this before, and felt as though the room was full of things she had never really seen.

There were four of the tall, arched Georgian windows as opposed to the dining room's seven. On the other side of the room, to the right as one walked in through the high oak doors, there was a row of portraits with eyes peering out towards the opposite windows. Each stern yet frivolous face resembled, in some way, her mother whose house this really belonged, despite her father's assertions. This room was also the only room without a fire, and so the idea it should have been cosier than the other rooms was quite absurd. Instead of where the fire should have been, there was a giant chest of draws made from polished cherry wood with gold handles. On top was an eighteenth-century Japanese pot of an aesthetically satisfying shape, partly resembling the pleasing curves of a violin, with rich blue dragons and blossom trees painted on its white porcelain. Next to this chest of drawers was a glass crockery cabinet that had for a long time past, it must be admitted, appeared to Edith too similar in shape to a double coffin. The plates inside were not pleasant either. On the window side of the room there were three Georgian chairs, placed against the wall between each of the windows, with big blue-clothed seats, long arms and short legs.

A Persian rug lay on the oak floor, running almost the length of the room, forming a path to the round breakfast table which stood upon its very end. Behind this table was a long, narrow table which stood up against the wall opposite the entrance. On it were three oval chafing dishes of polished silver. Edith walked along the carpet and around the table, nodding at her mother as she passed and got herself smoked mackerel and scrambled egg.

"Good morning Edith, sleep well?" Lady Norton asked her daughter as she sat and picked up her fork. She spoke as though they had been the closest of friends all her life. There was something slightly sinister in the change of character; from expiring on the green chaise-lounge and expressing deep disappointment, to this casual display of familial warmth. But the room was cold. Perhaps it was simply Edith, rather than the world, to whom something had happened; perhaps she was noticing, for the first time, things that had always been there.

She was hit by a sudden thought, almost a panic: could it have been that her brief slumber in the middle of the forest had been an irreversible process of transition, into which she had fallen from one side of reality, and awoken on the other?

"Your father wants to speak with you in the drawing room once you've finished breakfast."

Edith was not very hungry and it was not long before she and her mother went through to the drawing room where, to Edith's dismay, a fire had been lit. She had been freezing at breakfast, yet here she was roasting. Everything, all the furniture, ornaments and carpets, all that she had grown up with, seemed sickly. The feeling of suffocation was so strong that she thought she might be physically sick.

"So," began Mr Norton. "You have not told your mother or I where you ran off to yesterday. Not only were we concerned about your own welfare, but also how we were to justify the event for Lord Loehill. Not to mention what the gossip would have done. You did not think, I hope, that your actions would be accepted without explanation?"

"No—"

"Please *don't* interrupt! I really don't think you quite *understand* the consequences of your actions. I don't think you quite understand how *significant* your position in society is; how much people *observe* every move you make. You cannot *do* whatever you like, as some people can. You have *responsibilities*, and it's high time you learnt what those were and *acted* on them.

"Now, I *don't* actually want to hear why you ran off

yesterday. Gabriel said you were unwell, but you don't seem so unwell this morning, so I *don't* see the need for a doctor. Lord Loehill, however, might seek an explanation, as your future father-in-law. They *already* disapprove of your absurd commitment to music—it is one thing to play the piano, that is fine and good, but to go and *teach* in the village! No, no, *please* don't interrupt Helena. Your mother and I have put up with it because, of course, your happiness *is* our priority. Yet we *cannot* let this mar your position—we have to think of your *long*-term happiness and well-being *too*, something that you will not be able to *see* at your age. It is indeed a responsibility, *yes*, for those of our status to help the people, to maintain their *respect*. But you really have taken this *too* far, to the point that it is *disrespectful*."

"Yes, Edith," her mother took the opportunity to speak. She spoke smoothly, without the hard arrhythmic staccatos of her husband. "I've heard the comments among the villagers. Our servants wouldn't think of saying anything, but surely you must have realised how patronising they all feel it when you involve yourself too much. The villagers gossip about our negligence; they talk about how wayward you seem to be becoming as you approach womanhood."

"Thank you Helena," David Norton said turning from his wife to his daughter. "Yesterday your mother made me aware of something she has apparently known for weeks. She heard within the servants' quarters of your night-time wanderings and how you have returned, several times, with a *mud-stained* nightdress. I cannot stress enough how much this pains me. What, *what* have you been doing?"

Edith was about to speak but she was again cut off.

"No, no. I don't want to know. It does not bode well," he said shaking his head at her and then at the floor. His staccato speech returned. "It does not bode well *at all*. I'm going to have to pressure Albert into thinking you're still worth his while as a daughter-in-law. It's been four years, you realise, that you've behaved absurdly—not all the time, but on occasion since you were twelve. I hadn't noticed this at all until *Albert* came here last night to *question* me— he's noticed! He's been a keen observer, you see. He's been ensuring the arrangement is fair. You realise the gravity of the situation—he came here *last night*? And, what's more, he's coming to speak to you *today*?"

"I'm sorry, father. What do you mean?"

"What *do* I mean! I *mean* he's had enough of everything floating one way or the other. I *mean* he wants certainty—a final decision!"

"A final decision?"

"Oh don't act oblivious! You have always been aware of your future marriage! In three months' time, you will be seventeen; capable of making your own decisions, but needing a guiding hand with the more vital choices of life. We believe and always have, that Gabriel will be the perfect husband for you. As such, whatever age you are when you marry him, the outcome will be exactly the same and so time and place will not matter." (It would be pointless to print the staccato stresses here, since he spat every one of them.)

Edith had of course been prepared for this conversation by Gabriel, but she wanted to push it whole from her parents.

"I can't marry until I'm twenty-one, if that's what you're saying? You've always said that."

"That is precisely what I'm getting at Edith. It doesn't matter what age you are, since your happiness in marriage to Gabriel is inevitable at whatever time. Why the wait? Lord Loehill wants you to be married as soon as Gabriel is twenty-one, so what's the difference that you are seventeen and not twenty-one?"

"In short, in five months you will be Lady Loehill. Are you not excited, my dear?" Lady Norton interrupted her husband.

"I'm still not sure I quite understand … you've made this decision for me?"

"Well, you've known about the unofficial decision most of your life, there's no change there. And as I just said— some decisions require a helping hand. We cannot burden you with such a life-affecting choice."

"But I will be burdened my whole life with *your* decision instead."

"You are not pleased with our decision?" her mother asked.

"Pleased?" the suffocating sickliness of the room was suddenly replaced with an air of sinister maliciousness. It seemed odd to her that in all these years—all these years where this impending marriage had guided every aspect of her life—this was the first time her parents had spoken to her about it. Everything had pointed towards it: all her lessons, clothes, activities. Her life had been unquestionably dedicated to this one thing, until, about four years ago, she had given what there was of herself to music. Finally, then, marriage had become trivia, and her world had found a new core. But now here were her parents specifically making her aware of this fact *as fact* for the first time. Here were her mother and father attempting to throw her carefully self-formulated world off orbit. "I am not prepared to marry. You've never asked me."

Her father was silent.

"But you are fond of Gabriel?" her mother asked. Why was it, the girl wondered, that they were bothering to do this act of parental responsibility, apparently placing her happiness first?

"No. I won't say I dislike him but I am not fond of him. I am sorry, you will have to tell Lord Loehill that I refuse."

"You refuse?"

"Silence!" her father raised his voice over his wife. "You do not have such a say in the matter. I don't know why we are *bothering* to be so kind; this has been the problem all along. We've spoiled you! What more could you ask for anyway? You will have a name, land and wealth."

"Why not tell her, David?"

"I will—she'll soon realise her selfishness. You—you do not want to see us in a cottage, a cottage with one cook and maid—or worse, with your mother having to cook. It's about time you think of the others around you. Of the lives you will be affecting. Now, you will tell Lord Loehill that you give your consent. We have given ours. They have given theirs. Gabriel will be giving his. Do not think you can change it. You will answer—"

At just this moment, as if on cue, there was a knock at the door and Lord Albert Loehill entered the room with his wife.

"Hello, hello, good morning," he said hurriedly, without awaiting greeting. "So. I want to settle everything once and for all. I have, you realise, been worried on more than one account by recent events. Helena, David, you have given us your decision and assured us of your daughter's agreement. So, cutting to the chase—Edith: will you marry my son?"

"No. I'm sorry."

"Why, he displeases you? You don't like him, you don't like Gabriel, you don't like my son? Why?"

"No, no it is not that."

"You prefer someone else?"

"No, it's not that. I'm sorry. And … and I do like and admire Gabriel, do not misunderstand me, but I simply can't marry him. Again, I'm sorry, it will not work." Edith was confused by Lord Loehill's calmness, it almost seemed he did not really care, that he was a bit of an automaton (though she had always thought that anyway).

"You cannot give me a reason? What would you have me tell Gabriel?"

"What would I have you tell Gabriel? Well, why have you come? Surely it should be him here asking, and then I would tell him directly."

Lord Loehill raised an eyebrow (the first sign of expression) and turned to Mr Norton. "David, what is this?" he asked, but turned back to Edith before her father could respond.

"It is my understanding, Edith, that he has already spoken to you. It is not news to you in any case."

"Have you asked Gabriel if he has had a response from me? If so, why was it necessary for you to come and ask me again?"

"Edith! I'm shocked! How dare you speak like that! Apologise at once!" Lady Norton exclaimed, practically spitting.

"You know what this is, David, don't you?" he said still looking at Edith, now with an expression of mild amusement. "It's that damn music! You've been so very lenient, letting her take the piano much too far. It's gone to her head. It would happen to the best of us, but the soft and susceptible brain of a woman is especially vulnerable." He got up to leave. "There's no one to blame but yourselves I'm afraid. There's nothing you can do with a stubborn young woman, not a chance. It's over, I'm sorry David. I kept our agreement as far as I could."

Mr Norton ran forward, holding Lord Loehill's shoulders in unashamed desperation. Edith saw then that prominence in society was not all that her parents wanted, nor was it to compensate for the lack of a son. Just like Gabriel's family, her parents were bankrupt. Always money. What he had said about a cottage and limited servants was not figurative, they really were desperate. Perhaps the girl was selfish, because the only thought which passed through her mind, accompanied by a small wave of apprehension, was where she would go with poverty-stricken furious parents. What exactly was she getting herself into? She felt sick. It was so much easier not to think, not to think at all.

"Albert, please," said Mr Norton. "She doesn't know what she is saying, we all know there is no reason for her to say no when she and Gabriel are so perfect for each other. It is only that she is so young; she thought she would have more time and the prospect is a little daunting."

"If she is too young, then that is just too bad. We have

already waited too long, the marriage must take place as soon as possible. I believe Edith is old enough to speak her own mind (she clearly thinks so anyway), and if she has chosen, after all these years, not to marry our son, we must get to work and find a daughter-in-law. Believe me—we will not have to look far. There are reams of young and respectable women longing for Gabriel to ask their hand. So," he took David's hand from his shoulder and held it in both of his. "For your sake, and for old time's sake, I'll ask once more. Edith, this is your last chance. Will you or will you not take it, if not for your own sake, for the sake of your parents?"

"She will," said both the girl's parents at the same time.

"Please, let Edith. After all, you cannot say the 'I do'."

"I'm sorry, really I am," Edith's voice sounded so distant and sickly, even to herself. "I cannot help my belief that marriage is far too sacred to be agreed to for anyone else's sake. And since I can't agree to it for myself, I can't agree to it for my parents."

"There you have it friends. Too many books, too much music. Come Harriet, let's go—we'll be organising our last party tonight."

"Oh please reconsider, Albert. Come tomorrow," Lady Norton pleaded from the green chaise-lounge.

"I have considered quite enough over the last couple of months, your daughter going around the place as if the weight of the whole world rested upon her delicate shoulders. Well, it doesn't, and she has been offered everything and refused it. As I said, it is your fault she is spoilt. She doesn't begin to comprehend the privilege … anyway, that is enough, we must be going. And again, rest assured it will not take long to find a young lady willing to marry my son and gain a title, land and wealth."

They made a speedy departure and the room was drowned in sickly silence.

It seemed her parents were not at all averse to spitting their words at their daughter, as Mr Norton did just now, as his wife had done only a little earlier.

"You will go to your room. You'll think about your future, a future with no money and no family," he walked to the door which was still open. "Because, mark my words— unless you write to Lord Loehill before tomorrow night, expressing your deepest apologies and change of heart, you are no daughter of mine. If you are proud enough to reject our decisions, you are proud enough to reject us in entirety."

He left the room and her mother followed without a word, shaking her head in disgust.

Edith remained seated for a few minutes, trying to focus, but her brain was still made up of that tangled ball of string. To her, it seemed that this whole marriage, family business, was an unimportant side-plot to something of far greater value, but she simply could not work out what this something was. The trivia of money, family and prestige had too great a hold on her life. It had been pummelled into her thoughts for so long that even when, about four years ago she had pushed it aside with music, she had not removed it, only mindlessly distracted herself, only left it to stagnate. Mindlessness to the point of distracting herself from being distracted, from distraction. The weight and claustrophobia of trivia had followed her everywhere and she had never known what to call it. Music, art, literature—they had given her some peace of mind, some shadowy reassurance, but only in as much as they were abstractions, not thoughts in their own right. Now, for the first time, she was consciously aware of that very shadow trying to emerge, trying to prove itself the more substantial. But she did not have the strength even to name it, and so it remained an obscure shadow.

Thinking in this cloudy and disappointing way, she could only reach for this same mindlessness that had provided relief before. To read, to think, to focus on words; to try to immerse herself in the minds and worlds of others, would not work. To press down hard upon the keys of a piano, to be surrounded by sound outside oneself but being created by oneself—this would work.

She walked out of the sitting room, into the hall, and out the front door. She made her way along the familiar route to the village to the vicarage and their piano.

Mr Norton had given his daughter until the following night to sort herself out. He thought that would be safe; Albert would probably not have found a replacement in such a short space of time. They did not, however, need to wait long for a change to indeed take place, because that same evening Lord Loehill came back to their house. Edith had by this time returned from the vicarage and stayed the rest of the day in her room, unnoticed. And her helpful maid, Mari, had listened in at the sitting room door to this second coming of Gabriel's father. She did not fear being dismissed for putting her ear to the keyhole, since she was well aware that her dismissal was inevitable as soon as Edith left the house, if not because of times being as they were.

Shortly, with a little smile on her face, Mari went to tell Edith what she had heard. Apparently, Gabriel had been told she was no longer appropriate. He had been told that, as evinced by running from the car, there was something not at all right about her. They started their search for replacement suitors, drawing up the guest list for their 'last party', but Gabriel refused. He had left his parents no choice but to return and explain the awkward situation. There was nothing to describe the embarrassment in Lord Loehill's usually expressionless voice as he explained to her parents how terribly distressed Gabriel was, adamant that the fault lay with him and not Edith.

"Oh, Gabriel, the fool," Edith could not help but exclaim when Mari had finished. To tell the truth, she was surprised, more than anything, that he could be so independently strong-willed. She had never thought he had it in him.

It was strange, even to her, how far she did not have any particular feelings towards Gabriel—he just seemed very average and rather dull. When they were little, they had played together. There had been no sense of dislike; she had never judged him or thought him stupid or boring. It was only when she was a bit older that his slow and terribly careful ways suddenly became aggravating in the extreme. Then when he began doting on her, hanging on her every word, eyeing her with puppy-like eyes, her irritation intensified. And all of a sudden, not so long ago, her extreme irritation had simply disappeared to be replaced by indifference. This did not mean she wished to cause him pain, and she did find it troubling that she was unintentionally hurting him. His pain, though, ensured her a measure of power, of freedom, for the time being.

She could not think of any uncompromising solution. Something was missing from her life, she knew, and perhaps this stalling situation gave her the time to find it. This missing thing, this painfully present absence, was whatever was necessary to substantiate the obscured shadow in her mind. If the shadow could be focused upon, rather than simply pointed towards in abstraction, perhaps a solution would become apparent. Well, as things stood, she did not feel she had much choice but to continue following her instincts—the same instincts that had made it impossible for her to accept Gabriel.

Thoughts of shadows made her think of the lake, the purple velvet lake that had almost drowned her in her sleep. So—what colour were his eyes? She could not remember. It was tragic, but she could only conjure the vaguest image of that reassuring presence, and, the more she tried to recall, the fainter his image grew. His eyes were the least clear: a blur with only the dark lines of his lashes in focus. Perhaps it was not possible for her limited brain to capture the face of a god.

As Edith was falling asleep early that night, she tried to imagine, invent, the colour of this blur. The magical blue of a lake at dawn, the deep and dark blue of a silky night pricked with trillions of stars. Then the rich blue of a mid-day Mediterranean sky and sea, resembling the splendour of a stained glass window, sunlight shining through each piece, throwing their dancing colour onto old and worn cathedral slabs. Or were they not the soft brown of chestnuts or the golden hazel-brown of the majestic oaks, radiant in the path of the late afternoon sun? Or green? A most beautiful and vivid green like the dark of a leaf's underneath, or the light of a loving cat's? Otherwise his eyes were grey. No … Yes. Oh yes! They were grey! That powerful and stunning, most attractive grey of a thunderous storm cloud in April. And that was the gold, she recalled! The gold of the late sun glowing upon and behind those great clouds. Oh why was grey associated with dullness?

Sitting up in bed, she looked out of the window. It was still shade-filled evening outside and the dark line of the distant trees grabbed her attention. They were covered in a wispy, pale light which seemed to cling to the cold of winter as it pondered the summer question, creating about it an air of uncertainty. Those distant trees appeared to represent a beautiful and peaceful freedom; a place to escape all the world. It was incredible; when she closed her eyes for a brief second she could see herself looking up at the tall trees on the forest boundary and seeing them in a totally new way—a symbol of the edge of the world.

And they called to her. The leaves whispered her name and the last circulating birds waited to welcome her. Never before had she felt such a deep yearning. It began as a tight sphere in the middle of her chest and grew, like a dying star, expanding and expanding, drawing together all the feeling inside her until it become so big, and of such an incomprehensible density, that she was quite powerless. Then, without knowing it, without any conscious command for her legs to move, she was by the window and climbing out of it down the vine branches, still staring off into that distant horizon.

VII

There was one small cottage on Fleet Street that the local people knew nothing about. Fleet Street was one of twelve streets in the smallest district of the port, which could not itself be considered large. As the smallest district, it was well-known for its community-mindedness and conviviality, and this made the mysteries of No.6 Fleet Street all the more apparent and difficult for the locals to swallow. Along with all the other cottages along this street, it directly faced the estuary, and was heavily abused by the weather as a result. Yet, somehow, No.6 was the only one of the lot who did not bear this wear with jolly dignity. It seemed to present itself with such heavy misery that passers-by could not help but give a little shudder as they walked past its worn grey front.

It was known that there was a woman who lived inside, and there had been rare glimpses of two boys, presumably her children. But there was no sign of a father, and the house had been mysterious long enough that the current inhabitants must at least have been there since the children were born. No one could guess how they survived, since they probably only saw the woman outside the cottage once a month; they were never seen buying food or working or talking. She did not go to church with the rest of the congregation, and the local officials claimed they knew nothing more than anybody else. The only story came from one of the policeman's cousins, Phips, from another port not far from there, and that involved a murder, many unanswered questions and ancient superstitions. Apparently, the woman's name was on his police records, but most of them had been filed away under 'X' and the case dismissed as a sad event of Phip's youth.

This unsatisfactory story only encouraged other stories to be invented, usually around the fire on a dark November night, about the woman's misdeeds and her devilish children. Some people even suggested that all three of them were ghosts, while the more creative-minded thought it more likely that the mother was real, but was haunted by her two children, who had drowned with their father many years ago; the living mother's grief was so strong that the ghosts of her children could even be glimpsed by others. That solved the problem of the story being irritatingly recent (legends were supposed to be at least before great-grandparents). This version, as with every other, was debated, the rationally-minded claiming this would not work at all, since the children were certainly growing older with each sighting. The officials had the children registered as educated privately, and the documentation was supposedly all valid.

Whatever the truth of the situation (and the most

boring assumption was simply that she was a 'wronged' woman who had run off with her illegitimate children), it could not be denied that no one would have felt comfortable knocking on the door of No.6. Reports from the Harrisons of No.5 of unnatural noises were not even investigated by the officials and speedily dismissed as nonsense, since none of them would ever approach that forbidding door. To be fair to these officials, when they did try to get more from the Harrisons, asking them whether these 'unnatural noises' were loud or unpleasant, they received varying responses, and none of them were average noise complaints. Mrs Harrison said it was like church singing, frequently cut by a despairing scream. Agatha agreed with her mother, but added that the screaming had been getting less over the years, and that soft sobbing was more common now. Jonathan thought it sounded more like gypsy guitar playing, and was hypnotically haunting in that foreign way. Harry was convinced it was lullabies which penetrated his bedroom wall, interrupted every so often by the woman shouting hysterically. And Mr Harrison could not decide whether it was more like tolling bells or sinister organ. In this way, had the police wanted to, it would have been quite difficult to file a coherent official report.

Every day, from dusk until midnight, a small flame from a single candle shone from the bottom right window of this cottage. This, other than being proof that the place was indeed permanently inhabited, was more than a little curious and unnerving. No other light was seen from the cottage, and smoke never came through the chimney. The flame in the pit of the mysterious darkness was reminiscent of a sanctuary lamp minus its promise. Holy or sinister. It could not be decided. But since people are often more intrigued by the threatening possibilities of darkness, so long as it does not thoroughly involve them, it was pronounced sinister.

In this port of very little action, where even the main newspaper consisted of articles on fallen branches, the appalling state of that road off London Street with all the potholes, and updates on the condition of the eight-year-old who fell off their bike and grazed their knee, it was immediately noted when, for the first night in remembered history, the candle of No.6 was not lit. The sun had set an hour before Mr Harrison walked past on his way back from work, and he had to do a double-take to ensure he had not been mistaken: this would be big news. During this speedy double-take, Mr Harrison noticed something else peculiar. On the doorstep, blocking any entrance or exit, were no less than eight crates of pink lady apples. He hurried on to his front door and leapt in to tell Mrs Harrison. Not a sound was heard from No.6 that night, and in the morning all the crates were gone.

The people of the port liked to think that they were no longer superstitious, that they were adapting well to These Modern Times. However, because a series of awful events occurred after this day, and because it so happened that the very night before a massive purple storm had left several houses roofless and destroyed many fishing boats, the unlit candle and eight crates of apples were forever thereafter recounted as an ill omen. The first such hideous event was the beginning of Agatha Harrison's incurable and undiagnosed illness which was to cut her life miserably short: not three weeks later, before the institution could come and take her away, she was found lifeless in front of her mirror in the despairing pose of the dying swan.

It is unfair for an outsider to remain any longer in the confusion of all these people. It is, however, difficult, of course, to get inside the cottage, when there is no one from the outside who ever went in. As always, stories are pieced together by fragments; they might only flow through speculation.

In the corner of the room which usually held the single candle, a young boy sat holding his knees tightly to his chest. At the simple, rectangular table, his mother sat opposite his brother who claimed head of the table. She was shaking her head. "What have I done, what have I done?" she repeated, more to herself than either of her sons.

As the last remnants of dusk followed the sun into darkness, the brother at the table threw back his head and laughed in a manner not dissimilar to Don Giovanni. Its echoes seemed to push the already-disappearing shadows still further.

"What did you think Mother? What did you think I would do?" he said, his mouth still curved in the smile of the cruellest of cats.

"What have I done, what have I done?" she continued repeating.

"You thought I'd refuse? Thought I'd be like *him*?" he said momentarily losing his grin to curl his lip at his brother in the corner. "Thought I'd come up weak like him?"

"What have I done, what have I done?"

"Mother, that tiresome background recitative is really unnecessary. Though it has always been your motif hasn't it?" he threw back his head to laugh again. "No harm in varying it a little."

"What have I done, what have I done?"

"So Mother, how long do you think it'll take? How long 'til I'm of equal power to father?"

"What have I done? How has my body borne that of the devil?"

"Ha! There! You vary it! Well, Mother, you should be proud to have borne such powerful children—sorry, I mean to say *child*. He, *he* is an insult to father. Disgusting."

"If I have created it, how can I not destroy it?"

"Ah ha ha ha! Mother, how you make me laugh! But I'll pretend you didn't say that; it's not very kind. Where are your maternal instincts?"

"God! Oh God! What *have* I done?"

"Well Mother? Can you hear me at all?"

"I loved him so much, so dreadfully much," she cried, still shaking her head. "No one could possibly know how deeply I loved him. I loved him so much."

"We know what happened Mother. But you did it, you made a deal with the Decomposer. And aren't you proud that he remembered us, that he came back?"

"He wasn't supposed to be your father! Your father is at the bottom of the canal, through no fault of mine or his, through no fault but God! *He* did that, *he* did that to *me*, to *us*! Who else was there to turn to?"

"I'm not blaming you, Mother; I'm not blaming you at all. I'm having a civilised chat. You should be proud, you should be proud that though *you* have been given no power, it is *you* who has created *us*. And our father has chosen *us* to be his mirror mouthpieces here to draw everything he needs and deserves from this pitiful realm of humanity."

"The Devil is not your father! He was not supposed to be! He should never have been here."

"Just because he was not supposed to be our father, doesn't mean he isn't. Ah ha ha ha! I'm pleased to say he certainly agrees that we are his. But would you please stop calling him 'devil', it's so very tedious. We are the children of the Decomposer, and you are our mother. You cannot keep denying that responsibility. You begged him to give you the children you might have had with *your* man who lay at the bottom of the canal, 'our father'. The Decomposer answered your pleas—I see in your eyes how much we resemble your lover, but it is the Decomposer who is our father. A mirror was merely held up to your dead lover, and his features imprinted on ours—the Decomposer did as you asked."

"Responsibility! Do I not wake every morning aware of my crime of responsibility? The weight pressed upon my forehead like an iced towel?"

"Ah ha ha ha!"

"If I did think in that moment, in that instant I gave up to beg the Decomposer, did I ever think anything existed, anything at all? Did I think there was a 'god' figure of *any* sort? Did I even think I existed? Did I think the world was there beneath my feet? Did I ask for the devil?"

"You're talking to yourself again Mother. You must stop, or people will think you're mad—they'll take us away from you. Ah ha ha ha!"

The woman looked up at the beautiful angelic face of her son, which shone dusty silver as the half-moon outside chose a place of reflection in the room's darkness. How was his flesh made of hers? Like the flashing glint of a small shard of glass, she caught the veiled, sharp fragment of his attractive, seemingly soft, grey eyes. This fragment was nothing human; it was a black hole, not only dead to feeling, to life's songs, but magnetic in sucking out other people's lives, their songs.

"So, we were supposed to be mirrors. Mirrors being the two-faced illusion dividing dimensions; the simplest means to communicate between the Songbirds' veiled realms and here. Humans spend their lives searching and searching for something so very close, how deaf they are! Mirrors and song. Well. How hilarious! Don't you think? We were created by the Decomposer holding his mirror to your dead lover, but he also created the two of us *to be mirrors*. Ah ha ha ha! But he, my mirror, and the Decomposer's mirror on earth—pah!" her son was saying, again motioning towards his twin in the corner with disgust.

"My significance, my power, it will never cease to amaze me! Our father, the Decomposer, is so very clever. Don't you think Mother? Ah ha ha ha! All these humans would simply die should the Decomposer come down now, as he is, and their songs would vanish with them, reabsorbed by the Composer," he gagged theatrically. "But with us as his mirrors, his mouthpieces, we can do his work for him, we can gather people for him without them dying before we get to them! It would have been quicker had *this brother*, this *son of yours*, been my true mirror, because we could have faced each other, and our double reflections of the Decomposer reflect his power from earth immediately back to him. Well, now look! He has only had to turn the mirror round in my favour. Now, he is no longer our father's mirror. And yet he is, since he is still *my* mirror, but *I* am the one with *all* the power! Oh! It is marvellous, I shall crush so many people's songs, I shall gather so many for Father! Ah ha ha ha!"

The woman felt such a wave of hatred towards her own creation; she thought she was going to be sick. That would be rather anticlimactic.

"Did you not hear what Father said? I'm his only son now! But my dear brother cannot even go running to the Composer, he's forever in *my* grasp! Ha! Did you hear him, Mother? 'You were both my mirrors, and reflections to each other—a mirror to a mirror has all the more potential. You, my sound. You, my silence,' he said pointing to each of us in turn. 'Well,' Father said as he turned again to my brother. 'Now your gift will be your curse! You will be forever silent, trapped on the other side of the mirror you make with your brother. You will no longer be my mirror, but you'll remain your brother's reflection—you'll have nothing but him to hold you to your life!' Mirrors, mirror, mirrors, oh hilarity! Humans cannot cope with anything direct! They have *no* directness, it's insane! Ah ha ha ha!"

Tears ran down the woman's face, though she was not very much aware of them. Her son at the table turned to his twin in the corner.

"Well brother. You should have accepted father's deal. I haven't a clue why you didn't, except out of fear. Now if I'm destroyed, you are too; you bear no other reflection than to me. Like me, not created by the Composer, you still have no song of your own. You'll be trapped in your silence, the silence that would have given you such loud power! Why did you do it? You won't be able to speak to the Composer, and he wouldn't deem to help you if you could, and you can't speak to a single human. Oh it's tragic, brother! Hilarious! Oh Mother, you're crying, ha ha!" He threw back his head.

"My son," the woman said.

"Oh!" said the boy at the end of the table. "Now you call me son!"

"You'll never do it, you know. You'll never succeed."

"Ah ha ha ha! You don't have much faith in me, do you Mother; not as much faith as you had in Father that miserable night your lover drowned! Ah ha ha ha!"

And suddenly the woman was running at her son, running across the table like a gargoyle, screaming hideously, her fingers like claws at his throat and eyes. The boy was so shocked that his cat grin completely disappeared, and there was the smallest look of terror in his soft, attractive grey eyes. But just then the front door opened into the room, and a crate of apples were thrown by a gale force wind towards the table, the apples rolling on the floor and flying through the air, threatening like cannon balls.

The boy's terror left his eyes the instant it had appeared, and he grabbed hold of his mother's throat.

"Trying to kill me Mother? Hey?"

"Kill me now! Kill me now, I beg you!"

"Kill you? Now why would I do that Mother? You are my mother after all. Though you seem to forget."

"Please! Just kill me, I beg you! I cannot!"

"Cannot what? Hey? No, Mother, to kill you would ruin my fun."

She screamed, trying to destroy those beautiful grey eyes, the very imitation of her lover's. Her nails were long enough to scratch her son's mouth, drawing blood from his lips.

"Oh you bitch! You drew blood!"

He put his hand in her mouth to pull her tongue, but his silent brother was all at once on his back, pulling his arms away from their mother.

"Get away!" he screamed, biting the surprisingly strong hands of his mute brother. "Get away!"

Another crate of apples fell into the room, covering the floor, but they were ignored. The still-seated brother lurched out of his brother's grasp and put his hand back in his mother's mouth. Their mother threw her arms about hitting at both of her sons in an insane frenzy.

"You're both his! Take them both! Take them both! Leave me, leave me in my own misery," she shouted, as though to a fourth person in the room. "I deny everything! They were never mine, they're not mine, they're not mine! Take them both!"

She threw herself off the table, and slid on the apples onto her knees. "I can't destroy them."

The woman was indeed talking to a fourth figure, now apparent in his dark green cloak behind the remaining crates of apples at the open door. "Why have you come back? We've kept both sides of our deal; take them from me, I want no more in this," she said gazing at his hooded face from the floor.

"Father? Is that you? Come and take your disowned son from my back. He's trying to kill me!"

The cloaked figure kicked the crates of apples so that they split in one blow, missing the woman in the middle. But he stepped in as though he would trample on her himself, and the disowned son ran and dragged her from his path. She looked up at this son with such hatred, her lip curled, and he looked down at her in terror and mystification. Perhaps the cruel curl of his seated brother's lip did not come from the Decomposer, but from their mother.

He let go of her arm as though it were a heated iron rod. He ran to the now vacant door, avoiding the apples that covered the floor. But at the door, just as he turned back to briefly look at his brother, he realised he could move no further. He was stuck to the spot by his own will; his father, mother and brother had not done anything to keep him there, but he could not move. He was forcing himself to witness what was about to unfold.

His cloaked father, merging with the shadows about his brother, had his hand on his son's shoulder, and was motioning for him to be still and listen. He paused, whispered something in his son's ear, and then motioned for concentration once more. And, at the same time his brother heard it, the boy at the door did too: it was Agatha next door, humming. In a flash, he could somehow see her next door in her white nightdress, sketching by the light of a small lamp, and humming at a point of extreme, almost inexplicable happiness. No one would be able to say why the sketching at this particular point made her so ecstatic—she would not know herself, but there it was. And her whole self at this instant of serene happiness was laid bare, her soul at its strongest and most independent, was exposed.

Like a conductor, his father waved his right arm in the motion of a downbeat, and his brother began singing. The sound made the boy at the door double-up in a pain he could never have known existed, and as he stumbled out of the cottage to escape his brother's *noise*, he knew this was the start of the Decomposer's power. He knew that, what was torturous noise to him, was a honeyed angelic song to everyone else—except to his void mother who had already given all she could to the Decomposer.

Agatha would be the first of his brother's victims, sucked so dry that the mirror would be empty whenever she went to check, and she would go mad at its reflection of her own void self.

He could do nothing in his cursed silence and perhaps blessed pain, not even for his mother. She would be found in No.6 when it was finally searched after Agatha's unexplained death. His brother would by then have moved on, all the more powerful, leaving their mother mad and alone. She would be questioned and taken to an asylum.

The boy walked for miles, avoiding main roads, crying over his cowardice. He should have gone back, but he could not. He found comfort walking through the woods, where the creatures seemed to think him worthy enough to follow. After twelve years of silence to the world other than his mother and brother, it took him a long time to discover he was not a figure of silence to these faithful animals.

On the morning of the third day of his walking, however, he woke with a start to a blackbird sitting on his shoulder.

The blackbird looked at him sideways before gently pecking at the boy's ear and singing merrily. *Composer, Composer.* The bird seemed to be singing. *You'll meet the Composer, Composer, soon enough.* And he realised, astonished, that the bird was indeed singing with this meaning to him, and he could understand. But he could not sing back. *Your silence isn't a curse. It isn't a curse. He'll give you a voice; he'll compose you a life. You'll understand, you'll understand, soon enough.*

Not too long after, the tired and confused boy, weary in the knowledge that he, like his brother, did not have a song composed by the Composer (and therefore technically had no life) to be sung by a Songbird in the hidden mirror realms of the universe, came across a cottage beside a graveyard and round-towered church. If, because he had been written aside by the Decomposer and not the Composer, he had no song and no Songbird to sing it, no Songbird to be the vessel for the movement of his life, would he ever be part of that friendly-looking graveyard? He was a silent being, a lonely figure of suspension, with no supporting counterpart, no bird tying him with the mirror realm. What did that graveyard mean?

He stepped out of the trees, rustling past shrubbery as he did so, and heard someone call out, "Hello! Do you want a hand Mrs Rosamond?" before seeing the kind face belonging to the voice as it looked up from a bush of roses.

VIII

The logical thing would be to make for the lake. So, incredibly, this was how Edith began her search for the god. Having climbed out of the window as the last rays of light slowly dropped behind the most distant trees, the girl walked in the direction of the lake. Apart from her sleep-outings, she had not been there for many years, but the route remained familiar.

In the dim light, the trees seemed luminous and friendly, emitting a pale green haze which seemed to sing joyfully the promise of a plentiful spring. They were accompanied by a chorus of delighted blackbirds and the occasional high-pitch solo of an excited robin. She smiled to herself, feeling much less dazed and becoming more aware of where she was and what she was doing. Understandably, she immediately wanted a return to numbness, because her sharpened senses forced her to drop her smile as a wave of apprehension surged through her stomach. It was all too similar to her run from the car; she did not *really* know why she was here, and had acted on some strong irrational instinct. What on earth was she doing, allowing herself to be so totally guided by shadow-like emotions she did not even have names for? Perhaps, if she did not have names for these emotions, they did not really exist, other than by her own invention. Perhaps the god himself was a shadow of her imagination, an invented character.

It was best not to think, and continue as she had been. She picked up her pace and soon enough there was the lake, the very same purple velvet she had envisaged not more than two hours ago. Standing still a while, she looked about her, slightly out of breath. Here it was, the lapping waves, so peaceful against the bank. Those dark depths she had sunk into asleep. She shuddered.

She looked at all the towering trees with their branches overhanging the water, reflected in their dark, criss-cross way. Was he lurking behind one of these trees, in their shadow? No, lurking was not the right word for a beautiful creature. But quite suddenly her surroundings seemed truly sinister. Even as the word sinister came to mind, the lapping was no longer peaceful but frantic. And the trees really did conceal in their shadows unknown bodies of darkness.

He was here. Surely he was here. She would have to call out to him; he had to reveal himself, even if he wasn't here. He was here.

She felt the terrifying suggestion of one of her smothering panic surges, and had no idea how to prevent it. What was wrong with her, that she could not live normally like everyone else seemed to? It was a curse, a selfish curse, that allowed her so little control over her emotions. When she was younger she had been in control. Now it was as though someone else had bought that control and ordered her slave to foreign emotions. So, as though it were someone else's body, and she herself watched from afar, she saw herself collapse on the ground and crumble into some kind of ball, like that of despair. Despair for what? Not finding someone she had never actually *known*? She looked at herself in pity. Self-aware, she diagnosed herself: clearly she searched outwards for something inwards, a manifestation of her ideal, the pinnacle of her imagination, flesh of her creation.

There was a ticklish and teasing sensation at her feet and she spread her fingers slightly from covering her face so that she could see a small fragment of the ground. It was a bird! A small bird with wet and ruffled feathers. It pecked delicately at her shoes, as if it were nudging. She moved her hands quickly, making it jump backwards, though it did not appear threatened. The little creature stared directly at her and she stared back. They watched each other motionlessly for a long time and then she put out her hand. Without hesitating, it hopped gracefully onto the open palm. She brought her hand slowly back to her chest and touched its head with a forefinger. Its small beating heart could be felt vibrating though its feathers, but it did not speed at her touch. She had no experience of animals and yet she knew it was not at all scared. It liked her. And somehow—somehow, she knew it was female, had hatched less than a month ago and its nest was in the birch tree behind.

The young life she held in her hand gave her a strange sense of reassurance and belonging. When she raised her hand towards the almost black sky, the little bird flew off—

back to its softly singing blackbird parents in the very birch tree she had guessed. She got up quickly, and through the swiftness of this movement, she felt extraordinarily dizzy; all the trees swayed hysterically and the ground moved at unhelpful and extreme angles. Missing the birch tree's trunk several times with her hand, she eventually managed to lean her full weight upon it. She closed her eyes but the sickening movements continued in darkness.

The girl, surrounded in this dark confusion, opened her eyes towards the wide expanse of black sky which remained beautifully still. This void-like stillness stilled her own stomach and head so that, as she remained with her eyes fixed upwards and her fingers clasped tightly round the birch trunk, it gave strength to her core, radiating strange vulnerable security outward.

The trees and ground began to move with each other, rather than at antagonistic angles. She found herself letting go of the trunk and swaying a little more in unison until it was, almost, an unsteady metronome. She could not have said for sure that this stopped, but it was either that her dizziness did stop, or that she became so much in time with her surroundings that her movement cancelled all movement around her, creating the illusion of stillness.

Now, when she put her right hand on the same birch, she could feel its solid firmness and smooth ink-inviting surface. Her sense of touch and hearing seemed abruptly heightened—every whisper of every blade of grass, every movement of every bird—it all seemed friendly and airily at one. She discerned which sound belonged to the fledgling that had sat in her hand and she knew …

Three red squirrels lived on that branch in that tree and they were not on excellent terms with the owl which lived in the adjacent tree. There was a badger's den under that tree over there and half a dozen buck deers frequently visited the shrubbery that way. Everything revealed itself. And then she knew something else too; and as this discovery dawned on her like a cool summer morning, she began to hear it: a beautiful, single tone, encompassing everything about it. She was so overwhelmed she did not know whether to laugh or cry. It was him; he was coming through the trees playing a violin. And suddenly he was calling to her, by name. It was almost more than she could bear to turn and look upon the face which, last time, she had believed to be that of a God.

All night they sat together in complete silence, listening to the lapping water in front and the rustling leaves overhead. Neither felt any awkwardness, as is often felt in lack of conversation, especially in the company of someone little known or of the opposite gender. She did not want to wake up; she did not want to wake back in her bed, back in her boring life alone. The girl was leaning against the sandy bank, doing very well in supressing her temptation to stare at the god. She had learnt by her previous encounters that this did not work too well with her pathetic human mind; she would sigh and faint like a character from a Medieval Romance. But she wanted to memorise every detail of his face and neck and hands so that she could draw it, and feast on it whenever she was hungry.

Instead, as the pale blue and gold of dawn threw splashes of colour upon the water, she began to speak. The words, once in the air, sounded so disappointing and cold. "I didn't finish introducing myself the other day. Would you like me to tell you about myself? Formal?"

He didn't open his mouth; he only looked at her with eyes resembling the soft expression of a young deer or bird. Yes, he was rather like a bird, she thought, a small one, like a wren, a fledgling with slightly ruffled feathers.

She was embarrassed when she realised she had been watching his mouth so intently, as she waited for him to respond. There was a familiar curve of amusement playing about those lips, she noticed before he turned, stood up, knelt in the opposite direction and sat down again. She observed this with a comically quizzical look across her forehead, the tips of her eyebrows twitching. He's mad, she thought.

And quite suddenly, on turning back round, he produced a violin, placing it instantly, and with great ease, upon his shoulder. And then the bow, swiftly positioned across the strings.

There was a bird's breath of silence before that most ecstatic single tone rang out, the same that had announced his arrival. Edith immediately looked back at the lake, thinking it would be too much of a risk to watch him play— he, or she, might disappear. She felt herself surrounded by it, bathing in this one sound, soft and delicious. She could almost see it circling around her and just as she thought she had captured its wholeness it changed; at each point of grasping, it moved, teasing, like chasing dandelion seeds in the wind. As the third note rang, the girl was sure it would move her to madness—the slight nuances of tone gradually climbing so that she never could hold any one of them nor, because of its enchantment, could she escape, had she wanted to.

But her state of imprisonment was a happy one; she did not want to leave this circle into *that world*, though a floating faraway thought told her, faintly nagging at her captivity, that she really must go.

As in her sleep, when she had felt the warm cloaks of the dark silken lake fold over her, she felt inclined, or rather, totally succumbed to this falling away from herself (what she held to be herself). It was so much less effort to simply give in. It was just that note—that was the world: the only thing in the world.

Then abruptly, she twitched her head. There was someone or thing whispering in her ear. It wasn't exactly an annoyance, but it was a distraction; a pause in her absolute enthrallment which, as she made that slight movement of her head in an attempt to flick it away, only gained dominance over all other feelings and thoughts (or lack of) in her mind, as it slowly made its way to the centre. Once there, it drowned the singleness of the tone and replaced it.

Just as it was ruined by replacement, he stopped playing and began to speak. He did not stop abruptly, but let it fade out, just as his voice had seemed to fade in. In fact, the playing did not seem to stop completely at all, because she could still hear it in her mind—like a powerful tune that could not be erased from memory. In any case, he had stopped playing and was speaking to her. She had not heard him speak since he had called her name at the birch tree.

Now he said it again. "Edith."

She waited for him to continue, still looking hard at the lake. She must not wake.

"You will not wake up," he said with a laugh.

"How do you know? I did last time," she replied.

"Last time you were asleep; this time you are not."

"Well I wasn't asleep the other day in the woods and you disappeared rather too quickly."

"I don't think it was too quickly. You were there for a while before you were called away."

"Yes; a couple of hours I was told," she wondered how she could speak so normally to this god. All the more reason not to stop concentrating on the lake, she thought. "If it's all the same to you, I'd like to watch the light on the water."

"I don't mind," he said laughing again. The echoes of his playing in her memory became louder for a moment, so powerful that they almost pushed his voice away. She refocused on his voice.

"You met me before you were asleep."

The girl could not help laughing at this, and almost looked back at the god.

"If I was anyone else, I would find that statement very confusing."

"But you're not anyone else," he said laughing in return.

"No, I suppose I'm not," she said grinning, wondering if she would ever be able to tell anyone that she had joked with a god.

"Edith, you met me long before I found you asleep in this lake."

"You mean when you kept coming to our garden. That was you, wasn't it? Why was that?"

"Yes I did come to your garden a few times; your hedge is very comfortable."

"My hedge is comfortable? Are you *serious*? I don't understand you at all."

"Well I didn't come for your hedge—what I'm saying is I didn't mind staying in it. I came for you of course."

"Why would you need to stay in the hedge?" she thought it would be superfluous to add that he was a god. Anyway, he was clearly living in human form at the moment; perhaps it was part of his training to sleep rough too. "Why would you come for me? In fact, I don't understand at all why you're giving me all this attention."

"Because you're not anyone else, I suppose," he said, laughing again.

"You suppose? I could get frustrated at that: of course I'm not someone else, I'm me." She felt she was getting too brave.

He ignored her. "No you met me before the hedge. You met me several years ago."

"Several years ago?" she racked her brain for hidden memories. That would mean this god had been walking on Earth for longer than she had assumed. She wondered if he was becoming impatient at her stupidity.

"You were part of the audience; you were near the front row. You came to watch me play at a concert."

"A concert …?" she was trying to think of all the concerts she had been to in the last few years, with family, with Mrs Carey, with Elizabeth, but she knew before finishing the word which one it was. Something made her feel mistaken, and she continued attempting to recall all other performances. It had been at St Mary's where she had been ridiculously bored before a young violinist had started playing as an introductory piece. It was about four years ago, and it came to her in a flash, but not as too much of a surprise, that she remembered it had been after and due to this same performance that she had dedicated so much of herself to music, to some other life. Did this mean that, as a god, he had played to the point that he had hypnotised people to worship him? It did not seem too unlikely that this was the reason she had sought such solace in music. Was he the shadow in her mind?

"At the church—at St Mary's?" she asked him.

"Yes."

"Why were you there?"

"I don't remember, probably because you were there. No—I'm sorry. I keep teasing. Just the usual reason one plays in a concert—I was asked to play there."

"Asked? By who?"

"Whoever was organising it—some parish person who knew someone else I had played for."

"I think I'm too stupid to understand such an extended metaphor unless—unless … sorry, does that mean you're not a god?"

He laughed. "I'm speaking very literally."

"But that means you really are simply a violinist," she was completely confused. "But how then did you rescue me from the lake, and hide in my hedge, and, you know, *everything*?"

"'Simply'? One doesn't need to be a god to rescue someone from a lake or hide in a hedge."

"But …" This could not be true, he could not be human, normal. Everything was too strange, even if she could not explain exactly what was strange. Every question she thought of as proof seemed to have a logical explanation—why had she fainted? Her own stupidity. Why had she re-awoken back in her bed? He had taken her to the house and a servant had perhaps carried her upstairs and kept quiet. Why had time passed so quickly? Again her own thoughtlessness.

"But …" she repeated again.

"But what?"

"I don't know? I just …" she could not think what to say. Perhaps it was safe to look at him now. She wanted to see whether she now recognised him as the violinist.

She took her eyes away from the lake and turned towards him, but she was too late to ask any more questions because he was playing the violin again. She knew she could not interrupt. The conversation was evidently over for him, and so he must have very speedily picked up his violin. At least this gave her more of a chance to watch him, and remember him. To her own surprise, the knowledge he was not what she had thought did not leave her disappointed, and he remained just as beautiful.

When she arrived back home, she managed to return to her room unnoticed. At breakfast, her mother announced Charles would be taking her to the Loehills' house. She did not give an explanation, and had it not been for Mari's indiscretion, Edith would have been more than a little confused. She desperately wanted to speak to a friend, however, and the opportunity to talk to Elizabeth had just presented itself right on time.

Gabriel was apparently out of the house when she got there, and she had Elizabeth to herself in their drawing room. Elizabeth offered her a book to join her in reading.

"Do you remember the concert at St Mary's a few years ago?" Edith asked after pretending to read for a minute.

Elizabeth laughed, not looking up from the book she was reading. "Well, that was unexpected. I was waiting for you to ask about Gabriel. You realise you were called here because he was absolutely awful to Father and demanded that he saw you directly. Father wouldn't allow him to go to your house, so you came here, and now Gabriel evidently can't face his own anger—you know what he's like." She giggled again. When she did not get a response she glanced at Edith and realised her question had been sincere. "Let me think … there have been a lot of concerts at St Mary's." She looked back at her book.

"There was a child prodigy written on all the posters who was the first performer."

Again Elizabeth looked up from her book and frowned, trying to remember. Edith watched the memory arrive, pulling her eyebrows back upwards.

"Oh yes! That one who couldn't speak but played marvellously."

"Sorry? No not him, who was that?"

"No, that was definitely him, the one you're taking about. St Mary's. Prodigy. You remember that's how they introduced him, 'The Silent Violinist'. I remember feeling disgusted—the way the man smirked when he said, 'referring to the prodigy and not his playing, of course'. Don't you remember that? Hey, why are you crying?"

"I'm not."

"Fair enough, no tears on your cheeks, but water in your eyes?"

Why indeed? Why did she have to be so very sensitive? So sensitive to this violinist—he, after all, had forced her into a love for music. Who *on earth* was he?

"Really I'm not; it must be hay-fever. Well, they were wrong, they were all wrong! He speaks. I hear him."

"What? I don't understand what you're so worked up about."

"I'm not worked up. He speaks."

"Yes, you just said."

"Oh, it's so wonderful! You must hear him," Edith put her book down on her side table and folded her hands to control her excitement.

"I heard him in that concert."

"Heard him speak?"

"No, play—that's what happens in concerts."

"I'm talking of his voice … as in his speaking voice. Just as you speak to me now, I've spoken to him."

"Oh, that's nice! He learnt to speak? So why was he declared dumb before?"

"I don't know. They were wrong. He could always speak."

"That's interesting, but why do I need to hear him speak?"

Here Edith realised she did not actually know why Elizabeth needed to hear him speak.

"Oh I don't know, to feel the satisfaction that those people were wrong?"

Edith looked up from her folded hands to regard any expression in the big blue eyes of Elizabeth. There seemed to be nothing in those eyes. Only complete lack of understanding. She held her stare a moment longer than comfortable and felt, in that moment, a sense of utter despair. Complete hopelessness. Or exasperation. How desperately she had hoped for Elizabeth's support as a friend, but she knew that suddenly something had changed, and with it her relationship to all those around her.

IX

When she next saw the violinist two days later, Edith asked him to come and play for her parents. She wanted to hear him give another concert. They were sitting in the same place on the sandy bank of the lake, and there were several creatures sitting between them. Even if he was not a god, and she was no longer dazzled in the way she had been when she first saw the trail of animals follow him, it was almost unbelievable how strongly he attracted these friendly little creatures. They were so attentive, almost as though they somehow communicated with him and he with them. They appeared to respect the violinist's care for the girl, giving her kindly attention too. She was at that very moment listening to him play whilst stroking the head of a young red squirrel who looked up at her fondly. Edith still found it difficult to look at the violinist as he spoke, so she focused on the admiring squirrel when he quietened his playing to speak.

"There's no point, they wouldn't be able to hear me."

"Of course they will," she replied in confusion. "I hear you—you put your bow on the strings, they vibrate and there is sound. If I can hear that, they can. Why wouldn't they?"

"But Edith, I don't think you just want me to give a concert. You want them to do more than just hear my playing; you want to prove something too."

Edith gulped, knowing only too well that he was right. There was indeed something not too deep inside her which, for some strangely desperate reason, wanted to prove her discovery of the violinist.

"You want them to do more than just hear me play," the violinist repeated. "You want them to hear me speak too."

Here she realised that he must use the word speak as a type of musical synonym for 'understand'. Because of course she did not have any desire to bring him to her house to simply speak to her parents. She just wanted the opportunity to have him give another concert, that was all.

"They'll understand you just as well as I do. I don't see any reason why they shouldn't. Are you scared?" As soon as she had asked this last question she wished she had not, because it came out sounding awful and childish.

He shook his head, as though despairing at her lack of understanding, just as she had two days earlier with Elizabeth. Is that what he thought of her? She felt herself become increasingly frustrated, making her feel even more stupid, knowing that there was something she was missing of which he seemed to be refusing an explanation.

"It's alright Edith, in time you'll understand what I'm speaking about. Other people don't hear me as you do."

What was he saying? If he was using the same method of synonymising, he was telling her that, at some point, she would 'hear', understand, her *understanding* of him, because other people did not understand him as she did. Understand him? But she did not even know him; she certainly did not understand him in the slightest. She felt she had no brain—that this was it: she could not understand on account of her stupidity.

"Don't be ridiculous," he laughed (the most exciting and sweet laugh—like a flourish of notes sung by a young bird flying above a running stream). "It has nothing to do with your intellect. This understanding is different." (Had she said this thought aloud, then, that she had no brain? Or did he just read it on her face?) "Anyway, I will tell you truthfully that you really are the only one."

"The only one what?"

"The only one who understands."

"But you have used 'understand' both in a present and future sense! You have just said that I will understand "in time", and now you say that I am the only person who understands you—in the present sense! Understands what? All this talk of understanding, understanding and more understanding. I don't feel as though I'm doing a very good job of it!"

"You yourself understand it," he whispered. She continued to look at the squirrel. What mad nonsense did this boy speak? "Completely and as a whole. But you don't comprehend it yet. I realise this is a direct contradiction—what I am saying is that deep down (behind even your subconscious, but I will call it your subconscious) you know exactly who I am, what this is and how you are involved. It is for your own safety, I must add, that your conscious brain has not yet understood; if you saw beyond the surface just now, if you understood as much as your subconscious does, it would be most dangerous: it is beyond human capability—you yourself have commented on the limitations."

Have I? Edith thought to herself. Have I commented on this? The only time she had noted the limitations of physicality was to herself when she refused to look at the violinist in case she should faint, because the human mind could not bear facing a god for too long. That was common knowledge. But she had not said this directly to him. And anyway, he was not a god.

"I cannot explain. I cannot explain because I do not understand. That is why, when you see the horizon of conscious understanding coming from the subconscious self, you will still not understand, in terms of being able to put it into words for others—you can only accept a certain sense of *knowing*, rather than understanding … Alright, I have contradicted my own words—I say you are the only one who understands but that you will never understand."

The violinist let out a sigh. "God I'm sorry. I didn't realise things would get this complicated so soon. But—now I have started this, I will briefly say, or try to clarify, that there are two types of understanding. As I tried to explain, there is the physical 'human brain' understanding. Then there is that other 'deep acceptance' understanding which the brain will occasionally question but frustratingly never succeed in logically resolving. Your brain is no exception (do not be offended). Unlike many, however, there is a sturdier bridge between those two understandings.

"In this way, amongst other reasons that I don't know, you are the only one whose 'brain' understanding will comprehend it in a way that even I cannot. Unfortunately, even with this gift, it will still be trapped inside you because your language is your weakness. Words are too limited for you to be able to analyse the 'deep' understanding (using the forward understanding) and give it to others. To 'translate' it for the people, so to speak, is impossible. Well, at least, that is what I believe. I have been told differently. For that, we can only wait and see."

Edith was sure her right eyebrow could not drop any further towards her eye, nor her left reach any further up her forehead. She looked at him, just as he began playing his violin again. What was 'it', what was the *it* to comprehend? Who on earth was this? She asked herself for the umpteenth time. How was she here? She realised that she absolutely refused to believe he was not a god. Theoretically, if she could 'hear' him in a way no one else could, and there was no possibility of her translating this thread of language outside herself, such that she was only sedately accepting a mere *knowledge* of it internally, then that would be pointless and absurd. If he was a god, then all he had said was simply incomprehensible god-speak that passed straight over her ignorant head. But if he was not a god, it was simply nonsense, because that was how it sounded to her.

That afternoon she spoke again to Elizabeth. For whatever unstated motive, or scheme, Elizabeth, Gabriel and their parents were staying the week in their house, though they only lived an hour away. It meant she was not alone in the house with her parents, at least.

"Wouldn't you like to hear him play?"

"Who?"

"The violinist I spoke of the day before yesterday."

"Oh, him."

"Well?"

"He did play wonderfully, I said so before, did I not? But why ask? There are no performances on at the moment."

"No, but I can ask him to come here."

"You've met with him recently!? How?"

"It's of no concern. I thought I implied before I had met him recently."

"I don't know; I can't remember. Anyway, it would be rather impressive to have a private concert. Would he do it?"

"I could persuade him."

"You sound as though you know *him* very well. Is there something you're not telling me? Who have you been meeting him with and where, for example?"

"What do you mean? No, I don't know *him* very well and it doesn't matter where I've seen him," she echoed Elizabeth's pronoun emphasis.

"Edith," Elizabeth said narrowing her eyes and clearly enjoying herself. She was trying to create drama. "I'm not sure I like it when you're hiding something."

"I'm not; would you like him to play here or not?"

"I said yes."

"Alright, would you mind convincing everyone else …? You're good at that."

Edith quickly left to avoid further questioning.

Just before dinner, Elizabeth came into Edith's room. She quickly shut the door and ran up on Edith who sat by the window.

"They would all very much like to hear him," she said immediately, grinning, as though they were involved in a conspiracy.

"You've asked them already? They agreed so quickly?"

Elizabeth nodded vigorously, pleased with herself. "They did not even ask details, but agreed immediately. General Girding is coming on Saturday, and I think they were trying to think of some way to entertain him—and there I appeared with your violinist! They were very pleased; they want him to play in the hall for the General on Saturday."

"Oh yes, I had forgotten about him—our fathers' war friend. Is he coming on his own?"

"No, his wife and son are coming with him. You may've heard Gabriel speak of the son, Lawrence also called Blyth, who he is quite good friends with."

"Ah. Yes. Blyth wanted to go hunting with Gabriel, I remember."

"So, so, tell me Edith—what does the violinist look like?"

"What? Why? You've seen him."

"Yes, but I don't remember, and I think it's so exciting you've been meeting with him—*alone*. Please please, I want you to tell me everything! How did you meet? What do you do? What does he look like? Is he good-looking? Is he nice?"

"Gosh Elizabeth! You've definitely got the wrong idea— if I understand you right. We're not even friends, he's not at all like that. He's—he's different." She saw Elizabeth smile hideously as she said this. "Oh really! I will not bother, Elizabeth. You of all people should hear me better."

"Alright," said Elizabeth looking disappointed as she saw that her friend was serious, that there really was nothing exciting going on. "Whatever you say. If it's not what I think, it must just be for charity, which is nice I suppose. Well—we'd better get ready for dinner. I'll see you later." She ran out.

Edith sighed and dismissed her sad thoughts as she went over to her wardrobe.

At dinner no one asked her about the violinist's invitation. It crossed her mind that perhaps Elizabeth had not spoken to them at all and had made it up, until Gabriel approached her afterwards, as she was on her way to her room, her arm on the bannister two steps up.

"How are you going to ask the violinist?"

"I'll tell him that my parents want to hear him, of course."

"You know where he lives."

"In a way."

"I don't understand."

"Why are you worried about it? You don't particularly want to hear him, do you? It's fine anyway—he will be here on Saturday and you can meet him."

"You've already met him then."

"Yes."

"You like him? He is civilised?"

She laughed. "Of course he's civilised. And, yes, he is very nice. That is why I want you to meet him—not just keep him for myself, alright?"

She smiled until his worried eyebrows relaxed and his lips fell into some sort of grin and then she continued up the stairs. When she was safely in her room, she laughed and changed out of her dinner dress. She waited a few minutes and went back downstairs.

The hall was empty and no one stopped her as she got her coat and unlocked the front door. But ten minutes later, when she was in the forest, she knew she was being followed. Too light footed to be Gabriel, it must be his sister. She turned round, seeing the familiar navy coat poking out behind one of the trees.

"Elizabeth?"

No response. "What is it? What do you want?"

She watched as the girl stepped out from her hiding place. "I'm sorry Edith; it's only that I don't like secrets. I know I should've asked, so please don't be angry with me. I think it's unfair that you're allowed to have an adventure and be friends with someone I'm not."

Edith didn't reply because she couldn't think of a response, and so she simply watched in silence as Elizabeth stood for a while before sorrowfully turning round and walking back in the direction she had come. She had the urge to go after her, as her friend's slumped shoulders got further and further away, feeling the stab of cruelty. She was selfish perhaps? Well, they could never understand—oh how horrible she sounded to herself! But she was in the process of bringing him to all of them, wasn't she? Surely she wouldn't if she was selfish and didn't want anyone else to talk to him—no, she did want others to know him! He had something to give, and she would give it. She didn't want to be the only one.

Turning and continuing on her way, she decided it was far better not to dwell on such things and, successfully, in the space of about three seconds, she was barely able to recall having thought anything at all.

He was sitting on a large, moss-covered rock beside the lake when she got there. He was resting his chin on his hand and his elbow on his leg, looking off into the dusky distance. He dropped his hand and sat up as she approached. She smiled but he didn't smile back. He nodded. It wasn't the nod of greeting, it was that of agreement. How did he know?

"You know what I'm going to ask."

He nodded again.

"So you will come? On Saturday?"

He nodded slowly. She suddenly thought that she had done something very wrong.

"I'm sorry; I know you didn't want to do a concert for my parents. But you don't really mind, do you?"

He shook his head. He seemed so sorrowful. But it wasn't the invitation that was wrong, surely. It was something else. She could not help but apologise for that unknown something.

"I'm sorry," she said again, stepping further forward.

He gave one firm nod and then curved his mouth upwards, in grim acknowledgement. He tilted his head upwards and looked at her. His eyes were so sad, so disappointed.

"What have I done? Why don't you speak, why don't you tell me?"

Edith was confused, overcome with childlike guilt. It did not cross her mind that his distress might be caused by something other than herself. The violinist continued looking directly into her eyes, searching, before once more dropping his gaze. His gaze tore right through her, and she shivered. His nose twitched slightly and he refused to look at her again, intent on the distance once again. She felt that she would be better off leaving, and simply hope he would appear at her doorstep on Saturday. She turned silently and sadly, a little like Elizabeth had a few minutes before.

When she felt she was at a safe distance she looked back, instantaneously realising that the thing she felt 'safe' from at this particular distance was him. Him. But why would she ever feel danger in his presence? Surely she should trust him by the simple fact he had once saved her life. No, it was certainly his presence that held some extraordinary strength over her, that scared her, of which she had been unaware until she felt the relief of its release. Relief? Or was this simply what she told herself?

It suddenly hit her as to what she was looking back at, why she was upset, and why she wanted only to run further and further away. Run forever. How could one desperately crave company one day only to feel immense relief in its absence the next? She would have sung his praises as well as any worshipper might, and yet she felt burdened in his presence? Perhaps this was normal in any religion, this contradiction.

Under the dark purple, silver-streaked, dusky sky, she looked back at him. Possibly she only imagined all she thought she saw, at this distance, and with such detail, but she did not think so. He had a robin on his knee and a red squirrel sitting in the crook of his elbow. He was stroking the squirrel who watched his face as intently as the violinist had looked into the distance, and with a thousand times more love than the squirrel under her fingers earlier had even hinted at. And the violinist did not look into the distance now. He spoke to the robin. He was definitely speaking to that little creature, who she could see, even from this great distance, had its head tilted in such a way that it could only be listening with complete reverence.

That boy, who had once been a god, was sad in her presence, but now she had departed his sight, he sat happily nattering away. Fine. *C'est fini*. She was not to be used for his amusement. Make her feel in the wrong, make her feel as though she were always the inferior. Well if he was or was not a god! Why contemplate it! He wanted power over her … What right did he have? Who on earth was he? How dare he have had so much influence over her that she had given so much of herself to music. Reverend Carey, Mrs Carey, Mrs Baker's son Edward, those piano lessons—it was all through his power, not her own love. He had had such a manipulative influence that she had not even remembered him, and had sought solace in ideas and feeling she thought stemmed from her *own* passions, only to discover now that none of it had come from her. None of it belonged to her. Did he ever think about her? In comparison to the time she spent thinking of him? She did not want to care for someone more than they cared for her, it made her feel cheated. She would not cry. How annoying to be female! The ever-instinctive urge to cry. And she was not so different from Elizabeth: always he, he, he and him. Don't give in! Turn round. Walk.

That clarinettist, that horrible clarinettist at the concert. Edith remembered her now—she had laughed at the girl and told her the violinist could not speak. Edith thought about this in her anger. Was it through some sorry want of attention that he pretended he could not speak? Evidently he was disturbed—he chose to live without speaking to anyone. Mad. He spoke to animals to satiate his sorrowful and mistreated voice box.

Abruptly, she felt a slap across her right cheek, forcing her eyes to smart at its unexpected sharpness. It was her own hand that punished her, without her command. This was the extent of his cruel power over her; she had to hit herself when angry at him. The contact her hand made with her cheek emitted a tight, high and toneless sound which echoed through the trees, bouncing from trunk to trunk, rustling through the leaves. Quiet as it was, everything along its path went silent, and in the instant it took from her eyelids' automatic blink to the recognition of her own hand's disobeying action, the boy and squirrel looked up; and even at this vast distance, their eyes met. Why had she turned back round, and why, why, was time going so slowly that it was still light enough to see so well?

"Edith," he whispered. She could hear him as though he were right beside her. It was all so sharp and clear: the beetle under the leaves at her feet, the spider climbing the rock at his, the squirrel blinked. Just like that certain knowledge of the fledgling when she had gone looking for the god. She turned and ran.

She heard the squirrel jump from his knee as he stood and shouted her name. It was nightmarish, this terrifying clarity. There was an aching desperation in his voice that moved her almost beyond herself. There was something he needed to say. But why call for her now? He had not spoken to her when she was standing there. It must be that the girl imagined it all. After all, it was impossible; all this was impossible.

"Come back!" he called in a hopeless sigh, shouting her name again. Oh it was so loud, the whole world must have heard! She pressed her hands over her ears and carried on running but it barely muffled the echoes. The shouts were in front of her too, beside her, above her, inside her.

"NO!" she screamed. She could not help it; it seemed unbearable that any one person could live so many imprisoning nightmares as she had. "Let me alone," she sobbed.

She tripped on a root and took her hands from her ears to soften her fall. She heard leaves, birds and human footsteps but no voice. She was alone once again. There was no urgent need to get up anymore. Actually, the leaves were quite comfortable; their dryness caressing her bare neck and cheeks almost lovingly. So much relief this girl felt on the discovery that the leaves, birds and footsteps need not be listened to— they didn't speak verbally, they had no ulterior meaning in their sounds. They simply were what they were. A footstep was a footstep, it did not mean anything else; it was not a symbol for something else, a hidden universe. Leaf = leaf.

It was Elizabeth. Those were who the footsteps belonged to. She sat up, in control, calmly awaiting her approach.

"Your eyes are wild! And your hair! What have you done?"

"I don't know, Elizabeth."

"I was on my way home Edith, really I was."

"It doesn't matter; I'm not cross with you."

"Really? Then you'll walk back with me?"

"Of course," she got up and brushed herself down with firm, deliberate strokes. "Are there leaves in my hair?" she turned round.

"Yes, lots! Here, let me," she began releasing them from their tangled positions in her friend's hair.

"Did you hear him call, Elizabeth?"

"No, what did he say?"

"He was calling me."

"Obviously not very loudly; I didn't hear a thing—though I did hear you shout," she said dropping the last leaf. "There. All done … Why was he calling?"

"I don't know," she replied turning back round to face Elizabeth and shaking out her hair. "Thanks. Shall we go?"

They walked in silence for a minute, the elder enjoying the empty stillness of her brain.

"Did I tell you about the trip to Cornwall?" Elizabeth broke the silence excitedly. She replied that she had not. "Yes, well Mrs Lorton is taking us there at the end of the month so that we may see Cornwall in May, which is apparently essential for 'young ladies like us'. Oh, I'm so excited Edith! I've never been there! We're going to a small place called Porthgwarra where Mrs Lorton's niece runs a hotel and from there we'll be able to go to see Tol Pedn. There are so many legends about that place! So many shipwrecks! The village and cove and all the surrounding area is the most beautiful place in the country, if not the world! That's what she said, anyway. Mrs Lorton I mean. Have you been there …? Maybe I could persuade her to let you come too! There's only a dozen or so of us going."

"Oh thanks," she was irritated that a faint rustling had crept into the empty stillness of her mind. She must have imagined it, coming from an echo left in her mind, but she could almost hear the violinist again. It was some deep sigh directed towards her current conversation. But was he jealous she was with Elizabeth? Was a trip to Cornwall a problem? In fact, that was where the rustling had returned, when Elizabeth mentioned the trip. She shook her head to dismiss the sound, and said, "That's very kind of you but I don't think I'd be allowed. I'm supposed to be marrying your brother soon you know."

"Mmm. When's that supposed to happen?"

"Well, it was meant to be midsummer, the day after my seventeenth birthday, but since that's passed I don't know."

"Do you really want to marry my brother? Actually, don't answer—it's difficult for all of us. I know we always used to joke about it: the comical side of The Parents getting my brother to pay you compliments and all that. I mean, I think he does like you now, really. And I would like to be your sister—it would be fun. But it's still difficult. I do see your lack of choice, how it ruins things, for both of you: neither you nor he has had the chance to *discover* romance between each other, or to meet anyone else, apart from your violin boy."

"Of course you know that I am, and always have been, very fond of you and Gabriel."

"Yes, I know. But that doesn't mean that you want to

go and live in a big empty house with him in the middle of Norfolk."

"No." They were now in the grounds and walked the rest of the way to the house in silence, each deep in their separate thoughts.

X

The doorbell rang and George ran to answer it, slowing to a more respectable stride as he neared the door in case it should be the distinguished General Girding who still hadn't arrived, though an hour had passed since his anticipated arrival. His shoulders slumped as he saw that it was not him, but a scruffy and foreign-looking lad who held a violin in a grey cloth—no case. Was this the prodigy for whom he had ordered the servants to set up chairs in the hall? He who was to perform for the General? He asked for his name. Ah, no name, no voice. He was the dumb prodigy. Why did he get the feeling this chap was slightly impertinent, that actually he could speak, only decided it might be easier not to? That cheeky smile. He was hiding something, certainly, or maybe that was just young people in general. And gypsy-looking ones where always going to be suspicious.

George sighed as he realised there was no hope for the country, what with its unleashing of the young—letting them run wild. Good deeds and equality for all were all very well but, I mean, girls in trousers! What next!? Anyway, the boy would have to be scrubbed. He wasn't a child, but he couldn't be allowed in front of Lady Norton, let alone General Girding, like this. He stepped aside to allow him in.

"May I take that for you?" George motioned towards the violin. The owner put his head to one side. Perhaps he's an idiot too, George thought. He spoke slowly and as though in monosyllables: "May I take that for you so that you can get cleaned up before you are *put on stage* as it were. It can go here, on this shelf in the cupboard, yes?"

The violinist nodded and smiled again, handing the butler the violin. George took extra care as he laid it very slowly onto the shoulder-height shelf and was surprised to turn round and see that the boy wasn't watching … He trusted him? It made him feel irrationally guilty that his suspicion and dislike of the boy didn't appear mutual. Then again, that was how they made you feel, these sorts, to lull one into a false sense of security and then trample you underfoot.

Still, there was something charming about that smile, however provocative, as he smiled once again when George led him through the narrow servant's corridor to a bathroom. He had to consciously check himself as he handed the boy a towel and pointed to the bath, because he was automatically smiling back at those wild, gleaming eyes. There was a pause before he realised he was still in the bathroom as the boy unashamedly began to undress and George hurriedly forced himself out of the room, knowing that his intention had been to find one of the maids and instruct them on how to deal with the boy, but deciding that he himself would rather wait for, and on, the violinist.

He could tell that he was being spellbound by witchcraft; the boy was some kind of half fairy or nymph, or the result of an ancient Greek god falling in love with a human. Not that he had any time for all that pagan paraphernalia, of course. But the boy was not human, not entirely human—any rational god-fearing man could see that: his eyes were too pure, too free. Visualising them in his mind, the butler thought that each miniscule segment of his iris must have been formed of single crystal droplets, each encapsulating an individual revelation of astounding beauty which had transcended all time and space in the hearts and minds of any being that had experienced it. George could remember two such moments in his fifty eight years. He felt that if he could stare into one of those eyes, he would experience an infinite number of those instants, one after the other, each more overwhelming than the previous. The continual, powerful succession of them would leave him mad, he was sure.

He could hear the boy singing in the bath. The delicate notes complimented the sound of the moving water, coaxed out their musicality, touched their silent voices; voices which had surely been untouched since God first breathed life into the world. George felt his eyes helplessly fill with water, a feeling he had not had in at least half a century. The boy couldn't make a sound, he had doubted that before, but now he knew it was true. The singing was only the water made to sing in worship of the boy it washed. How did it all make sense to him in that instant? He shook his head and pushed himself away from the wall on which he had been leaning.

Going through to the kitchen, he saw clothes hanging up to dry. They would do. He took them back through to the bathroom, knocking and entering, the boy still in the bath. He laid the clothes on a chair and went to go and get the violin so that they could go straight to the hall.

He was thinking about the boy's neck, the way it curved so perfectly, so smoothly from his back. He must have held every most beautiful feature possible to have moulded in human form. The butler could understand now the joy of those artists when they captured an essence of the beauty of the world in that of their model. But this violinist could not be compared to any model, he was beyond any sort of earthly comparison. One could not, should not, touch him. He supposed that was why music had been handed to him as his gift, because it could touch people without the need of physical interaction. What would his voice be, if he could speak? Perhaps the wonder of it had been too great, it had made him too perfect, and so it had been taken, just so the world might have him.

But oh God! The cupboard was bare, so to speak. The shoulder-height shelf was absolutely empty. Why would they move it?

He ran back down the narrow corridor. "Ana! Mari! Charles!" The kitchen was empty. The whole servants' quarters were empty. The boy would be dressed by now. He would have to take him to the hall and then find the violin. God! Whoever had moved it would have a serious scolding afterwards. He straightened his waistcoat and walked as calmly as he could back to the bathroom. Once again he knocked on the door and entered. He was intensely nervous.

The boy had emptied the tub and dried himself. The high strip window was open, projecting a rectangle of sunlight across half the opposite wall, towel rail, and George's face. He shaded his eyes with his right hand, his left still on the doorknob. The violinist was sitting on the edge of the tub, his back to the door, facing the window. George saw a little wren perched in the corner of the window. It appeared to be listening to the boy who was plucking at the violin on his knee—slow, aimless, plucking, mirroring the pale pink blossom which fell past the window. The Violin!?

He was as sure as sure could be that his eyes did not deceive him, nor that he had been mistaken in the instrument's absence from the shelf. He knew, if not comprehended, that the boy had retrieved the violin through something other than physical means. The bird, the light, the petals? The boy was an angel.

Fortunately, the violinist stopped playing soon after George opened the door and so there was no need to commit the impossible task of interrupting. He led the fresh smelling boy through to the hall where the small audience had already assembled. They did not clap as he entered, but waited with an air of doubt. George stopped before reaching the chairs and walked back to the doors. The violinist stood calmly a short distance in front of the row of seats. The butler thought that the boy was the only one in the room who could not feel the terribly awkward silence. He knew the reason: this audience was used to introductions from a guest performer and, for this particular performance, there could be none. Yet the butler maintained his instinct that the boy was not silent in the way everyone believed of him.

The violin was raised to his shoulder, the bow placed on the strings. Gabriel could not understand why Edith had such an air of anxiety, her hands clasped painfully tight. Truthfully, she did not know any more than he.

A long, deep, rich note rang through the hall, vibrating through everything present. Just in this first sound, the audience was relaxed and compelled. More notes followed in quick succession, like the flurry of small wings ascending, before a whole passage was played in the very upper regions of the violin, though not only on the highest string, giving an unfulfilled, muted sound. Edith heard all this in much the same way everyone else did, probably even mirroring her neighbour's open mouth as she tried to watch the dancing fingers of the boy as they skipped upon different parts of different strings, as though there was an overlapping echo, or another player. It was here that she could no longer hold securely onto these notes as the mere sound surfaces her neighbours heard.

He was speaking. He was playing. His lips weren't moving. The bow was moving. The arm was moving. The fingers were moving. But there was no simple melody. There was simply that most wondrous voice of the violinist whose words flowed with all the beauty of every delicate essence of language, able to convey in its fullest sense. It was the violin that spoke. Or no, it was the *boy* who spoke, but it was as everyone said, he could not speak; behind the voice which demanded her whole attention, her thoughts fought in contradiction. Nevertheless she was able to formulate a sequence of the facts as they stood: he had no voice as she or her neighbours did, but he could speak. And it was through the violin that he could be heard; the violin was his voice. She could not understand why she hadn't realised that before, so absolutely persistent in her belief that he spoke through the same means as she, Gabriel, her mother, everyone. Well, who wouldn't assume that a voice came through the throat?

But, but, yet, Gabriel, and her mother, and everyone else … they could not hear! … oh! It was her along, she must be mad! The voice must be escaped; she could not think straight; nothing was coherent.

The boy knew her thoughts; he knew that she wanted to ignore him. Is it really so difficult to accept? He asked her. I know that you do comprehend. Stop trying to work it out. There isn't time. Stop trying to formulate a neat and logical solution. There is no need because I tell you in all seriousness that there is none. And you are not alone.

To the word 'alone', Edith got up and walked towards the doors. She was not sure if she said anything aloud in response, but no one left their seats if she did. No one appeared to notice. She pushed past the stunned butler and ran out of the hall. Pausing for a moment outside the hall, she realised how utterly terrified she was. He was wrong; she was completely isolated. She walked out of the house, not knowing what to do with herself. Everything was confused. The girl stopped when she got to the middle of a field on the Eastern edge of their land. Another twenty or so paces in the same direction and she could be walking into the cluster of trees on their boundary. She stood motionless, thinking what a relief it would be to burst into tears. But she wouldn't, she couldn't. The sky seemed to agree with her too; the clouds had gathered into an oppressive grey, but refused to allow its contents to fall.

A drop of blood fell on the grass beneath her feet. It came from her lip which up until now she had not realised she was biting so painfully hard.

It was quite some time that she stood there before hearing the footsteps of the violinist as he headed for the woods. She didn't know if he would approach her, she thought that was an awful expectation, as though she had come out here awaiting him and his attention. Thinking in this way, she turned and walked diagonally towards him in order that their paths might converge. As she got within a few steps, however, she stopped. He was ahead, facing the opposite direction, and she felt his presence so strongly that she could go no further. It seemed somehow like an invasion of his world that so clearly surrounded him. She *was* alone.

He stopped too, lowering his violin to the ground and turning to face her. His eyes were so bright, so very alive. She could not help but wonder once again if he really existed. They watched each other, not moving, until the girl eventually exclaimed "I don't know what to do with myself." A short pause followed before she added in a whisper "I'm sorry, I'm so very afraid." The boy tilted his head familiarly, in his bird-like manner. "I cannot determine or voice the reason, I don't know of what I am afraid." She wanted to go to him but her feet refused.

Suddenly, he looked very worried, concentrating on something on her face. He strode over in five steps and took her hand, lifting it to her mouth. Her finger felt the warm moistness of her cut lip, the object of his concern.

His eyes met hers, and his eyebrows quivered quizzically. Then, carefully replacing her hand to her side, he returned his fingers to her chin, softly placing his thumb on her lower lip. He held it there so lightly that it was as she imagined it must be to kiss a robin's silk head. He let it pass slowly to the corner of her mouth before letting it drop.

The long silence that followed felt so full of certainty to the girl that she could not help but smile. He grinned back and nodded once gently, like a deer. The silence was a confirmation of the violinist's outer muteness and the means of his communication. It allowed the unconditional acceptance that she was the only one able to hear his voice. She watched him pick up his violin and continue on his journey home. She had a strange sensation that they were both alone together, almost as though, in his all-consuming bubble of silence, he did not really exist outside the silence of her own unspoken thoughts; as though she really had invented him.

When Edith got back to the house and re-entered the hall, they were all still there, standing and talking. That is, all except the General's son who had not gone to the concert in the first place (much to the embarrassment of General Girding), preferring to familiarise himself with the grounds so as to better his chances of winning a hunt. It didn't appear she had been missed, so she walked casually to join them.

She stepped into the gap beside Gabriel in the conversing circle which quickly closed on the both of them, they being the only two not attentive to the General. They walked out, both wanting to escape and, as usual, when Edith extended her hand to open the door, Gabriel jumped in front to open it for her.

"My goodness! You haven't cut yourself, have you? Why is there blood on your hand?" he exclaimed as his eyes fell on her hand.

The girl automatically lifted her hand to her mouth where the source of the blood should still have been visible. But it wasn't. There was no cut there. She had not noticed its absence of pain as she had walked back to the house. Or before, when the violinist's fingers had fallen from her face. Blood could not simply disappear or skin grow back, in so short a space of time. Gabriel's legs felt a strange loss of stability as he watched her eyes grow extraordinarily bright. Why wasn't she surprised that the violinist's delicate touch could heal? For she felt no surprise, only joy. *He, silent, was real.*

XI

"It was the Earl of Sussex, wasn't it? Or the Lord Stafford? Someone with an 'S', anyway," Gabriel said upwards as he was serving the ball.

"I think it was Lord Stanley," Blyth casually replied, hitting the ball violently with his well-used racket.

"Oh yes, but his brother Sir William was more important wasn't he?"

"Yes, well their armies combined had something close to five or six thousand, so they were a pretty crucial family."

"Lord Stanley was very slippery. Wasn't he the one who didn't really care if his son was executed? Replying to the King's threats that 'he had other sons' or something?"

"I don't know. Could be. But he had been 'loyal' to every leader and King of the time. At the Battle itself, he was loyal to both armies. Did you know he was married to Henry's mother?"

"No … But, oh, that's quite telling. I still don't understand what he did, apart from having an importantly large army. So he came in from the North and killed the King?" Military history was not really Gabriel's preferred topic of conversation, but for years he had had to pay careful attention as Blyth laid out models of horses and knights and showed him every possible strategy, its advantages and faults, where and when it had been used, and to what outcome.

"No, no. That wouldn't have made any sense. Richard's army was coming from the North, going south to meet Henry's camp. The Stanleys were watching from the South, don't you see, and then—look there, your girl's making her way towards the woods."

"So she is," Gabriel replied, turning his head in the direction Blyth motioned. "Well, what's it to you? Stop trying to distract me, I'm trying my best to beat you," he added, turning back as the ball came flying past him.

Blyth did not say anything as he waited for Gabriel to fetch it and serve and there was silence for the next couple of minutes, save the hollow and systematic thud of ball hitting racket, until the General's son broke it in a voice too overtly careless.

"Doesn't that violin chap live in the woods?"

Immediately, Gabriel let the ball drop.

"Wow, you really *are* sensitive about her."

"What does it matter that the violinist lives in the woods? He's a friend. Don't you think she should be able to have friends outside the family's choice?"

"Just a friend?"

"Why can't they be 'just friends'? It might be hard to believe, it was for me at first, that a girl and boy can be close without being *your* kind of close."

"No, it's fine, I see what you're saying and I know how much you care about her. We're close friends, aren't we? That's why I only wanted you to know what I think—"

"What? What do you think, Blyth?"

"There's something more between them."

"You *think*? What on earth do you mean?"

"Alright, I don't think—I *saw*. I saw something more between them," Blyth waited for the anticipated question and was disappointed when the only reaction was a narrowing of Gabriel's eyes as he in turn waited for Blyth to go on.

The General's son sighed as though being the bearer of such news was a heavy and unwanted burden. To Gabriel, Blyth suddenly looked shockingly unpleasant. He wondered how he had never noticed the unfortunate curling of the upper lip, and was disturbed that he had thought of him as so good a friend for quite so long. He was not going to be the one to prompt the discussion further.

"Oh very well, I can see you're pretty stubborn on the subject of your girl," he said calmly as he bounced a ball up and down on his racket.

"She is not *my girl*! You know perfectly well that I don't think of her like that at all, Edith is not property."

"Ah, let us not get into a cat fight. I do not mean to be sour. I am actually trying to help you; to tread carefully on this very delicate subject. I do think it in your best interests to know. So, if I may, I will continue: while the violinist friend was performing here the other day, you might remember that I decided to explore the grounds a little, not much caring for the sounds a violin might or might not produce.

Well, while I was walking amongst the cluster of trees on the eastern boundary, I saw your… Edith in the middle of the field, roughly two dozen paces away. I was about to approach her (I had no intention to spy) when I saw the violinist walk through the field, apparently oblivious of her," Blyth paused a moment thinking he had reached a point important enough to stop with his ball-bouncing and walk up to Gabriel. "She walked up to him and then stopped. It was then that I realised there was something very serious going on between them. I mean, a girl doesn't walk towards someone and then stop within a few yards as though *overcome with a surge of incredible emotion* on a daily basis. He stopped too and turned round. In a moment their faces were this close," he thrust his hand towards Gabriel's face so that there was a distance of about two inches. "I hope you'll agree that isn't what friends usually do. Let alone put their fingers upon the other's lips as they begin to speak. I was momentarily distracted by a bird above me at that point, but when I turned back they were holding hands and had obviously just kissed."

"You're lying."

Blyth laughed. "That's what they all say."

"You're trying to create drama and make trouble where there isn't any. I've already asked her about him."

"I *saw* them."

"Alright. Perhaps you did. That doesn't mean they actually … kissed. Even if you're not lying, you were at a distance and …"

The response brought an irritating knowing grin. "Well, believe what you want to believe. I'm only telling you what I saw."

The rain fell heavily upon the lake, making little rings round each drop that hit the water, expanding into a chaos of intersecting circles. The violinist, sitting on the branch of the overhanging oak, desperately wanted to go for a swim while it was pouring but Edith, sitting beside him, preferred to stay above the water, inhaling the delightful smell of wet soil and sodden moss. Every so often, a leaf would have its capacity exceeded and the contents would pour upon the two young people below who laughed each time it managed to land on either of their noses. Three birds sat on the same branch looking eagerly at the ground where they knew that, when the rain had ceased, a scrumptious dinner awaited them; they could practically see the long, fat worms being pummelled out already.

The violinist was happy. It was the first time in his life that he had no sense of the oppressive isolation his stilled vocal cords had given him. He had been confused as to why it took her so long to acknowledge the simple fact that his voice and violin were as synonymous as light and lamp. The woodland creatures did not think twice about it, nor did the few small children and rare individuals who had heard his violin speak. True, young children did not need to worry about the indoctrination of 'reason', which meant they genuinely did not think twice: what they heard they heard, so there was actually no 'realisation' involved. And also true that the rare adult individuals heard his *violin* speak, detaching that object from his own person; it was the beauty of the music, composed by another and reaching out in its pure form to touch them. So it was not the same. She actually heard his voice as *his voice* from him *through* his violin. She was here beside him, beside his silence, and that was all that mattered for now. He forgot his other troubles.

But Esra and Marl, two of the thrushes sitting next to him, in unsolicited consultation, suggested the girl be told of the Songbirds and Composer. In other words, the 'logic' behind his voice-violin synonym, which expanded a metaphor far beyond him. He did not want to confuse her in her calm contentment. They, however, were so excited about the prospect of speaking with her: how rare it was, through all time, for a human to have her Songbird on the path's intersection that formed a connection between all languages, let alone two humans together, if the boy could be considered human which, for the sake of emphasis on the occasion, he could. The boy had wanted to wait until the rain softened a little, as it was so loud and so *pleasant*; so warm, so full, so *perfect*. They had never seen him this delighted and thought him a little light-headed in his relief to be understood by one of his own kind, but they were completely happy to wait for the rain; the worms were entertainment enough.

A squirrel, one the violinist did not know personally but was acquainted with its parents, thought the people were in need of refreshments for their arduous spectating, and brought them each an armful of nuts and berries from inside the oak tree. The female kissed it on the head, so it stayed beside her and called for its parents to join them too: the girl was just as kind as promised.

The rain continued to fall heavily until it began to get dark. The clouds parted in places allowing shafts of soft light to shine across strips of the vertical rain and gently heat sections of the wet tree trunks. The violinist tilted his head back a little to enable one such shaft to illuminate his face, smiling with his eyes closed at its gentle rays. When he leaned back, he looked directly as Esra who had jumped upon his knee. Some sort of communication seemed to pass between them. Edith watched in fascination as the bird flew down the trunk of the oak and a few seconds later, a badger came out of a hollow at the bottom, yawning and carrying a violin fastened to its back by reeds from the side of the lake. The girl could not help but laugh at the hilarity and impossibility of the scene (at this stage, however, she was not at all surprised by such an anomaly in nature). The violinist motioned to her as to whether she wanted to stay on the branch or descend to ground level to which she replied that she liked their current position. In accordance with her wishes, the parent squirrels scurried down the tree and untied the badger's load who, once freed of it, decided against going back to his peaceful underground slumber and lay down to witness what was to follow. The squirrels expertly looped the reeds around the violin's scroll and rib and then, with Marl's help, fastened the ends round their waists, so that they could carry it up the trunk with it falling below and between them, at the pit of the V-shape that their tails and the reeds formed.

It was duly handed to the violinist who personally undid the knots around their waists and took their paws in turn as though a handshake. The sight really was comical in its magical charm.

That these creatures had until now been the only true companions of the violinist was quite a sobering thought.

She did not consider it sad that he had not had a 'normal' childhood, with other children to play and communicate with. She assumed that usually in such circumstances, he would have been introduced and surrounded by children in a similar condition, and learnt sign language or something. Then again, he was not a common case.

It struck the girl as inevitable that, out of all possible life that could understand the boy's language, it would be animals that could. In his gestures and aura he was so much a part of the forests and fields, the skies and seas; it was interesting to question whether he had become so nymph-like in order to adapt to his environment, or that he fitted this world so well simply because it was his world; in a word, was nature the magnet to him or was he the magnet to nature? She secretly believed the latter. But her real question, of course, was why she was able to hear him, when no other person ever had.

She asked it now that he had his violin in place.

Well, I don't know much more than you do in that respect. I believed you may be the means to enable others to hear, to be a bridge between various languages, but I don't know why it is only you and why you in particular. Though I must add that, in all sincerity, I love the fact that it is *you*; I am happier now than I have ever been. I suppose it is the question as to why you ever met Gabriel or, more to the sensibly, why your fathers met. Why General Girding is a General, why a tailor is tailor, why a poet is a poet, an artist an artist, an athlete an athlete. Even, why some understand the constellations of the stars and others the movements of elephants, why numbers excite some and letters others. I mean to say, if other people don't know, at the very bottom of things, why they are what they are, and for what purpose they are anything at all, or whether they are, then why should we?

She waited a while before commenting, agreeing with him completely and thinking now that her question had been a pointless and rather pathetic one. She knew that he understood her thoughts; she was pretty sure he could read her mind to a certain extent. It was nice not always having to respond, or explain everything she said. Conversation with the boy sitting beside her was the most excitingly tiring but effortless form of communicating she had ever known.

"So … um … how is it you know their names—Gabriel and all of them, and that it is through our fathers that we know each other?"

I could say I heard it while I was playing at your house, but no: I do know a lot about you—not in any way suspicious. It is that I can hear you all the time. It is not altogether strange, as I have lived in my own silence for as long as I can remember. I have only had the trees, animals and elements to speak to and that, in a way, is silence. And when there is no one to confirm one's language, one cannot know that they are communicating with anyone or thing, or whether it is all in the mind. In this lengthy silence, I have learnt to hear a lot; either through my own ears and the delicate vibrations sent from where you speak to the ground and air all around you, or through the messages of the trees and animals and what they choose to tell me.

"Alright, I think I understand. It sounds like some ancient secret, folklore. But I can ask then, since it is impossible to answer *why* it is me that can hear you, *how* you knew it was me, in order that you knew to listen out for *me*."

That is what Esra and Marl wanted me to tell you today; they are very keen to know your response as they've never witnessed someone being told before. Don't worry, it is nothing drastic.

"Never witnessed …?"

It is probably best not to think of this literally, but as a tale, a tale you are somehow a little caught up in. As you said, an ancient secret or folklore. You see, every life is a song, composed by the Composer and sung by a Songbird. These birds sit in a mirror realm, upon infinite threads of language; imagine Arabic joined letters stretched outwards to form a musical stave, with the birds sitting like notes among the lines. A Songbird is born a hundred and twenty days after conception, when the foetus is first able to hear sounds from the world outside, and sense the vibrations of their song. The song will have fast bits and slow bits, interesting passages and dull ones, complicated parts and simple parts. Some songs will modulate more than others; some will have long passages in the minor and others in the major. Some have more loud and dramatic phrases in the dominant and others have a higher frequency of touching and haunting phrases augmented or diminished, as though just out of reach. A fast passage may reflect an exciting time in a person's life; a dominant culmination may reflect a period of immense joy, and so on.

Relationships are formed on the basis of these songs: when people's lives are sung in a matching key, they will naturally have an understanding, and when two songs are dissonant, they will not. If a song modulates in a way that cannot be matched by a song that had once been matching, the two people will no longer be solicitous with each other, and their rapport will be at an end, or completely changed. And of course, if two people's songs remain harmonious throughout, despite modulations and vastly varying passages, they will remain congenial.

I have heard a small part of your song, though I was not meant to; nobody should ever consciously hear their own song, let alone someone else's. Sometimes, however, the layers of language intersect and a person may catch a glimpse of a part of their song that has not yet been sung, that they have not yet lived—this is how one may recognise, or feel unusually comfortable with, a certain moment or event they later experience. Extreme anomalies must occasionally occur, perhaps the Composer wrote a song at a slightly different frequency from the rest, or maybe a Songbird got lost, or simply decided to stray into a different layer of language. Your Songbird must be at a point of several intersections, which is how you hear me and how the animals are able to communicate with you too, as though you were of their same language. And so, yes, I am not able to tell you *why* it is *you* that is in this position, but I have told you *how* I believe you were able to come to such a position. Esra and Marl are desperate to express their excitement, as you can imagine, that you can speak to them and as well as to humans, and what such a link (so ancient and established but mostly misunderstood, trivialised or severed) might enable.

The boy stopped playing and looked at the girl. She was watching him very intently with a completely open expression.

"Well, I … I think that is a most beautiful idea. That my life is a piece of music intertwined with the music of others is an absolutely wonderful thought," she spoke softly, with a slightly deeper tone than usual and then added, placing her hand upon the boy's forearm, "What is it that you heard of my song then?"

It was in a dream many years ago that I heard it. The tune was so familiar to me that it was as though it was a fond childhood memory of a mother's lullaby. The feel of it brought me through various levels of consciousness until I was awake, at which point I could still hear it. I was living in a port at the time, and there had been a series of miserable events in my household about to culminate in the last. Walking over to the window, I saw a massive storm was approaching and the distant rumble was a supportive accompaniment to your Songbird's singing. The clouds were so purple and rich, and the rumble so perfectly deep, that I could not stop myself from opening the window and sitting on the sill. With the first strike of lightening, your song disappeared, but in that instantaneous flash, I saw your face most clearly, as though imprinted on the fast-approaching sky. I did not understand it at the time, I thought it was my desire for my own absent Songbird … But it was the first time in my life that I had a sense of courage.

"You don't have a Songbird? How if, as your tale suggests, lives are *sung* by these vessel-like birds?"

Ah! It appears I keep falling into telling you a part of my story rather than answering your question: I think I shall express this part of my life that concerns you, then your question shall be answered in the process and other things may become clearer. No, I don't have a Songbird, but don't think about that now. I'll go on.

The following night, as I witnessed the most hideous scene pass between my family, I knew I could go. My family ... well I think I have a bit of time before I must tell you about them. That night I ran away into the world. I walked miles and miles before I became fully conscious of the fact I was able to understand the animals, when no one else seemed to. They seemed to find me worthy enough to follow, and I was touched. I soon came upon a beautiful cottage at the edge of a small village. I remember the image very clearly: a graveyard and round-towered church, and dark pink roses surrounding a small turquoise door. A man was clipping roses when I stepped out from the trees into the garden, and he had the kindest face I'd ever seen. He gave me dandelion tea and ginger biscuits and asked me many questions I obviously could not answer.

Anyway, from then on, until quite recently, I lived between him and the woods and was considered his son. It was he who gave me this violin and I would often take it into the woods to play to the animals, so that I was no longer voiceless. One time, I played the tune I'd heard that purple thunderous night, not fully realising that I was doing so, and I was shortly surrounded by more creatures than ever before. The trees bent terrifyingly close. A small buck deer broke the awkward, slightly sinister atmosphere and asked me where I had heard that tune. It was then that I was told in full detail about the Songbirds and you, and how it was the tune that defined me, your tune, the tune that told all who heard it that the layers of language were not static. Before, I'd only been given dark fragments of the tale of Songbirds, and their position in the mirror realm.

I performed at various church concerts for the priest and he taught me to read and write to an extent I had never deemed plausible. I really did love him… Anyway, it was at one of those concerts that I first saw and recognised you— you remember?

"Oh yes, yes, I do, most certainly! I did not know why you looked at me in the way you did. I first heard you in that church, but I couldn't understand what you were saying … if only I had! Just think of all the years we could have been sitting like this!"

Well, I was distracted and confused myself, with ten million thoughts and doubts in my head. I was actually rather scared, but excited to *see* the face I'd seen on the sky during that storm such an age before! And to identify it with the song—it gave me such a surge of happiness.

"I have to say that to think of my image upon the clouds is quite a horrifying thought, especially during a flash of lightening! There's something about lightening, the way one is blind and then momentarily able to see again, that I've always found unnerving … Doesn't it remind you of a Brontë novel, though? Storms, clouds and impossible communication through powerful emotions … I'm sorry, I'm not suggesting anything by that, apart from everything about you being so beautiful!" She sat meditative for a while stroking the young squirrel who was on her knee. "I have to comment—there was of course never any need for you to be upset about your own absent Songbird. There can be nothing absent about it (except so far as zero and infinity might be linked); your Songbird must be at a point of boundless intersections at the very centre of the mirror."

The badger thought then that he had not been wrong to stay out in the light at this untimely hour: the girl was a good as promised. But the violinist had misjudged in avoiding, delaying, the darker news of warning for next time.

XII

Before dinner that evening, Gabriel went in search of Edith. She was in the summer house, watching the evening sun. A few rays of the soft golden light shone through a window, bathing her right side in its beauty and darkening her left side so that her on-looker could see every detail of her profile in the form of a silhouette. He had to stop and watch for a moment; she was so beautiful. There was a rush of feeling for her, rising from the pit of his stomach, making him feel he wanted her to stay there, as a part of the landscape, forever. Her gaze was pensive and calm as her eyes took in the various shades of orange from the sky and quiet last calls of the content blackbirds and thrushes. It reminded him of the story of Endymion and the moon goddess, only he was the moon goddess and Edith the youthful shepherd. He had always thought it so awfully cruel to have cast eternal sleep upon the shepherd, just for the selfish pleasure of a goddess, but the beauty of Keats' poem on the subject and Sir Joseph Paton's painting came rushing back to him and he felt guilty in his empathy for the myth. The pain struck him hard at that instant in supposing she didn't care for him at all and, not only that, but that she actually cared enormously for, even loved, someone else. Surely it could never be, though, that he felt so deeply about her and she felt nothing? The image of him only crossing her mind once in a while as the memory of a slightly irritating childhood friend. If there was anything he was certain about, it was that his love was not forced or imagined on his part, it was not a fantasy based on reading too many books or going to the cinema too often. Perhaps their difference in age was finally showing up, that would explain any strong, unhelpful feelings towards that violinist, because she was merely experiencing childish romance; nothing substantial could possibly be between them, no. Anyway, he began to feel pathetic standing and staring, he had come to ask her and that really wasn't so difficult.

He stepped into the summer house, careful not to block or interfere with any of the light that fell directly upon the girl. She had just closed her eyes to appreciate the sun's warmth and she seemed to appreciate the sensitivity in which Gabriel entered to come and stand, then sit, next to her. She opened her eyes and turned to him, smiling.

"Hello," she said in such a soft, almost foreign voice, that it was as though she hadn't spoken in such an age that speaking was a forgotten art to her. "It's a wonderful evening, isn't it?"

"Yes, it is very."

"We forget very quickly how cold and dark it is in winter, at this time of year—oh look! Did you see that tiny little rabbit? Its tail was so white! Look, there it is again! Just there by the oak!" She pointed excitedly, looking younger and fresher than ever. He was young himself, but could he really marry this young creature so soon? "Do you remember when we would play hide and seek and you would count under that oak and I would hide in it. You looked all around but never looked up! How worried you got!" She turned to face him again and saw that his attention wasn't entirely focused on what she was saying. "I'm sorry; did they ask you to fetch me?"

"Oh no, no, I wanted to come and speak to you … I wanted to ask you about the violinist."

"Yes, of course, he's pretty astonishing. What about him?"

"Well … this sounds ridiculous … but are you close?"

"Yes."

"Oh. In what way?"

"Not in any way that would upset you, I'm sure."

"Please tell me about him then … and exactly what your relationship is."

"I like him very much, and I feel we are very close, as I said. It seems odd, but I see him as I see no one else and, in the same way, I feel something towards him I do not feel towards anyone else. It can't really be explained, I've only just discovered it myself, and please don't take it in the wrong way; you've always been such a good listener, nevertheless it is in his company that I feel that everything has purpose and I am content with who I am." She stopped, slightly breathless, perhaps a little anxious. "That sounded childish didn't it."

Despite her compliments and reassurances directed at him, his eyes had become wet with anger or jealousy.

"How can you love him when he doesn't speak to you? How do you know what he thinks or … or anything?"

"I don't love him. Alright, perhaps I do. But one can love a brother or a cousin immensely too, one can love a friend, without having to be romantically involved with them, without wanting to be married, can they not?"

During his outburst, Gabriel had stood up and now she joined him.

"I do know what he thinks though. I realise it is difficult to understand how, but it is because despite everyone and everything, he *does* speak. He speaks to me all the time."

Gabriel looked at her with an expression she had never seen on his face before—horrible bitterness. She was about to question him, to tell him it was uncalled for, this reaction of his, when Blyth came walking in, whistling.

"Oh, I say, I'm sorry. Am I interrupting something? I was told by your mother to come and fetch you," he said looking at Gabriel with an expression that was somehow pitiful and jovial at the same time.

At dinner, the conversation gradually progressed from a discussion of the weather and season (the sport and hunting appropriate as such and Elizabeth's trip to Cornwall) to the changes and furthering of General Girding's position, until eventually the topic arose once more of the young violinist who had performed so well for him.

"He can't be much different in age to Lawrence, it's really quite incredible. Then again, one can never be absolutely sure as to the age of a peasant; they seem to mature in a very confusing way. I recall occasions when I have been both ten years over and ten years under in my estimations of our maids' years," said the General.

"Yes, I should say he was probably the same age as Lawrence and Gabriel—give or take a couple of years. I think it is rather a shame that someone of his social standing has such a gift. Perhaps those charitable schemes we put so much into do actually serve the poor. I suppose this is the evidence that all those Education Acts and Benefits and Curricular Additions did actually work out for the best," Lady Norton pronounced.

"Wouldn't you agree, though, that he had not all the looks of a working chap? He was not too scrawny or shabby, and his skin and teeth were pretty healthy-looking. Of course being a mute will mean that not all areas of employment are open to him, but that's not to say he can't work in the fields or do something that adds some roughness to the skin. I wonder what's keeping him," Girding said.

"Some might say he doesn't even have muteness as an excuse," Gabriel murmured. "Edith, for one, claims he's not a mute."

"What was that, Gabriel? You must speak a little louder," his mother said to him.

"It is nothing; only that Edith says the violinist is not mute—he does speak. It came to me, as General Girding was speaking, that if he does have a voice, then perhaps he is hiding it for reasons of laziness or something similar. I mean, it probably is easier for some, under some circumstances, to decide that the world should consider them silent," he continued to speak under his breath looking at his plate.

"Edith? Is this true? Does the violinist speak? Is he living a lie?"

"Yes, he does speak," she replied, looking over at Gabriel and catching his eye. It was only for the briefest of seconds, but is succeeded in making his cheeks flush painfully red. "But he is not lying when he says he doesn't."

"I'm sure I do not understand you. I don't suppose it really matters—" Mrs Girding said lightly before being interrupted by Gabriel's father.

"Oh, but I think it does matter—if not for any other reason, then simply on moral grounds. A man should not be able to go around his daily business with everyone living under such false impression. It is not as though it were a small lie either, no, if this is true, it might be quite serious, the effects could be far-reaching for all we know."

There was a sparkle in Lord Albert's eyes as he spoke: a sure sign to any who knew him that he had an idea. Something had set his quick and intelligent mind at work, and he was evidently instigating the start of a strategic plan, a plan that really excited him. Mr Norton spoke carefully, as though already resigning himself to a scheme he did not like.

"Well, I do see what you are saying, but I don't think we should discuss it anymore now. Let us uncover the facts tomorrow, and not allow it to interrupt dinner."

XIII

In the morning Edith came downstairs to check the tray in the hall which, as she had expected, had a postcard to her from Cornwall, written in Elizabeth's fast-maturing hand. It did not convey much in substance—simply that she was enjoying her time there immensely, particularly, it seemed, because it was the first time she had been away from her family. That the air appeared purer there, the colours brighter and the weather good (she wished to return there with Edith sometime very soon), was the only extra, informative information, written as part of an excited postscript. She allowed a little sigh as she grinned: as dismissive as she had been of Elizabeth's attention, she genuinely noticed her absence and missed her. She must remember to ask the violinist today what he thought of Cornwall; she vaguely recalled an unclear sense of his distress across the woods when Elizabeth had first excitedly mentioned the trip. But, since she had not been 'fluent' and open to his language then, it was like remembering what someone said in a foreign language before learning to understand it.

Her father was in the library with Lord Albert Loehill and the former, being thoroughly acquainted with the nuances in sound that defined individual footsteps within his household, held up his right hand to silence Lord Loehill, knowing his daughter was passing by. When they heard her ascend the stairs and get out of earshot, he let his hand drop and allowed his friend to continue.

"You see, I have no doubt that the violinist is a mute. Absolutely no doubt. The point is, your *daughter* believes he isn't."

"Yes?"

"I know this is going to be difficult for you, David old chap, but what would you say … or rather, let's detach ourselves … What would *one* say of someone who believes in something that isn't there; that they are utterly convinced about the existence of something that no one else is? What if it was also given that they had recently gone through sudden and dramatic changes in emotion—mood swings, complexion changes and irrational impulses …? Or say they had been hearing imaginary voices and were determined against them being imaginary?"

"Well, putting it like that—"

"Putting it like that *would* (still in the conditional) show it to be nothing less than *schizophrenia*! You've no doubt heard of schizophrenia or dementia praecox and its symptoms?"

"I'm somewhat familiar with what it entails, yes."

"Then you will know that your daughter is showing many of the signs?"

"I don't think you can really say—" Gabriel's father interrupted him again.

"*Shh*, hush. Don't speak quite so loudly! You always work yourself into such a fluster!"

"Look, Albert. You know I respect you immensely. Please could you simply *say* what it is you *want* to say? You never speak directly—I think you're worried over what my response shall be, that's it isn't it? Well, listen, it's not going to change, however you put it; whether you ask me after half an hour of talking in circles or right now, my answer will be the same, so just get on and say it *please*."

Albert looked at him in silence for a moment, evidently slightly irritated at his friend.

"Alright. Going straight in, short and sharp! Gabriel's being a right nuisance over your daughter. He's totally set on the idea—I don't altogether know why, but it's *incredibly* irritating. Whatever the case, we can't do much about it in the present situation. I'm trying to keep this simple, really. The situation at present, to reiterate what both you and I already know, lies like this: Gabriel has been left the Norfolk estate, with a condition attached—he cannot get the estate without marrying, due to some hair-brained scheme of his great, great uncle's cousin's nephew. I wanted it to be your daughter he married because I have owed you that since the war, but she is impossible. Of course, there are plenty of decent girls in the world to replace her, but then Gabriel won't have it, and since the estate has been left to *him* and he is of age, *we* can't do anything about it. I, like you, have a somewhat decayed purse, and if we wait for your daughter, or threaten her, or try anything in that line of things, we will be on the street, or dead, before the Estate is ours." He walked over to the mahogany table, poured himself a glass of brandy and, after throwing it back in a single motion, he continued. "Last night, Gabriel unintentionally gave me the solution; if your daughter was declared mad and taken to a nice place for help, which we would support of course, my son would have no choice but to look elsewhere for a wife."

Edith's father sat down and put his head in his hands, eyebrows furled, looking at his knees. After a few silent seconds in the pose, he heard Lord Albert pour himself another glass of brandy, without replacing the stopper in the decanter. He looked up and met his gaze, and Gabriel's father visibly faltered for the first time. He put his glass down to minimise his shaking.

"I do know this is a lot to ask of you, David. But I need your support. I don't know what I shall do otherwise, I don't see another way. I—"

"Why should I, Albert? What is there for *me* to gain?"

Albert drank the rest of his brandy. "Both of us are in an unfavourable economic situation. This will secure our family's future and I will most definitely ensure that it secures yours."

"How secure is secure?"

"You will have twenty-five percent of any gains."

"Sixty-forty, your family to mine, and I'll consent."

"That can be done. I don't know how to thank you otherwise. We may shake on it?"

"Yes," replied Mr Norton, standing up and taking Lord Loehill's hand. "Of course you'll have to get her mother to agree too."

"Ah," Albert considered his feet before looking up again and smiling. "Yes, of course. Do you know where I might find her?"

"She will probably be in her room writing her letters."

"Alright. I'll go at once. Do you think we could talk with Edith in the drawing room later today?"

"I don't see why not; today is the same as any day."

"Straight after I've spoken to Lady Norton, then. Good."

Exactly one hour after these last words were spoken Edith was called into the drawing room where her mother, father and potential father-in-law were seated expectantly.

"We would like to continue last night's conversation—your comment on the young violinist's ability to speak," said Gabriel's father, immediately wanting to get started.

"Yes, I—"

"No, let us ask you the questions—we believe this to be rather a serious matter. Of course, we do not wish to interrogate or frighten you." He motioned for the girl to take on a seat opposite him. "So, first things first: were you speaking sincerely when you said the boy could speak."

"Yes; he can."

"And why did you say that he was not lying by saying he didn't speak?"

"Well … he does certainly speak—I have spoken to him on numerous occasions. But his—" She was interrupted by someone entering the room: it was the doctor. He seemed slightly embarrassed.

"Good morning, or afternoon actually," he said, glancing at his watch. "I was told to come straight in here."

"Ah, yes, yes, take a seat Dr Frank; you don't mind Edith, do you? The doctor is interested in the violinist too," said her father.

Lord Albert Loehill spoke again before the girl could reply.

"You were saying that he was not lying …?"

Edith looked around at the four faces watching her and very slightly raised her eyebrows.

"No he is not lying." She sighed and looked downwards, saying very quietly, as though to herself, "He said you would not understand; that you couldn't, not in this way. I don't—I *refuse* to believe him. I really can't believe it."

"Sorry, I can't very well hear you, what did you say?" asked Gabriel's father.

She looked up at him. "Oh, it's of no consequence. It is a complicated matter."

"Well? I'd very much like to hear what the 'complicated matter' is. Please," he replied, motioning for her to continue.

"He can speak, yes. But he does not do so in the way we do … It is difficult to explain; you see, it is not really *speaking*, though it is a voice, and I can hear it, if no one else can."

Lord Loehill could not help but glance momentarily at the doctor whose eyes had suddenly widened.

"You can hear a voice?" asked the doctor.

"It's not *a* voice. It's *his* voice. And I hear it while he plays the violin."

"Ah," the doctor leant back in his chair, his eye returning to their usual shape. "That is nothing to worry about," he said turning towards Mr Norton. "Listening to a good musician playing a beautiful piece of music, one often hears a sort of added dimension which can sound very much like an angelic voice amongst the layers of sound. There's a passage in Marcel Proust about a piano … well, it's of no concern. I've experienced this myself." He smiled kindly at Edith, knowing her family and friends were not terribly understanding in such matters.

"It wasn't only my imagination."

"No, no, I wouldn't say it was only imagination. It is some emotion, I think, that can't quite be pinned down."

"Oh, yes." Edith looked at the doctor properly for the first time. "Yes, I think you do understand."

"Well, thank you."

"No, no. I don't think you do quite," said Lord Loehill, rather impolitely as he thumped the arm of his chair. "We're not discussing music and its properties. We're trying to discover how, with no proper voice, Edith was able to actually *talk* to the boy. I don't mean simply hearing some kind of godly voice; I mean really having a *conversation*. One-to-one. That's what has previously been implied."

"Ah," the doctor leant forward again, appearing slightly irritated. "So Edith, is that true? That you have really and truly *spoken* to the violinist? Question-response and such? Do you hear him say words together, with coherent meaning?"

If the girl had been in a completely logical state of mind, with all her attention focused on the situation at hand, she almost certainly would not have responded as she did. She would have taken the escape the doctor had offered and been thankful for it, and her future might have been altogether different. But she didn't. She was tired and hopeful and had been pleasantly distracted from processing anything other than the spoken words themselves, not their potential consequences, as a bird very like Esra had passed by the window and momentarily perched on the ornamental cherry tree.

"I hear words said with coherent meaning, and when I say something, he responds appropriately, and vice versa. He's told me all about himself; not in writing, not through any other person, all through his very own words. But it's his violin that is his means of communicating and that is why he does not speak in the same way we do. I don't know, one could say it was as if his voice box was outside his body as the violin … There is nothing wrong with him: he is not deceitful or psychologically disturbed. In fact, the only aspect that appears wrong is that everything about him is so *right*. I know that doesn't sound at all reasonable."

"So … So what is his name?" asked the doctor.

"I don't know. But I know where he comes from and how he came to be here and everything like that."

"And has he told anyone else? Has he been heard by anyone other than yourself?" asked Lord Loehill.

"No; that is to say, not another person. But he talks to the birds and other woodland creatures, and they understand him."

"Ah," said the doctor, as though he were about to speak, but thought better of it.

Lord Loehill spoke instead. "Alright. I think that's all, Edith. We can probably make a judgement now. Thank you."

Edith knew this was her cue to leave. "Don't do anything to him, though. There's nothing wrong with him."

"Oh, no. Nothing wrong with *him*. I'm quite sure of that. Thank you," Lord Loehill smiled.

Edith left. Mari was passing by the door, and the girl asked her for some water.

She drank the water outside the door, and her brain became suddenly hyperactive again and she could hear all that they said on the other side of the door.

"Well, doctor. Surely that's enough to go by?"

"I … I don't honestly think there's anything wrong with the girl. She appears completely in control of her senses. Really, it's healthy for girls that age to speak romantically; she will get married without too much thought and then be a woman. In my opinion, it simply sounds she is impatient to be married—a natural female fixation with masculinity. It is a difficult age."

"I don't want to risk it, I'm afraid. I respect your opinion, but I don't wish my grandchildren to be tainted with imbecility."

"I assure you with absolute certainty that there is no taint, in any mental or physical capacity, to be inherited by your potential grandchildren, from her anyway."

Lord Loehill then spoke so quietly that Edith couldn't catch any of it. When Mari passed by again she gave her the glass and went back up to her room. She had heard enough, however, to realise how fateful her words, and how distinctly purposeful their questions, had been.

Gabriel's father had not taken the doctor's subtle hint on the incapacities that were perhaps to be gained from his side of the family, but had simply whispered to the latter that no grandchildren, no future, no *nothing* for *anybody* was to be had if the girl was not removed from the scene.

"Ah." There was a pause, then, "You do know that for certification (as I believe this is your intention) two doctors' signatures are needed."

"Damn! Yes, I did know, of course. That can be dealt with soon enough, with your helpful persuasion," replied Lord Loehill.

The clock struck one and the doctor rose.

"Ah. I shall have to leave you. I have an urgent matter to attend to."

"Of course, of course, urgent matters as always, yes. You realise that we are wanting to be absolutely … *proper* in this situation. We want the very best of care and treatment for her. And … this is the best, the *only*, way for everyone," Lord Loehill said.

The door opened and the doctor came out, followed by Lord Loehill and the girl's parents.

In the front hall, Mr Norton held out his hand without speaking and the doctor shook it before having to take Loehill's, whose grip was painfully firm.

"We'll be in contact shortly then, doctor," he said.

"Ah, yes, indeed," replied the doctor, casually reshaping his hand.

XIV

"Is she safe?"

"Mr Norton, I certainly wouldn't put any of my patients' lives at risk. I mean, it is not my preference to have two in the same room, but unless you wait for the new wing's completion, it is the only way I can accommodate your daughter. The lady is harmless; she has never caused any trouble. So yes, your daughter is as safe as she could be in the circumstances," Dr Tarten, head doctor at Barford House, was standing with his hand on the doorknob. "It is entirely up to you. We have the correct papers, and I would be most pleased to help."

Mr Norton adjusted his coat, giving himself as much time as possible to find the right words. "Er, yes, I suppose it is for the best. For my daughter, that is. When should she be brought here?"

"Whenever is convenient."

"She's … Well, she's downstairs now."

Dr Tarten, raising his eyebrows slightly, opened the door.

"Then by all means, bring her up now." He held his hand out of the door, motioning for Mr Norton to take its lead.

When Edith came up, she came alone. "Your father is coming?"

"No, he said he had to leave."

"Alright. So that's how it is. Shall I show you to your room now, or would you prefer to sit and talk here a while?"

"I don't think it matters to me much either way. Though I might ask how long I am supposed to be here?"

"There is no fixed length to your stay with us: your parents think it a good idea for you to have a holiday; a break from your usual duties, and has asked us to help you use it to your utmost advantage. Neither we, nor they, mind how long it takes for you to recover … or rather, become fully rested."

"What is your view of my health, then? What do you think of this situation?"

"It is against our rules to confer any such information to our patients … or guests."

She looked out the window behind him; there was a small bird on the nearest branch of an English Oak observing her with interest. She tilted her head in response to its questioning gaze.

"Is there something more you want to ask?" she heard the doctor in the distance.

Thinking about it, she thought it could be Esra. She couldn't quite tell, but the face and movements were definitely familiar.

"Oh, no. There doesn't seem to be much point. I might as well go to my room. Thank you."

Dr Tarten rushed her down the corridor in as fast a speed as he could muster without seeming too keen to be rid of her. "Here. It's here," he held the door for her. It, the door that is, was painted a slightly scary canary yellow with a small, circular window about three quarters of the way up, like the porthole of a brightly coloured eighteenth-century ship.

Once inside, with the doctor still holding the door, the first thing the girl noticed was the blue velvet chaise-lounge in the right-hand corner, reminiscent of her mother's one of green velvet. Its legs were a rich dark brown and shaped like the curved paws of lions. Upon it sat a middle-aged, grey-haired woman, chin rested on cupped hands.

"Good afternoon, Miss Thomas. How are you today?"

Miss Thomas allowed her eyes to leave the position of their pensive gaze and rest casually on him. She made one subtle nod without moving any other part of herself before her eyes rolled back off him to land in their former position.

Dr Tarten turned to Edith. "This is Miss Thomas. She will be your room companion for the next little while." He stepped into the room, closing the door. "Come. This is one of the best rooms, let me show you round."

He walked towards Miss Thomas. "This room is your sitting room, you see it is well furnished." Edith did not see how it was well furnished; there were two uncomfortable-looking wooden chairs, an empty writing desk, a small side table and the chaise-lounge. The walls were white, the two windows had blue curtains matching the chaise-lounge and there was one big Indian rug covering most of the wooden floor. She wondered how the worst of the rooms were furnished and who these were inflicted upon. She did not know the precise nature of this building. "And here," he said walking back across the room and opening a door in the left wall, "this is Miss Thomas' bedroom. We will be transforming a corner of the sitting room to act temporarily as your bedroom as soon as my assistant gets back from … never mind … Through that door there is your washroom. Yes. And your meals will be taken with a few other guests in King's Dining Room. Someone will call for you."

The girl had a wave of nausea at the idea of sleeping in a sitting room next to the bedroom of a strange woman she didn't think she knew. What sort of place was this, to have to share? It seemed so cramped; the ceilings were low, the rooms pretty small, and no privacy, it would appear. She prayed the woman would be nice and that she could go home as soon as possible, preferably in the next three days, since she knew she wouldn't sleep for at least the next two nights.

"Alright, that's all, I think," said the doctor with a nervous laugh. "I'll leave you to become acquainted," he nodded at Miss Thomas and then left the room, as though he couldn't get out fast enough.

Edith watched the door for a minute and then took one of the wooden chairs across to the window opposite and sat looking out. In the window, she could see Miss Thomas' reflection, and could tell that this woman was regarding her. The reflected image wasn't clear but she had the faintest idea that she did know the lady. Perhaps she had been a visitor at their house once?

"What have they told you?" the lady suddenly asked.

"Sorry? I don't understand."

"I mean, what have they told you you're here for? Have they explained to you the nature of your visit? Etcetera …"

"No. Well, they've only told me I'm here temporarily as a guest."

"And you believe them?"

"No; of course not. I know I'm not a guest, but I do believe I'm here temporarily."

Miss Thomas smiled slightly. The girl was not sure whether to think it sinister, wry or genuinely friendly.

"How old are you?" she asked.

"Seventeen."

"Only?"

"Yes?"

"What have your parents said?"

"About being here? They have not spoken to me about it; not extensively anyway. They want me to have a change of scene, a rest, or something."

"Why?"

"I don't know! Alright, I do know … But, I don't mean to sound rude … do I know *you*?"

"Fair enough. I didn't mean to interrogate you. It's only … Oh, don't worry. I'll find out soon enough. I feel I will. Nothing happens around here."

Edith didn't know what she was supposed to reply, so she didn't. At the same time, she felt sorry for this woman who seemed rather melancholic. She needn't have worried about struggling to find a way to break the silence before it grew uncomfortable, because Miss Thomas suddenly put her head in her hands and then flung them back on her knees to push herself up and walk briskly to her bedroom, shutting the door loudly behind her.

She did not come back out: Edith was very much aware of the silence. The windows seemed more a reminder of the room she was in, than a means of looking out into the world. It was like a barrier, separating her from all the songs of the birds outside. She experienced an instantaneous surge of remembrance of her hours spent in her room at home, when her parents had refused her freedom. It made her feel sick and she was upset that she had not been stronger and more practical about it all at the time. Then again, she told herself, she had not understood the violinist at that point; perhaps it had all been down to a subconscious battle.

She sighed: to the matter in hand. Right. She did not have any of her belongings; nobody had told her to bring anything, so she assumed luggage would be brought sometime later today. It was all a little vague and strange.

Was there anything to read in the room? Anything to do at all? It didn't appear so. The girl tried to look through the porthole window in the door but she was too short to see anything other than the corridor wall opposite. She counted the number of birds passing by the two windows, and told herself both the English and Latin names of the trees she could see. She got to such a point of desperation that she tried to calculate the distances and heights of the trees. She tried to tap out the first movement of Rachmaninoff's third piano concerto on the windowsill, remembering looking out of Mrs Carey's window while teaching Edward Baker. Then she walked around the room so many times that she felt faint with dizziness. The silent clock's hands moved smoothly through the minutes, yet the hours did not seem to move at all.

She was called to dinner at five-thirty: a terribly uncivilised hour to dine. Still, it could not really be described as dinner without an incredible, and generous, stretch of the imagination. There was an attempt at civility and elegance, with table places laid out with decent crockery around a medium-sized circular table, but there was no choice of food. There was bread with leak and potato soup to begin, followed by salty beef stew, and baked apple for dessert. No one spoke, save to ask for the salt.

Miss Thomas had not come to dinner and when Edith got back to her room (where a bed, dressing table and suitcase had arrived in the left-hand corner of the 'living' room), she was still in her bedroom, or so the girl supposed, since she was not on the chaise-lounge. She did not want to go into the bedroom and check, or have to speak to the woman, which meant she could not go to the washroom and prepare herself for the night. She opened her suitcase and emptied it onto her bed and then wondered where she was to put her clothes.

At least the lack of choice in clothes suggested she would not be there long. She looked round the room and saw what they expected her to use, an object which had not been there before dinner. It was a back-stage theatrical costume stand, a pole placed horizontally on vertical sticks. A generous amount of red and yellow coat hangers hung somewhat tragically on the pole. Sighing, she reduced the tragedy of the hangers by placing her dresses upon them, and then took off the clothes she was wearing and got into bed in her slip. As she had predicted, she passed a very restless night. The gap in her usual evening routine of cleaning her face and hands contributed to her discomfort, but the loud breathing of Miss Thomas and creaking floorboards of someone pacing up and down in the room above made sleep all the more unlikely. However, shortly after the first high twitters of the birds outside, while the room took on a blurred, dark-purple glow, she fell into the upper layers of unconsciousness.

XV

A week passed with no definitive events. Miss Thomas sat in what was obviously her favourite position, the blue chaise-lounge, and did speak to the girl, but the conversation was minimal, monosyllabic. Meals were the same and most days Miss Thomas would miss breakfast and dinner, declaring one meal a day perfectly adequate.

They took daily walks outside though, like meals, Miss Thomas often missed hers. Edith wanted to be alone outside and try to talk to the birds but she had yet to be granted this opportunity; she was only ever alone when Miss Thomas isolated herself in the bedroom. Dr Tarten had come to see her once during the week to ask her somewhat jovially if she was still alive and tell her the new wing would be ready before she knew it. This brief visit had upset her because, if it really was true that the new wing would be ready for her to move into, it must mean she was staying in this place long enough to see the completion of the new wing and need her own room in it. And so it looked like home wasn't planning to be home for quite some time.

It was on the second Sunday of her stay that a soft-faced nurse ushered Edith's corridor into the hall. She did not say what this non-routine calling was for, only looked very jolly and said that everyone would enjoy it. The sour expressions of the people making their way through the corridor and down the stairs made Edith herself become so melancholic that she told the nurse she had to return to her room for her scarf, though it was not at all cold. In her room (or their sitting room) she sat on her bed for a few minutes with a completely blank mind: this was a pleasant experience—like a wakeful deep sleep.

Then, her mind focused back on the clock and she saw enough time had passed for them all to be down and ready in the hall. She grabbed her scarf and made her way downstairs, looking around and humming slightly, relieved to be alone outside her quarters. As she arrived at the top of the flight of stairs that would take her down to the hall, she paused. There was someone else humming, someone at the bottom of the stairs, she thought. She craned her neck to see who it was before going down—she did not want to bump into anyone, particularly not Dr Tarten.

There was no one there, not anywhere near the stairs, or down any of the corridors. She shrugged and continued towards the hall—perhaps she was going mad after all, imagining noises in her head. On the other hand, it was not surprising with all the silence she had grown accustomed to: it had probably made her hearing so sensitive that she could hear the faintest electrical hum of the lights. Perhaps she was getting closer to understanding an aspect of how the violinist felt.

But the humming got louder as she approached the hall. At twenty steps away from the doors, she was sure it couldn't be the lights—it modulated too much. It was almost as though someone was singing a song with a bandage tied tightly round their mouth.

Oh! If this were the case, what precisely was the nature of this building? They could be torturing people here; people could be tied to chairs with their mouths silenced to prevent discovery or unwanted attention, whilst awaiting interrogation. Dr Tarten could be head of an underground spying mission! Then what was the purpose of all the other 'guests'? She knew they were pretty much all insane to a greater or lesser degree, but apart from suspecting that they had all been the victims to extreme psychological torture, she could not compute the relevance of her own position. She could not genuinely believe that *she could be thought insane.* Was she? Alright. Of course, her poor bored mind had run away with itself. She should go and see what they had been called into the hall to see … any distraction was welcome.

She put her hand on the large knob of the right door and was about to open it when the left door opened and Dr Tarten appeared. He gave a small yelp at the sight of her and closed the door with sudden alacrity.

"Good Evening, Dr Tarten," the girl smiled at him, impressed at this effort of hers.

"What are you doing here?" he asked, looking flustered.

"Oh … well the nurse, Nurse Fitson, that is, came …" She inclined her head slightly towards the door—a word spoken from within the room had grabbed her attention. The mumbled humming was becoming more pronounced.

Ah, you are outside now, aren't you? Outside those doors at the end? Why don't you come in?

"Oh, oh! It's him! It's him inside, isn't it?" she tried to turn the handle but saw that the doctor had placed himself in the way. "Oh please! Please let me!"

"Who? Who's in there? Try to speak calmly Edith, I'm trying to help you."

"I *am* speaking calmly! You *know* who's in there! The violinist! The one in whom my parents were so interested!"

Edith, if I could only see you! There's something, some things I haven't yet told you and I think I know a way out. Let's leave! I can't wait to run through the long grass, the overhanging leaves, the open sky and wind! Run towards the river with you! Yes, I should laugh, I know, the imagery is absurd, but I am desperate. I thought we had more time.

"Tell me now, I can't get in!" She spoke with her cheek against the panelling of the door.

"He certainly does have some extraordinary skill, how full and loud a sound he is making, and how passionate his playing has just become, and the staccato following …! I quite understand that you find his performances exceptional."

"I don't need you to understand. If only! But don't try."

"How did you know it was him …? No, sorry, I see your expression. Stupid question. This playing has his very own special signature on it—you could recognise it anywhere. Is that it? Well …" Dr Tarten's voice blurred into the distance as she focused on that of the violinist.

I can't tell you now, Edith, with the door between us. I need to speak to you face to face. It is too serious … I can hear the doctor out there. He is the doctor, isn't he, the round-stomached man with spectacles and a chequered handkerchief? Well, don't worry. And don't tell him anything about me. It won't work. I'm going to come back and get you soon. We need to go.

"But when and how? I will be waiting in such suspense … You know, I really don't miss anything, not even having my own room, decent food, and the freedom to roam about the grounds at whatever hour. May I say though, without feeling I sound too French, how much I've missed you! I didn't realise hearing your voice would make me feel so homesick!"

"… and so I completely see why you should think that … Ah. You were not speaking to me. Come, though we are quiet, we should not speak so close to the door—it may disturb the violinist," the doctor's voice had come back into focus and she allowed herself to be guided away from the door, down the corridor and into Dr Tarten's study.

"Please, take a seat," he stepped behind his desk and before deciding against it and taking a seat in the pale green armchair opposite her. He folded his hand in his lap. "Who were you speaking to through the door?"

The pointlessness of telling the truth in such a situation and to such a man would have been evident even without the words of warning from the violinist.

"Oh, no, I was not speaking to anyone through the door. I was speaking to you, but I was tired, so I rested my head against the door."

"Hmm. But you asked me to tell you something because you couldn't get in to the hall, and then you said you missed me but that my voice made you feel homesick?"

"Yes, well, you see, it was only that, because I couldn't get into the hall, I wanted you to tell me why it was I shouldn't go into the hall. That is quite simple you see? And, in speaking of your voice etc., I meant that it was reminiscent of the comforting tone of my parents."

"Yes, yes. I see. This is perfectly logical. I am sorry I have to ask these questions—"

"No, no. It's absolutely fine. I know how confusing I can be when I am tired. I was probably mumbling terribly unclearly."

"Yes, alright. I think it would be better for you to have an early night. There's no point going into the hall now anyway, they'll be finished quite soon. You should go to your room now."

"Alright. Thank you, Dr Tarten. Your hospitality is very much appreciated. Do you think I am better? When will the new wing be ready?"

"Very shortly, very shortly. You must be patient. Now," he stood and opened the door. "I'll say goodbye and see you tomorrow."

She stood in the hallway for a moment and then decided to go the long way to her room past the hall. Before she got there, she saw Nurse Fitson outside the doors, waving her arms in her direction. She was not waving in greeting, so Edith stopped and waited for the nurse to run up to her.

"You can't come this way. You're not allowed near the hall, Miss Norton. Dr Tarten just spoke to me very seriously."

"What's there to be so serious about?" the girl asked.

"Oh, I shouldn't say, even if I knew, and I don't. He's got your best interests at heart. That's all I know. But he's angry at me for arranging this concert without his consent. I shouldn't be saying … I was only trying to help—"

"Don't worry; I'm sure everyone has enjoyed it, so you have helped, of course. I'll go straight to my room the other way, thank you."

The nurse nodded and smiled and Edith went on her way, arriving at her room a couple of minutes later. She took the novel from her bedside table and carried it to the window where she sat in her wooden seat and looked outside with the novel open upside-down in her hands. The sky was gradually edging its way towards the start of a long, purple dusk, and the birds were singing their slow evening songs above the dewy grass.

She opened the window to smell the dusk air. As she took one last deep breath of damp grass and smoke, she became aware that Miss Thomas had quietly entered the room and was standing a respectable two yards from her. Edith closed the window.

"Please don't close it on my account," said Miss Thomas. For some reason, the gentleness with which it was said made Edith feel slightly nervous.

"Oh, no, I was just about to close it anyway, thank you," she sat back in the chair.

Miss Thomas gave a small and motherly smile. "Do you mind if I bring a seat and sit beside you?"

Edith made a hurried effort to hide her unavoidable surprise. "No, no, of course, please do."

Sure enough, the other wooden chair was beside her in an instant. They sat in silence for a minute. Then, "I didn't see you in the hall."

Why this sudden interest? Her expression must have clearly reflected her thoughts since she made no attempt to conceal them, but Miss Thomas, if she did notice, pretended not to see.

"No I wasn't in the hall."

Miss Thomas did, however, see that there would be no point in waiting for the girl to volunteer more.

"I was close to the back of the hall; I could hear you speaking."

"Oh?"

"I think Dr Tarten was with you; he had just walked out when I first heard you. I wondered why you wouldn't come in, or why he wouldn't let you."

The girl watched Miss Thomas who openly regarded her in return. "It was no great problem," Edith said.

"I hadn't noticed that you didn't come to the hall with the rest of us. It is strange; I know you find this place quite depressing and all the people deeply oppressive. When I first came here, I was so much in another world, I never noticed anything. You see, there are two types of people here, or two types who are rightly here. They can be assessed on their arrival: the first type is how I was—going about like an automaton: no senses, no emotion. The second arrives hysterical. I say it is strange because you don't fall into either of the types. I did wonder why you were here at the start, though I think I realise." Miss Thomas paused, and the girl saw, in the depths of the woman's eyes, the first promise of a spark.

"Perhaps I don't *think* I realise, I'm sure I know why you're here. One can never be sure of anything—apart from life's inevitable end, of course. But, I think I'm as sure as sureness goes about this. After all, it has affected my whole existence, for one thing, let alone the existences of many others."

Edith wonder what this had to do with anything, the poor woman was rambling. She had become an amateur philosopher, a wise woman, in this house of madness.

"You did recognise me when you first came, didn't you? You asked me, and you were not being impertinent. No, don't worry, yes."

The girl was suddenly very cold. Why was she here?

She looked behind her to check she had shut the window. But no, it was shut: she had not fancied it. She went over to her bed and threw her thick woollen scarf about her shoulders. Miss Thomas seemed in no hurry and waited patiently for her room-mate to come and sit back down.

She had changed the subject. "He's a very good violinist, isn't he?"

"Who?" Edith asked, shivering slightly, and knowing full well the answer.

"Oh, why, the one playing in the hall, of course: you could hear from outside, couldn't you?"

"Oh, yes, him."

"Him?"

"Him, yes: you said *he* was a very good violinist."

"Ah, yes, I did. I couldn't understand why you were speaking outside the door, why you wouldn't be curious to come inside and see whilst listening. There's something very different about seeing people play, being in a room with them, and hearing it behind walls."

Though Miss Thomas' voice revealed nothing, Edith somehow knew she was crying. The light had dimmed more rapidly, or to a greater extent than usual it seemed, as the room had now taken on a translucent dusty grey. The girl looked into the face of Miss Thomas and, even in this light, she could see the shining paths the tears had left on her cheeks.

"I'm sorry," said the girl, though she was sure she wasn't the cause of upset, "I wasn't able to come into the hall."

"No, I know: Dr Tarten wouldn't let you. He wouldn't have let me either, I shouldn't think. But then, he can't know everything. He doesn't actually seem to know very much," she let out a small laugh. "He taught me to speak as I do now, you know. Ah, if you had heard my voice when I was first here, you would probably have run a mile at the least!"

The woman now rested her chin on her hand which was propped at an appropriate height with her elbow on the arm of the chair. There was silence for an uncomfortable length of time. And then suddenly,

"But it wasn't him I heard you speaking to."

Edith did not know what to do. Without knowing why, she was terrified of this woman who sat beside her. She knew she was insane, but not to what extent. Did she know anything about anything? The desire to turn on a lamp was great, but the idea of getting up and walking past the woman in order to do so with her back to her …

She shivered again. The woman sat up straight. "Get ready for bed," she said. "I need to tell you a story. My story."

XVI

*T*he crying continued. It began as quiet and sporadic sobs which mounted to become a howl one might mistake as that of some tormented animal of the night. Eventually this became a long, deep moan like a foghorn. The slumped figure, from whom this noise came, was sitting by a wall beside the docks and in front of her lay the body of a young man whose hair was covered in the grim river water. He was motionless.

A man dressed in a suit and tie, who himself was not completely sober, mistook the two tragic figures he walked past as drunkard beggars and kicked at them with his pointed shoe, shouting insults. His day had not been the best and he wanted to cool his head by letting his anger out on any creatures more helpless than himself. The woman mourning the stillness of the man lying before her stopped her wailing and hit and kicked the attacker with all the wild power of a woman in pain, leaving him to run off yelping and wake up the next morning ashamed of something he did not know.

But he, although a few bruises and a headache remained, could leave for his business the next day as usual, be breakfasted by his maid and have all the comforts of his daily routine, with the vague memory of a bad dream, forgotten as his headache left. The tragic figure, though, still lay at the side of the man who had been everything; hoping, praying that she would wake. When these prayers remained unanswered, she prayed for the eternal sleep granted to her lover to be granted unto her too.

She was deaf to the noises of the dock. The creak of the abandoned 'Three Sisters' pub, whose sign was moved back and forth slowly by the wind accompanied by a thick, sickly fog. The forbidding sound of metal clanking against metal, as the harboured boats swayed into each other and the occasional cold, sharp whistle of strong busts of wind travelling through the alleyways which boatmen long ago had named, for some past and forgotten reason, 'Devil's Walk'. These eerie sounds made even the bravest and stable of people shudder and quicken their pace, avoiding memories of all those campfire stories and thinking instead of the kind face there to greet them when they arrived home.

The darkness was such that it was not dark. In the alley, not a glint could be found; there was no friendly lamp to reveal its sinister corners. It was of such depth that if one closed one's eyes, what they saw would be exactly as when they left them open. If feeling vulnerable, as one did on such nights, the question was sure to arise as to whether their eyes were actually open. This lack of sight was like hers of sound. To her, there could be no difference in her utter silence or complete and deafening noise. If she screamed, there was no one to hear, so, did she actually scream? No one was there to assure her of her existence, not after the drunken man had gone. But the pain loudly assured.

A passing policeman forced her up and called for help in the early hours. None of the local people would enter the Walk and so eventually he had to deal with the body himself, after taking the woman to the station where she sat as if she too were dead. The young and unusually jolly policeman took a car to the dark alley he had found the woman and, as he wondered how the body should ultimately be dealt with, he realised that in his normal, absent-minded way, he had turned into the wrong alley: it growing so dark and all. But he had been sure that the alley was called 'Devil's Walk'. He remembered smiling at the name when he had originally walked past, before spotting the heart-breaking couple. And the alley he was in had, indeed, got an old and rusted street sign bearing that name.

It could not, however, have been that alley, because there was no dead body. He smiled once again on thinking of the local people; they had probably once been spooked in a storm, or someone had claimed a sighting after having one too many, and it had been decided that all the alleys should be named something thereof. He was finding his move from the city highly amusing.

Then gradually, his smile wore off, and his cheeks did not hold the same boyish, red glow. He had looked at every other alley in the street and none had a body slumped on the cobble.

"Excuse me, which alley is Devil's Walk, or is there more than one?" he asked a man who was wrapped snugly in an old hat and scarf with his collars up. A local man.

"Oh no, sir. There be only one alley with that name. I'd not go there if I were you, sir; many a one's had too bad a time there. It was so named for a reason." The man looked at him with an expression which seemed concerned and then continued on his way.

The policeman was a level-headed young man who realised that it was a bad idea to spend any time dwelling on the warning in the local man's words—he was much more concerned about what had been said before: there was only one Devil's walk which meant that either his eyes had deceived him or the body had been stolen. No one would steal a body. Surely? Unless it was a case of murder and the body had been taken away to conceal the murderer. But he also knew this was unlikely, given the fact that the woman he had found next to the body was in the police station right now.

He went again to Devil's Walk and turned into it, peering through the darkness. It was still completely dark but for the moonlight bouncing off the water into the alley. He was glad the fog had passed. His eyes grew accustomed to this light enough to see that he had been mistaken, poor chap, and that the sad body was still there. Then, he rubbed his eyes. There was a second figure there also, standing, looking down at the body.

If it had been any other alley, he might never have questioned another's presence—people often stopped and stared in such events. But no one would dare walk here, no locals anyway, and there were few visitors in this part of the port. It wasn't only that. The standing figure had a presence, an atmosphere about him that was not comfortable. There was something unnatural in the way he stared … He told himself not to be quite so pathetic; he needn't become as superstitious as the local people just because he had been transferred here. His job was to protect, not involve himself in the petty fears of the locals.

Having turned away, he looked once more at the two figures. Or … where the two figures had been and should have been, only, they weren't. Not anymore. Both the corpse and the staring figure had vanished in the moment he had looked away. Oh. They had been there.

He was suddenly aware of the chill the breeze brought to the centre of his bones. His senses were heightened to the sounds of the dock, the sounds which, before, had seemed friendly and romantic. Now the metal clanked, getting faster and faster with each further gust of wind as though in hysterical warning. He stood mesmerised, not able to move and then, with a rush of adrenaline he had never felt before, he ran. Ran until he had reached the security of the inside door to the police station. He barely noticed the faces, crossed with the shadows of window frames, looking onto the moonlit street as he ran.

After collapsing onto the waiting bench, recovering his breath as much as his nerve, he decided not to reflect on the situation. As was his theory, it was best not to dwell on things for too long because in most cases one would be the worse off for doing so.

"Gone, you say."

"Yes, sir. Gone."

"And do you know how? Or why, even?"

"No, sir. Well ... "

"Yes?"

"There was a person ... a figure standing over him, his back was turned."

"Then this person ran away with the body and you stood and watched?"

"No, sir, I certainly would not do that."

"So, we have now established the fact the body was not taken when you brought her here. How would you suggest that the body then went, in front of your very eyes?"

"Please sir, don't take this is the wrong way. The body was taken whilst I was here but was then brought back. That is when I saw it and the figure."

"Constable, I know that you have only just come here, but surely you don't expect me to believe that a corpse was lying in an alley, disappeared, reappeared and then disappeared once more, this time right before you … It would be better if you told me the facts straight; I will not be blaming you."

"Sir…" the policeman was about to protest, to assure the rather ancient Inspector that he was indeed telling the truth, but then he realised that it was not the truth that the Inspector wanted to hear. The truth could never be solved, and would cause nothing but fear and confusion. "What I meant to say—that is to say what really happened was—I turned into the wrong alley and when I eventually arrived back at Devil's Walk, I did see someone standing in the place I remembered the body to have been but the corpse itself was gone. I called to the person but they ran and when I chased them, they disappeared into some dark corner I could not find."

"Thank you, Phips, I am glad that is now established, you needn't have looked quite so pale when you came in. Alright. As soon as you have brought the girl to me you are dismissed for the night. It was in Neville's Walk that you found her, wasn't it?"

The thought of the Inspector's mishearing cheered the policeman, "Devil's Walk, sir. Devil with a 'D'," he said, closing the door behind him. As he did so he heard the smash of crockery from inside the room. Reopening the door, he found the Inspector looking quite pale with his coffee cup in pieces on the mauve rug.

He called to a fellow Constable to get the girl ready. She must have been sitting on her own for some time and this was *usually the time of a change in shifts, only he hadn't seen anyone pass to take the empty desk sergeant's place. And it was not good to leave anyone for too long in the state she seemed.*

When he originally tried to speak to the Inspector, to ask him if all was well, he did not receive a reply, though when he bent to pick up the broken cup, he thought he heard the Inspector mutter to himself. On a different day, Policeman Phips would have believed it to be old age. He would have left chuckling to himself. But now, after having a local man's warning and the shock of his life witnessing a disappearing trick, he could not help but notice that the reaction of his senior man had come just as he had heard the alley's true name.

The supernatural was not here. No, it definitely was not. Phips made sure of that. He, at least, would not consider that. But there must have been something. And evidently something which was not good: a story to be told one day, perhaps. A story passed down as a myth from parent to child, or a true event even, distorted as it went through the generations, or maybe a recent tragedy; a tragedy happening to take place somewhere with an appropriate name, a name like Devil's Walk. Whatever it was, he could not discover now, certainly not from the shocked yet now embarrassed Inspector before him.

He was almost knocked over as he quit the room, colliding with a fellow Constable who was rushing into the office with a dreadful panic-stricken face. It was not at all becoming of him, Phips thought, brushing himself off.

"She's gone!"

"Who's gone where, what do you mean, Lodes?"

"The lady you ast me to make ready. No one saw her leave, burt she ain't where she spost to be."

"Oh God—you've sent someone to chase her?"

"Little and Hodsy are on the look now. She can't have got far; it mus've been, why, barely five minutes since I walked past her."

"What is going on out there?" came the Inspector's voice. He had once more assumed his authority, his voice strong and steady.

"The girl found by the body, sir, she's gone. No name was given."

"You mean you let her go? Do you realise she could be a murderer? A murderer?"

"She won't have got far, sir, there are men gone to get her now."

"If she's not found … "

"I will go, sir and see if she has been found," Phips interrupted the Inspector.

"I will go too, sir."

She had wailed and sobbed, but no salt tears had fallen. She had yet to be aware of anything or anyone around her. She was now silent. When Phips and the other Constable found her, it was in the place they would certainly not have assumed her to be for it was in Devil's Walk. The girl or woman (they could not identify which) had walked calmly and slowly away from the station, and her stillness filled them with such fear that at first they made no attempt to get a hold of her, or even make an advance into the alley in her direction.

Her lips, blue with cold and hunger, began to move, forming small shapes. Gradually words could be made out before finally, her voice rose to a shout, or perhaps a hysterical scream. *Phips and the Constable stood there like rabbits in front of car headlights.*

"God does not hear me. God does not do as I beg. God has taken him from me and left me with nothing. It was him …

"You second Him in His almighty greatness, if not be the same power. May You do as I beg You? You can create no more darkness than that in which I stand. I cannot suffer more than I do. Please. Give me something, anything. Anything that could have been from him. Anything that could give hope to the life I must now live …

"You saw it, You saw everything. Surely You must pity me. I kneel before You and plead to a side of You I do not know exists. Show God that You have mercy. Show me mercy. Give me what I must have or watch me die, too. I am desperate. I will never be satisfied again. I have lost what I believed I'd have forever, never questioned my content and against my will I have learnt…

"I know what I am doing; I know what I ask. And I beg of You."

Shaken from their shock, they managed to get her back to the station, though they did not need to silence or calm her because as soon as her arms were grabbed, she fell towards them, silent and limp, though fully conscious.

XVII

Edith sat propped against her pillows stunned but utterly confused. Beside her, Miss Thomas had dropped her head forward so that it rested upon her chest in an unnatural, doll-like way. She very soon became aware of the heavy silence and could not help feeling the need to swallow, which she did awkwardly loudly, as though afraid. In all honesty, she was afraid. Though this dominating silence had nothing creepy about it, it disturbed the girl because her mind now had space enough to reflect on what she had heard. She did not understand it.

The impression it immediately left on her mind was of the tragic situation of a young woman finding herself with nothing left to live for. The situation in which a person is so raw that reason does not exist. In such a case, one might easily find themselves swearing allegiance to mysterious and insubstantial beings. She knew that the young woman was Miss Thomas, but apart from that had no idea why it had any relevance, or at least enough relevance to be told to a young roommate.

Miss Thomas looked up and stared into the face of the girl for slightly longer than was comfortable (which, in the case of Miss Thomas, was for about five seconds). Then, without a word, she got up and went into her room, not to be seen again until tea-time the following day.

She thought about her roommate all the morning before dismissing it from her mind at lunchtime. She wondered if Miss Thomas had borne any children after her plea to the devil to have something made of her and her dead lover. She had understood that much. Obviously, she did not think the devil himself (insubstantial as he was) would directly grant that wish, but strange things do happen, and perhaps Miss Thomas had previously conceived a child anyway. Deep down, Edith hoped, even believed, that there was a child somewhere whose mother was in the room next door. She told herself this conviction was perfectly natural, since surely the story would have been pointless if the conclusion had been left unfulfilled. A child born in such a situation would make a good story. Ah well, she could let it all go with lunch, otherwise it would only keep repeating itself as a circle in her head.

Gabriel came to visit her after lunch. They sat together in a sitting room near the hall where two nurses were knitting in a corner, pretending to be wholly uninterested in the two people they were clearly observing.

"I am so sorry you are here," Gabriel said.

"Oh, no, well, you shouldn't be. I'm enjoying my holiday here."

He sighed. "Why aren't you serious with me?"

"What do you mean? I am always serious with you."

"You can't be enjoying yourself."

"Why not?"

"Oh come on, Edith, look at it!" He motioned with his arms, flapping them wildly in all directions of the room.

Edith laughed. "Shush, don't make such a fuss; otherwise they'll think you should be here!"

Gabriel let his arms drop and looked at the floor for a moment.

"At least … you don't think I think you should be here, do you?"

"What does it matter if you think I should be here or not? It doesn't much affect me." She saw his expression and added, "Of course it is good and comforting to have such kind support, but I don't see much practical benefit—since I am here, and here to stay as it would seem."

"They are trying to convince me, you realise."

"Sorry, no, who is trying to convince you of what?"

"The Parents. Our parents, I mean. They are trying to convince me that you are insane, or at the very least, too unstable to bear the possibility of … well, anyway, they are constantly throwing young women at me. They want me to marry, and marry quick. I don't really understand what's in it for your parents, but they're in on it too. I suppose it's money; it's always money. Well, they have a problem, of course, because I will always have the upper hand in this matter. That is, they can never force me to say 'yes'…"

Edith remembered thinking exactly the same thing not so long ago, but that had been in achieving the opposite to Gabriel's wish.

"… Inevitably, they could disown me. But then, where would they be, since it is all in my name? They could get neither the house nor status—just the same as if I remain a bachelor under their roof all my life. So you see, no threats have the potential …"

Why was he so desperately keen? The girl wondered. He was so terribly sweet and sincere, she almost felt like crying. Ah, if only he had never had the pathetic notion of marriage—they could have grown into adulthood together, in the same manner that they had journeyed through childhood. They could have remained unmarried, or had families of their own, and had jolly family gatherings at Christmas and New Year. She would have been delighted to speak with him regularly on such terms; discourse with him could certainly be interesting with his certain level of insight. They could have met in his would-be well-supplied library and sat in large, high-backed armchairs by a grand and roaring fire, like those pleasant occasions with Mrs Carey (she sighed, feeling nostalgic). Or they could have had tea every so often in London.

"… Edith? Are you listening? I could get you out of here. Do you understand? I could get you out."

"Are they holding back letters from me?"

"What …? You're not listening."

"No, I am. I don't mean to change the subject. But I just wanted to ask because I … have you got any letters from Elizabeth? It's only, I haven't since I've been here, and I thought she would have kept me informed of her activities in Cornwall. I miss her."

"As far as I know, no one is holding any post from you.

I have heard from Elizabeth, yes, I got a postcard when she arrived there."

"Nothing more recently? That was almost two weeks ago, I got a postcard then too. That is strange."

"Two weeks? Really? Oh, I hadn't realised. Well, yes, I suppose that is strange … But not to worry, we're sure to hear every minute detail when she gets back! Mrs what's-her-name will be keeping them thoroughly occupied, as she always does … you are evidently in need of company, or you would not get yourself so concerned."

"I am not concerned. I have lots of time to think, and I just thought it a little peculiar."

"I will come again tomorrow. You do not have enough visitors."

"Oh dear, you are obviously worried now. You're trying not to get yourself in a panic, I can see, Gabriel! Look, don't worry—that would be nice to see you tomorrow, but about Elizabeth … just tell me if you get a letter from her. I would like to know how she is finding Cornwall."

"Yes, no, yes, alright. Oh, I really can't stand this place, Edith! It's making me all hot and irritable!" He pulled at his already loose collar as though it was choking him.

"You don't need to stay any longer. I'll see you tomorrow, if you decide to come again."

Gabriel suddenly became completely sincere again and looked straight at her, all thoughts of his collar apparently forgotten. It made Edith feel embarrassed.

"I will come again tomorrow, Edith. You must never believe you are alone—while I remain me, and you remain you, says Robert Browning, 'So long as the world contains us both, Me the loving and you the loth, While the one eludes, must the other pursue'—you will never be abandoned. I cannot leave you here."

And with those last words, he took her hand and squeezed it before taking his leave. Edith felt she wanted to cry but found she could not. The boy's (no he was a man, wasn't he? Yes, well, by any culture's standard he should be) sincerity really did become oppressive. She was absolutely certain he had not always been this heavy.

At tea time, which arrived shortly after Gabriel had made his escape, Miss Thomas brought a cup of tea over to her roommate as their section sat in the common room.

She stood behind the girl as she lowered the cup into the girl's hands and then pressed her tea-warmed hand upon the exposed part of the girl's shoulder. The firm feel of the woman's fingers on her skin made Edith's heartbeat become inordinately pronounced, such that she could see her legs move in time with it. She was sure that when Miss Thomas had released her from the pressure of her steamed hands, everyone would be able to see the remaining imprint, left prominent and permanent-looking, on her right shoulder.

Before she came and took a seat facing Edith, she lowered herself slightly as she let her hand fall to her side, and whispered into the girl's ear. Her whisper was so hushed and breezy that it made the lock of hair that fell beside her ear tickle her cheek, slowing her pounding heart and sending a shiver through her instead.

"Vous comprenez tout, chère enfant. Il n'y a pas besoin d'expliquer plus, alors c'est votre choix—c'est tout à vous maintenant."

The voice was disturbingly unlike Miss Thomas' and left Edith with an immediate cold headache. She responded quietly without turning to look round.

«Quoi …? Je suis désolée, mais comment? Je suis certain que je ne comprends rien ou, au moins, c'est certainement vrai maintenant—je suis plus perdue qu'avant. Que voulez-vous dire?"

Miss Thomas stood up straight and stepped in front of Edith.

She shrugged as she sat down and said, "Sorry, I don't speak French. What are you saying?"

The girl thought it best to concentrate on her cup of tea rather than reveal the frown that threatened to form across her forehead.

"Nothing. I'm sorry. It's only that I am confused, as usual." They were silent for a few minutes, each sipping their tea. Then Edith began, "Miss Thomas, by way of conversation, do you have children?"

Miss Thomas put her cup back on its saucer as her eyebrows fell low and angry, her eyes forever fixed on Edith's. And just as suddenly as her expression seemed accustomed to its change, she released her eyebrows from their uncomfortably crinkled position so that they dropped diagonally sideways and tears ran down her cheeks. It was like speed-theatre.

"Oh why? Why? Why do you ask?"

Edith felt like throwing her cup at the woman, she was so infuriating! How was one meant to react to someone who did not seem to know what feeling they felt and what feeling they showed?

The sobbing woman brought Edith the attention of the observing nurses.

"Was that appropriate, I wonder?" a large and middle-aged nurse asked Edith who decided the question was rhetorical.

An older female patient decided her opinion had evidently been called for and came over to give it. "I suppose you don't realise that it is highly offensive to ask a lady titled 'Miss' whether she has children. Perhaps you do not understand the connotations, but you might as well openly insult her with explicitly rude phrases."

A woman of a similar age came and stood by the patient who had just spoken. "But do you not see, Felicia? This generation do not understand anything of the sort. It is most probable that the young lady believed she was simply making polite conversation. After all, it is getting to the stage that women can have children whenever, wherever and in whatever position they happen to be in. In fact, I'm of the belief that soon men will be having children *instead* of women—men being far superior to women in practicality and intellect, they will realise that they would be better without the idiocies of womankind—because the women will refuse to do their duty in their desire for 'equality'. Well, that is *my* opinion, but, in my passion, I seem to be drifting off-topic …"

Edith could not help but wonder whether this woman was ever able to be 'passionate' about anything: her eyelids weighed heavily over her eyes and she spoke in such monotones that the girl was sure that any time spent with her over five minutes would be dangerous, particularly if one happened to be standing.

She stood to leave, passing Miss Thomas on her way out. "I am so sorry if I have caused offense, Miss Thomas. I have said nothing with malign intent."

Miss Thomas looked up at her with her wet eyes and patchy face. (Those eyes really were familiar, weren't they?) "Oh, Edith," she said, grabbing her by the elbow. "Don't leave. It is not through you that I am upset."

The girl looked down at the hand holding her arm in mild disgust. She was a firm believer in personal space.

"I am sure that I will see you back in our room," she said and left.

Gabriel was right, she thought, she could not stay here much longer. She had not properly noticed the insanity of the situation and, most particularly, the insanity of the people she was being pressed against, or, rather, who were pressing themselves against her. It might begin to rub off on her; she really would become that unspoken family secret, that daughter locked away.

She could not leave now, however. The violinist had said they had to leave before Gabriel had. There had been a level of urgency in his voice, too, which haunted Edith. Something had been left unsaid, and then she'd been kept away here. She sincerely hoped he would be quick in coming, though she had not the slightest idea how he would get her out. In that sense, it seemed more realistic to have Gabriel getting her out.

In the room, she lay on her bed. She tried to divert her thoughts by attempting to recall the face that was at the tip of her tongue. The face of whom Miss Thomas reminded her. She must either have met Miss Thomas previously, as she had first believed, or a relative. Otherwise, it could only be that Miss Thomas had a look that was common amongst the people of her region. She was just deciding that the similarity was perhaps best paralleled to their previous cook's daughter-in-law (or was it her niece?) who had cracked a score of walnuts for her one Christmas when she was about five, when she dozed and her mind lost all direction of thought.

As she fell into a deeper state of unconsciousness, she dreamt in a similarly muddled fashion. She was at the breakfast table with Gabriel who was reading through a huge pile of letters as he ate. At the bottom of the pile of letters, there was a worn and yellow-edged postcard which she knew was from Elizabeth. She called to Gabriel to ask for it, but he appeared not to hear her, so she got up and went over to get it. She tried to pull it from its position, and this proved impossible because it was as though the pile was instead made of bricks. She pulled it with all her strength until it came loose, causing all the other letters to fall. Gabriel suddenly turned on her and started shouting hysterically, his eyes wide in such a terrifying manner that she ran from the room. As she ran to the door, which was much further than it should have been (though this did not seem at all illogical), she felt a tickly sensation under the base of her foot and then a sickly wet one. She looked down and saw that she had squashed a large black spider and that two larger and more orange spiders were running towards her blackened foot. At this point, seeing her bare foot, she realised that she was also naked, and she felt the overpowering vulnerability of such a situation.

Though it appeared she had run in a different direction

to the spiders, she felt her other foot squash first one and then the other of the dark orange spiders, making her feet look as though they were covered in human blood. Then, rather than getting through the door and into the hall, she found herself on grass-covered granite cliffs, looking at the rich blue sea unevenly striped with snow white foam.

She thought she saw Elizabeth in the cove below and called for her. The figure was wearing Elizabeth's straw hat with the yellow ribbon and her white dress with the blue sash. She thought she could also hear her humming, softly and beautifully, to herself. She called again, less desperately though a little louder. But there was no response and, presently, the hat blew from the figure's head and she saw that it was not Elizabeth at all, but a sharp and hideous rock dressed in her clothes.

The sight made tears full rapidly down her cheeks, dropping onto her feet. And, though the human-like blood on her feet should not have been hers, the salt tears seemed like drops of acid, as if her feet were covered in deep cuts.

"Here," a mellow voice said from behind her. "Have a drink." And a hand came over her shoulder, giving her a tall and slender crystal glass filled with delicious-looking water. She suddenly realised how thirsty she was, and smiled, still a little tearful, at the beautiful glass she held. It was comfortingly familiar, perhaps reminiscent of the dinner glasses at home. Stained red with transparent patterns elegantly carved into it, it made the sunlight dance playfully upon her hand. She turned round to thank the speaker, but instead of the human figure she expected to see, a squawking black raven flew into her face.

XVIII

"Oh, that's strange; I had a dream about Elizabeth too," said Gabriel the next day.

"It's not really that strange; we were talking about her yesterday. What did you dream?" Edith replied.

"Have you still not heard from her?"

"I asked you that yesterday, why would I suddenly have heard from her before you, over night?"

"Yes, I suppose, I just wondered because—"

"I can see you're worried Gabriel. What did you dream?"

"It was most peculiar dream."

"That isn't so rare for dreams—I bet it is not as peculiar as mine."

"I dreamt that I was on a beach … it must have been Cromer beach because I saw Elizabeth trying to climb up one of the columns underneath Cromer pier. At first I thought it was funny; she looked a little like a koala hugging a slippery tree. But then I saw that the centre of the horizon had an ugly swell and a hideously huge wave was coming our way. I shouted at my sister but she would not look my way to the point where I was not even sure it was her and instantaneously thought that I had been mistaken all along. I began to run away from the sea in the hope I would outrun the wave. When I momentarily turned round to check if the girl had climbed up to the pier or swum to the shore, I saw that her face was turned in my direction. It was Elizabeth. I remember the overwhelming weight of my hopelessness—it remained even as I woke.

"She turned back to the fast-approaching wave and appeared hypnotised by it. I knew she would not move, but there was nothing I could do—I would never be able to swim there in time.

"In that instant, I was aware that there was someone standing beside me. It was your friend—oh!" he stopped suddenly and hit his forehead with his hand before leaning on it upon his knee. He had tears in his eyes.

"What? Why do you look so wretched all of a sudden?" Edith asked after Gabriel had been silent a couple of minutes. She knew he was 'sensitive,' but crying over the re-telling of a dream was a little too much.

"You do realise that it is all my fault … This, I mean. All of *this*," he said looking around the room in desperate kind of despair. "You are here because of me."

"I know that. But it is not your fault. It is only for the simple reason that your parents want you to have that damn estate. I am in the way—a mere obstacle in your path of getting it—by my refusal to be your wife. Anyhow, they do not want me to carry their grandchildren with such a 'vulnerable' disposition; my psychological inadequacies might be passed on to your children … I'm sorry to speak so brusquely, I see you are uncomfortable, but we rather are in this together so I might as well speak out the truth, wholly and plainly."

"I know my parents are at fault too, but it was I who gave them the idea—so it *is my fault*. I spoke out in jealousy of your attachment to your musical friend, and they lapped it up in a way that was hideously similar to inexperienced vultures …"

"'Inexperienced vultures', really?"

"Alright, that is not quite the right simile; you were not dead, so you would not be their prey. They were hideously similar to young hounds that had developed a taste for blood—better? Well, what I mean to say is they wanted to find a way to turn my attention elsewhere, and they saw the opportunity of removing you by having you certified as officially unstable. They cannot be blamed though—I might as well have given them the knife to stab you by."

"This place is not that bad! I have not been murdered."

"No, but your honour has been."

"My goodness Gabriel, stop being such a fool! What have you been reading? You're starting to speak like an eighteenth-century play! You said you could get me out of here … well then, do it! I admit that you were wrong to blurt out what I had told you in confidence. But you know what? I would have told them my thoughts sooner or later anyway—in fact, I was planning to do so within those few days, despite advice to the contrary—you only beat me to it. Actually, the only fault I can find in what you did, or did not do, was not speaking out for me when they started making their diagnosis. It would not have made a difference, but it would have made me feel less dejected."

"But that is precisely it. What if I had intentionally not spoken out, so that I would have the upper hand in getting you out of here?"

"I don't think you would intentionally do that. Did you?"

"Well … I don't know. I don't think anything *actually* crossed my mind. I think, if anything, I thought it would get the violinist out of the way—as in, they would forbid you to see him or something."

"I think you should stop thinking about it, and carry on telling me your dream."

"So you forgive me?"

"For what you either did, did not do, or partially did? Yes, I forgive you. Of course I do. I'm here now, so there it is. Now, continue with your dream."

"May we shake hands?"

"Go on," she said, holding out her hand for him to take.

"Thank you, I will endeavour never to give you reason to think badly of me," he said after shaking her hand. "The violinist said—"

"'Said'!? Is that why you've suddenly questioned why you told everyone what I said? Has he spoken to *you*?"

Gabriel looked slightly taken aback by Edith's enthusiasm. "No, no; I'm going back to the dream … He 'said' in the dream."

"Oh, yes, of course. I'm sorry; I get slightly carried away at times." She saw Gabriel look at her as though waiting for her to expand on this statement. "Perhaps I'll explain at some point."

"Well, so, in this dream, the violinist came up behind me and said that I must go to Elizabeth. He said he would come too, that we should go along the pier together now. I felt so ashamed that he seemed to care more for her than I did, and I felt the full impact of my potential cowardice. Then, with the strange logic one sometimes has in dreams, I wondered why it was that the wave was still fast-approaching, but still hadn't arrived. The violinist knew all my thoughts, as well as if I had spoken them aloud, and he told me that the wave would only move as I moved. And, if I would only trust him, if I would only listen to him, the wave would never engulf me.

"Don't laugh at me, this is only a dream, but when I turned and looked straight at him, I was so drawn by the fullness of his expression and the softness of his voice that I felt like hugging him, and I took his hand like a little child.

"Then his voice, the sea and birdsong all merged to become indistinguishable and I woke to the sound of blackbirds outside my window—this must have been the source of the sudden birdsong in the dream. Anyway, so, I don't know what happened to Elizabeth, but I suppose we went and got her. I tried to go back to sleep to finish the dream, because it was only just past dawn, but I couldn't sleep. So there we go."

"It is nice to hear you dream of the violinist, but why exactly did you want to tell me your dream?"

"I'm, well, I'm worried about Elizabeth now."

"That is probably my fault from yesterday."

"You are not at all worried about not hearing from her?"

"Yes, I am. That's why I asked before."

"I don't know what to do with myself, I feel so guilty. I

need to get you out of here and I should make sure Elizabeth is alright. I know she will be, but I think I should prove that I do care when I have not heard from her. Perhaps I should go to Cornwall—no, that would be far too drastic—I would never live it down—oh, I really don't know—only—" he stopped and looked at the girl strangely.

"Yes? Only what?"

"Only … I do know how to get *you* out. That is why I feel so cruel, because your way out advantages me."

"And what is that?"

"Well—"

"Stop *well*-ing! Please, just get on with it."

"… You can be free of this place if you … on the condition of marriage."

"Marriage?"

"Yes."

"Swear to it?"

"Yes."

"Of course, yes, of course. I see. Of course. Do you mind if I see you tomorrow?"

"No, I'll leave now. I'm so sorry. I don't know what to do anymore. I feel all is lost. I simply don't know."

"It is alright. Please don't speak in such a way. What's done is done. I'll see you tomorrow."

He left and Edith was alone.

She did not think about Gabriel at all; it was Elizabeth that occupied her thoughts for the next couple of hours. An ominous sensation. It was stupid and unfounded, but she felt there was something to her niggling fears, and it coincided with the violinist's urgency.

The sky was sympathetic to her feelings, and heavy, dark, thunderous clouds began to take their places, ready for battle. When they had reached their blackest form, and were to be seen in this instant of contemplation before releasing their bulging contents, a sharp, determined tap was heard against the girl's window. It was a strange and surprising sound against the deep and full rumbling accompaniment.

Shaken from her trance, Edith opened the window to allow the fluffed-up sparrow to enter. The bird leapt onto Edith's hand, stood on one leg and began to chirp.

The girl's heart made a little jump with joy at the warm sense of life in her hand and the delicate, sweet and earnest chirps coming from the bright little beak. But she did not know what it said.

"I'm sorry. What are you trying to say?"

"Oh the tragedy, oh the tragedy!" said the little bird.

The girl tried not to laugh, but it was difficult. The frantic little bird spoke so quickly, and at such a pitch, that it seemed slightly pathetic.

"Tell me. What's the matter?"

"Oh the tragedy! I never wanted to believe it was true— that it existed. Oh but it does, they do, they do!" Edith was gradually becoming more and more aware of the sparrow's accent. She could not quite place it, but she realised this was the reason she had not understood the bird at first. It reminded her of the little children in the village school.

The bird shook itself, ruffling its feathers more. "I've seen it for myself! His smile was so beautiful! So beautiful! Oh it would make the cruellest of cats cry!" It shook itself again and looked at the girl's lips.

"I'm sorry, this sounds like nonsense, I'm sure. I'll try to be clearer—you would not believe the amount of time the others tell me to stop my mumbling repetitions. Alright, the short of it is this: the violinist, as you say, told me to come here and tell you to be ready when he comes for you tomorrow."

"Is that all? Why are you in such a panic?"

"Yes, that is in essence all that I came to tell you. I was put in this state of upset because of the meeting this morning. You know about the intersections, I'm sure."

"He spoke of it briefly—do you mean the intersection points of language?"

"Yes, I do. Like little speaking pockets of silence in a song they are, ah dear. I digress. So you know that it is because of these that we are able to speak to each other—oh! Is it true that I am the first to speak to you? You have not yet spoken to any others?"

"No, yes, I suppose you must be the first bird I've spoken to, or understood, at least."

"Oh what fun! Now *that* is something to tell the grandchildren!" It shook itself so that its ruffled feathers began falling into place. "Anyway, the tragedy is when these intersections are abused."

"Abused?"

"Ah, you probably wonder why or how they could be abused when no one seems to know of them. It is so very sad and difficult. But yes, the intersections are abused. Sometimes these are minor abuses, sometimes these are critical. Fortunately, critical abuses are very rare—they are incredibly difficult to achieve. However, at a meeting a little while ago, they spoke of a major intersection which is being abused. Damage; lots and lots of damage. They spoke of where this abuse was coming from and, in my naïve curiosity, I sought out this place and flew to it.

"At the meeting this morning, they affirmed their deepest and most dreadful suspicions. I knew it was bad, I knew that after I came from the place. The most terrible thing is that you cannot realise how bad it is, or if is bad at all, *while* you are there. Oh! But his smile was so beautiful! And so warmly familiar! That is what I cannot understand. How can such beauty contain such ugliness? Ah! The problem is, such power needs such power to destroy! It is such an insult to everything good!"

"I think you should go and cool down; all this flapping about isn't going to help anyone! Perhaps you should have a bath or something?"

"I couldn't possibly! Oh! It's such a tragedy! Well, I suppose that little fountain outside doesn't look *too* bad … maybe I will take your advice. Ah! But I want to be able to do something! To stop the monster before he does any more damage!"

"Well, we'll see. For now, anyway, don't hassle yourself. The violinist will be coming tomorrow, you say?"

"Yes. To be sure, it is beyond a doubt he will defer with you on the subject!"

"Defer?"

"Yes, infer; talk, you know. No, wait, I think that's confer. Well, in any case, he will—oh! And there *was* something else I was supposed to tell you … let me see … yes, marriage, yes! That was it! You need to accept Gabriel's proposal. Yes, that was what I was told to tell you; if Gabriel comes before the violinist, you must accept marriage, on the condition of however the violinist decides to use him."

"I don't quite understand that?"

"No, neither do I. Oh, it is such a tragedy!"

"You'll go and have your cold bath now?"

"Yes; yes, I will. See you." And he flapped out.

XIX

abriel did not come before the violinist. The girl
had not slept at all that night in expectation of
the two men who were sure to be coming for her
the next day. She was greatly relieved when, as the grey of
dawn cleared and the light was on the edge of being full, she
sensed his presence and knew she would see his face at the
window by the time she had moved over to it.

And there he was, expected, yet unexpected. Despite
this, the girl started with surprise in the instant that she
recognised him.

"Hello," she said.

He smiled. He did not have his violin with him.

"Come in," she said, opening the window for him.

Swiftly and silently he swung his legs onto the windowsill
and was beside her, landing on his feet with the delicacy of
a cat.

"Are you taking me now?"

Putting his head to one side in his bird-like fashion,

his eyes lit up in amusement at some private joke. Then he smiled and nodded, motioning for the girl to collect her things. She began to put everything onto her bed in order to pack it, but he shook his head. She shrugged.

"Well? Am I coming back?"

He shook his head, and gave her a rucksack he had somehow procured. He folded up one of her blouses and placed it neatly into the bag. Looking up at her standing motionless, he motioned towards the clothing earnestly and held up one finger. Unlike with the bird, she understood him.

"Nothing else? Just one change of clothes, is that right? Why? Ah well, I suppose I'll find out soon enough." She was aware of the aura he gave; the complete contentedness she felt herself surrounded by in her trust for him. This sensation reminded her how she never could quite get over the idea of him not being real; perhaps she was asleep after all, or this asylum was the right place for her, chasing these figments.

He nodded and took the blanket from her bed, folding that up too. She was very slightly perplexed, but as it was him, she accepted.

"What was that about me having to agree to Gabriel's proposal? Why do I need to do that if I'm leaving now anyway?"

He shook his head and smiled. She did not mind. They were leaving; she was escaping, and she felt the impending freedom.

At that moment, the door to Miss Thomas' room opened and its occupant stepped out in her nightgown.

"You were speaking?" she said to Edith. She had not yet noticed the boy.

"Was I? Oh. I'm sorry. It sometimes happens," she thought perhaps Miss Thomas might just go straight back into her room without seeing the violinist. She did not think it would matter if she did see him, but it would probably slow their getaway.

The girl tried not to look towards the boy who was fortunately cast in the shadow of the wall. However, for the first time, she was aware that he was … uncomfortable, or something, so she could not help but look at him through the corner of her eyes.

He was clearly affected by Miss Thomas; his face said it all. So, they knew each other. Alright. What did that matter? It shouldn't. But Edith remembered very vividly her roommate's tears the night she had spoken of the violinist. She had known there was something between them then. In a split second, the girl was ashamed at the realisation that she was jealous. Though she had been placed in this very room as the result of her desire for people to hear and understand the violinist, she had refused to think, actually properly *think*, of people truly knowing the boy. And so she had not thought about the possible acquaintance of these two people standing before her. Christ! There! She had thought it, despite herself: she had wanted people to know the *violinist*, but she had never wanted anyone other than herself to know the *boy*. No, surely no, she could not be that superficial! That selfishness would mean that no one could have him as the boy *or* violinist. Did she really only want to know him because he was male, would it have been different if he had been female? Perhaps there was some substance to Gabriel's suspicions, perhaps she was only pleased to be able to pour her attention on the violinist to get away from Gabriel and their families. That would mean she was using the violinist; she did not actually care for the beauty of his voice.

She knew that was not true. Ah, but suppose it was true, and she was forcing herself into a state of denial. No. No one could fake the immensity of the joy she had felt in understanding him. That in itself, surely, was evidence. Nevertheless, she knew she could never be *sure*. But she could only do what was logically possible and accept the truth that she designated as truth. In general, first instincts seemed to be truest, so, circular questioning put aside, she knew her care and love for the violinist was not superficial. Her immediate and natural intimacy with him would always remain inexplicable, but it was there, sure as sureness could go. Unconscious understanding was never false.

His eyes had an odd look of confused yearning and, above them, creating small shadows across his already shaded forehead, the ends of his eyebrows had drawn themselves together troubled. She could see that his jaw was tense, though his lips were a little apart.

And then Miss Thomas came forward and saw the boy. He stepped out of the shadows. A pause.

"It's you. I knew. I knew. I've always known." She put out her hand to touch the boy. He took a step backwards so that her hand fell without coming in contact with him. She fell on her knees.

"Oh, you *do* hate me! It's as I suspected!" Tears were again streaming down her cheeks. "It's not my fault, I tried to destroy him. I thought that would be possible: I should be able to destroy what I create. But I couldn't! I *couldn't*! Oh, do forgive me, please! I am lost as it is! I tried, I did, I tried."

Her words met silence.

The disturbing tension which had replaced that most satisfying contentedness of the room was almost unbearable and, had the silence lasted an instant longer, the girl felt she would have been forced to scream or grunt, since no comprehensible words were at the forefront of her mind.

Then the violinist came forward, his eyebrows and jaw relaxed, though his eyes still contained that peculiar look. He put his hand on the kneeling woman's right shoulder, lifting her head with his other hand so that her tearful gaze met his. Once the silent tears had ceased and she looked at him without the barrier of salty water, he put his left hand on her other shoulder. They remained in this position long enough for the girl to be reminded of a painting she had once seen of a knight kneeling before a queen, or was it a woman at the feet of an angel? Mary Magdalene before Christ? Well, she could not quite remember, but it was oddly familiar and otherworldly. She almost felt an intruder.

The violinist's expression did not change from the moment he came forward to the moment he lifted the woman to her feet. Then, in one movement he took hold of the packed rucksack from the bed and, taking Edith by the hand, climbed out the window, gently pulling her through after him. As she looked back at the standing woman, she understood in a flash why she had felt like a stranger. Why she had been so disturbed by Miss Thomas' story. Why she had recognised her roommate from the very first. The resemblance was undeniable. They were standing on a narrow stone ledge about ten feet from the ground. He closed the window and jumped down, still holding the girl by the hand.

Edith looked up towards the window as she was led away, but could not see Miss Thomas. She could not see the violinist's mother.

"I didn't know you were capable of being so cruel," the girl said to him as they disappeared from the building's site. He didn't stop walking. She was sure this was the first time she had been irritated with the boy.

"When are you going to explain at least *a little bit* of what's going on?"

He looked at her but did not stop; instead, he increased his speed, so that she had to take three steps for each of his strides in order that she was not pulled over. There certainly was an air of urgency about him.

It was not long, however, before they got to a country lane that she knew. They did not walk on the road, but stepped alongside it, by an old and crumbled lichen-covered stone wall. A few minutes on and they arrived at a large English oak which had weaved itself through the wall several generations back, so that many of its knotted roots were curled around individual stones.

Gabriel was there, waiting for them. She stopped dead in her tracks, making the violinist, who still held her by the hand, stumble slightly.

"Hello," said Gabriel.

"Good morning."

"I came here with your friend," said Gabriel by means of

explanation. "He seemed to suggest that I should wait here, so I did."

The violinist nodded at him, and then pointed at the ground.

"Ah yes, yes, of course," Gabriel said as he bent over to pick up a violin lying there. "Here."

Have you two spoken to each other then? The girl wanted to ask, but thought better of it. She knew they had not.

"I have to admit, I am a little confused," Gabriel said to Edith.

"Well, you wouldn't be the only one," she replied.

The violinist was unwrapping the violin and walked over to the back of the broad tree, out of sight from the road. He briefly adjusted his strings, making no more than a whisper as he did it. She did not understand how the instrument survived through all weathers wrapped in only that rugged piece of cloth.

She and Gabriel went over to join the violinist behind the tree. He began to play.

I am sorry that I appeared cruel before you, Edith. As I know you know, she was, is, my mother, but I do not sincerely say the word 'mother' in its usual sense. Before I explain myself so far as I am able, I must deal with the matters closer to hand. Gabriel is here because we need him for your escape.

His playing suddenly grew more nervous, impatient, staccato.

In all honesty, his sister, your friend, is, I fear, in danger. I feared as much when she told you she was going to

Porthgwarra; I'd already heard news from there. We need to ensure she is safe, and I feel it is my responsibility to do so. I had to take you from that place—you were not supposed to be there. This is not as I once planned, but we have little choice. Gabriel needs to prevent your families, and any others concerned, from taking you back, from stopping our journey. Whatever happens, you cannot be returned to that cage, insanity, my mother. I know what would happen there, even to someone with as strong a mind as you. Especially now you know the nature of the woman you slept so close to. I assure you, it would be far from safe. You would be turned; you would cease to be the 'you' you have finally grown to understand.

His tone grew a little humorous, so that she smiled, in spite of herself and his words.

By accepting Gabriel's proposal, you will make a vital and secure ally. It will also appease the enemies. In any case, in agreeing to this one condition, you can make as many conditions thereafter as you please. Now; you should tell him now.

It was true. The violinist was right. She could make all the conditions she wanted to. Marry him, yes, in the eyes of the world; no one need ever know how they chose to live. The Norfolk estate was, it had to be said, incredibly beautiful and luxurious. In fact, marriage might not have been a cage at all; it might mean freedom. It *would* mean freedom. She would be able to do just as she pleased, see who she wanted, and never again have to feel that heavy, suffocating sensation she felt when surrounded by their families and houses. Perhaps the violinist would come and live there too. The orangery could be used for Esra and the others, they could have a space for all the woodland creatures who cared to congregate around the violinist. A lake. A music room. A huge open fire. Life, freedom. Yes.

She nodded at the violinist and turned towards Gabriel.

"Yes," she said. "I accept your proposal of marriage."

"Really?"

"I wouldn't say so otherwise."

"No, of course, it's just—oh, never mind."

She let him take her hand in both of his. "We will need to talk more about it, of course," she said after a pause, looking seriously and directly into his eyes.

"Of course," he said with a little curious quiver of his left eyebrow, though his eyes contained a seriousness that matched hers. A brief look of sadness crossed his face as she freed her hand from his and took a step back towards the violinist who had taken to his playing once again.

You must tell him that we're going to Cornwall for Elizabeth, and that he needs to cover for us. Rather, he needs to cover for *you*, and make sure you don't ever get dragged back to that place. I am not sure how long we will be gone from here for, so it might be quite a task for him. Also, he needs to be sure that he trusts *me*, because if he doesn't, it might get complicated. If he has lingering doubts, this will become apparent to your family—just as an animal senses fear. We don't want anything to interrupt us. Stability is needed at base, with Gabriel, so that there is some solid core in *whatever confusion of oblivion we might find ourselves in.*

"You seem stable enough to me," the girl said to the violinist, even if she thought his words theatrical. He smiled.

It is not enough. You can never tell how circumstances change, how people change, how there is no certainty in language. No; Gabriel, in his present world of unknowing, is good ... Quickly now, for we must be on our way.

XX

She was irritated and flustered: that feeling that everything was wrong. Usually, detecting the emergence of such a sensation, she would strip herself of all her clothes and have a bath. Alternatively, in the rare absence of this convenience, she would run until she felt her chest would explode, by which time she was too worn and aching to remember the unknown prompt of her frustration.

No, actually, that was not entirely true; this time, she did know the prompt of her extreme anger. She could not have articulated the *reason*, but she knew the prompt: the violinist's unkind lack of explanation as they continued their violently-paced march along the road.

Her bag caught a protruding branch which, as she carried on walking, succeeded in releasing itself before whipping her across the back of her neck by means of thanks. She threw her bag off and sat in the middle of the road, bursting into childish sobs. The violinist was ahead and stopped, visibly letting his head drop: he seemed a different person. Too human, she thought. Nevertheless, she was deeply embarrassed by her tears. To her they did not only feel childish, but also manipulative in an irritatingly typical female way. Despite all her efforts and attempts to focus on stopping the flow from her eyes, though, she could not stop these unsummoned tears.

Of course, the violinist did turn. She saw his blurred feet as he approached, and his hand as he picked up the bag and offered the other to help her up. She sat there awhile looking at that hand. That beautiful hand. The urge to trace each of those long, delicate-boned, perfectly proportioned fingers with her own, was incredible: it was the desire to form a replica which would do them justice, to keep them in that perfection forever. How feeble she was! She stood up without taking his hand.

The violinist waited a moment before following her. He tapped her on the shoulder and pointed, smiling, to a young female blackbird flying overhead.

"And? What of it?"

She knew why he was pointing to it; he was trying to cheer her up, to lighten the atmosphere. But she had decided to be grumpy, and she did not want to change her mind so easily: the female sex might be the weaker of the two (she was beginning to believe, given herself as her nearest and most reliable example), but that did not mean she would give herself up to this fact and be so irresolute as to change her mood in an instant, through the power of a little smile from her male companion. She took the rucksack from him.

It was impossible not to grin, however, when he unwrapped his violin and began playing it as they made their way down the road. A funny version of Orpheus. She was imagining the look they would get from any person who happened to meet them on their way. A girl with a rucksack, led by a boy skipping as he played the violin down the middle of a country lane, would certainly look a little out of the ordinary. If they were foreign to these rural parts, they would probably assume it was a tradition that refused to die, something akin to morris-dancing. Otherwise, they would do a double-take, shake their head, and think them offensive or insane.

He was, in fact, playing folk dances. They were notably gypsy in style and rather humorous. She could picture campfires and clapping, laughing and chattering. She wished the violinist would stop somewhere so that she could sit, watch and listen. So that he could explain, as a parent to a child, in unadorned clarity, their situation.

And not just *their* situation, it seemed. Though it sounded ridiculous even as an unborn thought, she knew that '*their* situation' reflected '*a* situation' that was much broader than them. The whole idea of the Composer, Songbirds and Lines of Language—whether it be a mere concept, a reality, or a combination of the two—was such that she knew it unified all the chaos of ordinary existence. It was an impossible thought, really, like so many things; she could not have begun to articulate it. This unity of multiplicity, concord of discord, it was not the dull and ultimately scary mass unanimity of a crowd. It was not the unquestionable neatly ignored, or the beauty of the void pressed into those box-shaped arguments that seem so satisfying to the human mind. No; rather, this unity of language, the point at which all the layers and Lines intersected but were not intercepted, symbolised the wonder of the unknowable. It epitomised the inexplicable moments where individual perception becomes objective and rational consciousness becomes unobtainable.

Elizabeth. That was, essentially, what they were doing. They were on the way to Cornwall to check her welfare. But based on what? They had not heard from her, she had had a nightmare and a few concerns—that was all. There was some person that had got the birds in a flap, a person who would 'make the cruellest of cats cry'. Something like that. And there, behind it all, was her roommate Miss Thomas, the violinist's mother.

"Can we stop?" she asked the violinist.

What? Forever? The violinist replied, his tone exaggeratingly questioning.

"No; well, I don't know. Perhaps. I'm pretty sure I haven't a clue as to what is going on. But can we stop for just a while so that you may explain it all to me?"

Explain it *all*? I'm not sure *that's* possible, even for me. You will understand in your own good time.

"My goodness! You sound like an oracle of the most irritating variety!"

How many oracles have you met recently, then? Alright, I'm sorry. I can hear how annoying I'm being; it will irritate me in a while too, so I'll stop. Hey, but why do we need to *physically* stop for me to talk to you?

"I probably won't be able to concentrate if we're on the move. I can only do so much at once. Like most humans. I don't know about you."

Are you suggesting that I'm not human?

"Well, are you?"

I look like one, don't I?

"Yes, mostly."

Mostly?

"Alright. Look. You cannot deny that it is quite rare for someone to speak through their musical instrument."

Is it?

"Come, you said you would stop being irritating."

Hmm. Right. Of course. But tell me, how do you define a human? Do I not fall into your definition?

"… I don't know how I'd describe a human in any other way than the uninspired dictionary way. And yes, I'm sure you *would* fall into that definition. But that does not stop the fact that you are not just a little strange. I mean that in a very good way, of course. I'm sure you will not be offended when I say that you possess an atmosphere of something otherworldly."

I would take that as a compliment. You certainly seem to be gaining confidence in my presence, however. Not that that is a bad thing either. Only, before, you did look at me as though I was Zeus walking in human form, which, as I'm sure you realise, I am not. Now you do not seem to hold me or question me in that same kind of awe. I own I do miss it a little.

"I will admit, as with everything, I become familiar to your differentness. I am not afraid to say, though, that I will never cease to be in awe of you. And however much I get used to your presence, as with a beautiful piece of music or literature heard or read again and again, my feeling towards it changes but is not lost. There is not the same delightful surprise in the sensation it brings, but that initial sensation is never forgotten, and new sensations are brought through its familiarity, no less beautiful."

Thank you. I always like to be compared to a beautiful piece of music or literature that is heard again and again. So, I am like a good poem, then, offering more with each further encounter? That suits me fine.

"Alright then, since you appear to have everything sorted, are you human by your own definitions?"

Oh. Now that does offend me. I'm sorry that you have the impression that I 'have everything sorted.' That makes me feel very cold and arrogant. I am content, I am stable in my current person, but *nothing* is ever *sorted*. No. I'm sure you did not mean what my ears heard and my mind interpreted. I must re-invent your question to suit my answer: do I think that I am human? Well, I'd rather you did not test my physicality by seeing whether I die at the hands of the usually fatal methods. The problem is, Edith, that I could ask you the same question: do you think you are human? I know that's not quite fair, but you must see that, since I am not 'omniscient', I cannot really know the actual truth of the situation. Have you ever considered that perhaps I exist only through you?

"What do you mean? I might be the only one, of a kind, who can hear you, or understand you, but that doesn't mean you don't exist outside of my sight: lots of others have at least *seen* you. Your mother, for one, must have *given birth* to you."

She did, in a way, of course. That is beside the point. I know, as far as knowing goes, that other people *see* me. What

I mean to say is, perhaps I only exist *because* of you, and it is because of *your understanding* that others *do* see me.

"I see you are trying to turn the tables: now you are trying to call me Zeus in human form. If I understand you correctly," she laughed "you are saying that all mankind's perception is one with a part of my perception; what I see, they see. In that case, why can't you speak?"

He laughed; she could hear a thrush excitedly hopping from stone to stone over the delicate and crisp trickling of a friendly stream. Tears came to his eyes through the heartiness of his laugh and, in his rapturous smile, she suddenly understood the clichéd descriptions of legendary creatures, teeth and sunshine. She could not help but feel her own eyes become watery in sympathy with his.

Ah, I do not know how I lived before I finally met you! You are so unconsciously wonderful! No, it is that perhaps *your understanding*, which in a way is *my voice*, is representative … Anyway, let us not go into that any further right now; you want to know what we are doing going to Cornwall, and you would like an explanation of my attitude towards my mother. If you don't mind, though, I'd prefer it if we continued on our way.

Edith nodded. They were now walking along open road; there were no trees laying shadows across their path and the fields stretched to the horizon in all directions.

The violinist resumed his playing. I am going to tell you a story now, he said. Please try not to interrupt, so that I may get it all in the right order. I'm going to begin with a gypsy legend, you may have come across it before.

The girl realised the violinist was incapable of being 'to-the-point'; he would never be able to give a straight and simple answer. But then, she knew this is one of the many things that made him so uniquely beautiful. She nodded again, looking up at the wide, wide sky, as he began his tale.

There was once formed a glass of the most pure crystal … Before the knife had even touched its delicate sides to create the swirling lines which would seduce passing light's rays and cause shadows to dance out of their darkness, it held clear reflections of the sky. Not the simple versions of the sky that you and I see now, but visions of the sky containing all those threads of music. The threads along which the Songbirds sing and dance, determining the direction of our lives. Each person that saw these reflections in the curves of the crystal glass went mad, and many blind too. They became known as the children of Diana, the 'moon-touched' ones. At first they were thought sacred, enlightened, and were revered as such. Few people dared to venture near the glass, and it was placed in the centre of a mountain temple, guarded night and day by trusted soldiers. The few years the glass stayed in that temple, the kingdom experienced no bad harvests, no devastating illnesses and no unfruitful marriages. The people went about irrationally kind and happy. All this goodness was attributed to the influence of the moon's glass. Travellers come from distant places, believing the glass had healing properties of every nature, and the kingdom so cherished it, that it became a national symbol, drawn onto the flag and placed in the national anthem.

Relatively quickly, however, this superstitious awe was replaced with suspicion and the glass was looked upon as cursed; the 'moon-touched' ones as dangerous. These suspicions were confirmed when, one day, a guarding soldier, who happened also to be the King's son, heard a strange noise and walked into the temple, his hands half-covering his eyes, to find paths of the most intensely beautiful golden sunlight throwing itself in organised chaos around the temple. He could not help but take his hands from his eyes to see the morning sun rise behind the temple, sitting perfectly upon the rim of the crystal glass that had become blood red. It was as though the light itself had carved those patterns now dancing their way round its sides. The streams of light were said to find their beginning from those delicately carved lines, here began their whispered command to run free all about the temple and tickle darkness from every corner, transforming it to light.

The King's son was to be the last 'moon-touched' one. The influence of Diana's hand had been too subtly severe in this instance. You see, none of the others touched by the glass had been able to speak afterwards, or at least not in any language that was comprehensible to the rest.

The King grew angry in his confusion as his son returned to the palace, smiling as openly as any child in deep delight, and declared undying love for one of the men in his command. The Prince told the King that he must marry the man directly, and on being refused his father's blessings, he swore he would become a monk in a distant land, as he would not put his lover in an uncompromising position. Here he relinquished all claim to the throne, his family and his country, leaving that minute to walk off into the mountains.

His father ordered that the glass be destroyed, and its

creator found and punished. Inevitably, whoever it was who had moulded the crystal and carved those lines into it never came forward. And, also not surprisingly, it was found to be impossible to destroy: blind-folded men and women made their way into the temple with sticks, stones, and eventually boulders, but no one was able to smash it.

That summer solstice, when all hope had been lost, their prayers were answered: the glass had disappeared. For a short while it was hunted after, just in case it was still amongst the people, but their minds were soon occupied with the first bad harvest in years. Incredibly, it was the first time no supernatural or superstitious explanation was sought to explain this bad luck.

Now the glass is forgotten among all people; it is one of the few unnerving myths that have conveniently been removed from folk history. The owls, though, never forget. It is they who have kept the story alive, such that all 'dumb' trees and animals have it ingrained in their psyche: the cranberry-stained crystal glass that maps all the Composer's Lines.

"It is a very beautiful story," Edith said, taking his pause here to be the end of the story. "But I must confess I cannot understand the relevance it has to our going to Cornwall and your mother."

The violinist sighed.

Of course you do not, he said. That is because I have not finished, not through any deficiency on your part, or in my telling either, if you don't mind! However, since you *have* interrupted me, and I am of an eternally forgiving nature, how about stopping for lunch a while? It is midday, and I know you are hungry: your rumbling stomach is vibrating through the ground.

"Alright; I'm sorry. You must remember that the concentration span of humans *is limited*, and I am no different in that respect, whether or not *you* are. And yes, lunch would be very nice, what did you bring for us to eat?"

Bring? No; of course I didn't bring anything. Come. Let's find ourselves something to eat. We have helpers!

As though on cue, the violinist and girl soon found themselves surrounded by a multitude of blackbirds and squirrels. Behind these creatures were four hedgehogs whose spikes held up the four corners of a mat weaved of long, foreign-looking grass. Each bird and squirrel appeared to have a nut or berry of some kind which they ceremoniously dropped onto this hedgehog-held mat. There were large leaves too, and dandelions. The girl did wonder for a minute whether all the food was edible for humans. However, this thought was of course speedily dismissed. The creatures, 'helpers', went on their way after they had donated their item, leaving the violinist and girl to their lunch.

They were in silence as they ate, but he did not eat much, and was soon playing to her again.

You understand why the crystal glass could be essential for the protection of these Lines?

"I suppose if a map of the Composer's Lines got in the wrong hands, something could go wrong? A little bird was absolutely frantic in the belief that someone was abusing some major points of intersection, and intercepting the Lines, something like that."

Well yes. The little bird was right to be frantic, though

it will not do much good. There is a heaviness in the air that cannot be felt by most people, but it weighs greatly on the heads and hearts of the animals and trees. This heaviness is a result of interference with the Lines above and, unfortunately, it is not a very helpful warning signal. Rather, this is only felt once a lot of damage has already been done.

To get to the point, there is someone out there using the glass abusively. It cannot be an 'average' person because, as I have said, the glass 'makes fools of men'. Previously, the general consensus was that the glass *had* been found and destroyed or had simply disappeared, because although every creature and plant living on, above and beneath all seven continents knows of its existence, its whereabouts have never been uncovered. Perhaps the Prince had taken it off with him to the monastery and disguised it as a Communion Chalice. However, it is not unspeakable that these past centuries have formed the wrong conclusion in our minds. In any case, the heaviness which weighs upon the stars in such a way that makes them appear somehow white and sharp, as they try to burn as brightly as usual under the strain (you have noticed they seem colder, smaller?), this must be through use of that crystal glass.

Cornwall is said to be where he is based; the birds have flown to check. News arrived from Porthgwarra a while back, which is why I felt it when Elizabeth told you she was going there. I do not think it any coincidence that no one has heard from Elizabeth while she is supposedly staying at this very place. Though the glass maps the Lines, it takes more than the glass to actually act with power enough to intercept the Composer's songs, to destroy the beautiful points of intersection. Just think what would happen if a Songbird is crushed as they cannot make their way along their prescribed path; the *person* whose life they sing has not been crushed, no earthly murder has been committed, yet their song has been stopped. What happens to the person? What happens to the unfinished song?

A nut seemed unable to make its way down Edith's throat, and she suddenly felt rather vulnerable.

She swallowed again. "So are you saying something's happened to Elizabeth's song?"

I could not say but, as you might imagine, I have not the best of feelings about the silence coming from Cornwall. And I don't just mean silence in the way of Elizabeth's lack of postcards. Rather, there seems a hole, a gap in music coming from that direction. The animals who have come back from there have been in an uncomfortable state of shock, each stuttering something about the unnerving stillness of the trees there, the lack of birdsong and the absence of cheerful barking.

"What are we going to do when we get there? Surely it should not just be the two of us?"

It is not just the two of us; we have all the world's support, in a way. We cannot plan what to do when we are there, until we see and understand the situation ourselves.

"Can you not speak to the Composer about it? He must know that someone's interfering with his music?"

I have tried. The problem is, say what you might, he summons, I cannot. It is rather a one-sided relationship; he must always speak first for me to know for sure that I am being heard. In general, he calls to me when I have nothing very useful to say. He seems uninclined to listen in this, but perhaps my path of sound to him has also been intercepted. I cannot tell.

"Right. Alright. I see the situation now, I think. Shall we get moving?"

XXI

s the sun began to think about making its way more distinctly towards the horizon on the third afternoon of their travelling, they reached the village of Porthgwarra. There was only a small cluster of white-painted cottages so it was not difficult for them to find the guest house in which Mrs Lorton and her girls had been staying. The small, comfortable-looking lady at the reception told them that Mrs Lorton was not due back until that evening; she had taken the girls to Penzance. She was very willing to enter into conversation with the two young visitors; she told them that there had been nothing odd with the girls, no events out of the ordinary. No. But that did bring to mind the time when, a few years ago, (or was it a few decades ago? Ha ha! Well, never mind …) a similar set of school girls stayed here under the care of two respectable ladies. About a week into their stay, the usual delivery had come from Mr Bens the baker. He had told her about the raven he had opened his curtains to that morning. An ill omen, he had said, and he never had been wrong, had Mr Bens, nor his father and grandfather before him. Ill omen he said, and ill omen it was. Never was there so bad a year for the fishing, for the …

They nodded, and nodded, not registering a word she said. They wanted to get out. Edith could tell the violinist was agitated; it made her agitated too. She was not entirely sure why he should be in such a hurry since there was enough light left to last them several hours, and the receptionist had just reassured them that nothing odd had happened during Mrs Lorton's visit. If Elizabeth had truly gone missing, as the lack of correspondence suggested, it would *certainly* have been noticed; this was not exactly the most crowded and active of places. And so, this could only mean that Gabriel's sister was safe, playing with the independence achieved by sending no word to family and friends.

Annoyingly, this logical thought processing did not do much to reassure the girl, who could not help hearing the echoes of the violinist's words. *No earthly murder has been committed … no earthly murder … no earthly murder … yet their song has been stopped … their song stopped … What happens to the person? What happens to the unfinished song …? What happens …?*

She shook her head, trying to dismiss her repetitive thoughts, like a dog shaking water from itself after a surprisingly cold swim in the sea.

"You alright there, dear?" the receptionist asked her.

"Excuse me? Oh. Yes. Sorry. We have travelled a long time. I think … I think I need a little fresh air. Thank you."

The two of them walked out, openly relieved. They took to one of the coastal footpaths.

"Well?" Edith asked. "What are we doing now?"

She knew he would not bother to answer, because he knew that she knew what they were doing. She knew what they had come here to do, and what they were doing now: seeking the source of silence; the creature contaminating the Lines' convergences.

The violinist pointed ahead of them at the sun. It was truly spectacular, as though they were walking into the sunset itself, off the edge of the Earth. It was one of those occasions when she wished she could take a photograph with the eyes—a photograph that had all the colour and sensation attached. She had experience enough to know there was little point actually *trying* to remember the scene exactly as it was; its essence would stay with her if she simply allowed her whole being to soak in its fullness. And, at that precise instant, she was aware, somewhere at the back of her mind, that she was being hypnotised out of consciousness by the warm, blood red of the all-encompassing, sinking sun. There was a sound too, like the sun was softly singing to her. She was becoming detached from her body; she was becoming two distinct yet indistinct selves. In this state of mind, she did not feel it an idea at all terrifying, or even unpleasant, to walk off the edge of the Earth into the dark and full oblivion of its light.

The girl was snapped out of her trance by a silent scream.

It was silent, so of course the girl did not hear it. But she did feel it. Goodness, she did feel it; she felt it tear right through her body, as dramatically as any chilling cry heard in the silence of night. She turned and saw the violinist crouched over himself, as though in immense pain, his hand tightly placed over his eyes, his teeth clenched. The girl went over to him and stood beside him helpless, not knowing whether or not to hold him. He was so perfect; she was confused to be standing above him. He was the one who held her, who cured her and satisfied her. How could she now be in the stronger position? How could *she* help *him*?

With great effort, he straightened himself out a little, so that he could look into the girl's face. He did not take his hands from his ears, nor unclench his teeth. The pain in his pleading, searching eyes made the girl's heart freeze. He was trying to say something; he was trying to place words in her very soul through the interaction of their eyes.

And she understood him. She did not know whether he had achieved his attempt at communication without music, she certainly heard no words, but in his eyes she saw the literal reflection. She turned and saw the sight as it was: black and jagged rocks which formed an ominous dark island against the red sky, like an opaque shadow in an empty, fire-lit room. That was where some hideous noise was coming from, the noise which was torturing the violinist here. It was there that the creature was. Why, though, could she not hear it? Not only could she hear no painful sound but, to her, it was as the violinist had reported a couple of days ago; she heard as the animals who had returned disturbed by the cold hole of silence.

Save she was not disturbed. Rather, as she stared more closely out at those rocks, they began to look more attractive to her, and she again began to hear the soft singing of the sun. She turned briefly back to the violinist and nodded: she would go to the rocks alone. She saw the recognition of her intention in his tortured eyes, and his reluctant realisation that there was no choice; he was frozen to the spot by the agony it created in him. Deep in those questioning eyes, there was something new, as though he was, for the first time, understanding the full extent of danger and tragedy. Out of the cause of his pain, he had discovered something; some deep knowledge had clicked into forward focus, a missing puzzle piece had fixed into place. And the new picture filled him with fear and concern at the girl's going out alone. Of what was he so afraid? Why should she not go? If she was strong enough not to hear the noise which physically crushed the violinist, she was strong enough to face the creature.

Ah yes, now she remembered! The violinist had taken her out of her peaceful trance. That was the reason she had stopped hearing that perfect singing. Now, as she let herself hear it, her petrified, frozen heart began to melt, and she was again alone in the world. Alone, but not alone; drawn to the single other life out on those rocks.

She walked along the sloping cliff edge until she got down onto the rocky shore. The rocks were dark grey with sharp points, such that the lower ones might have passed for sharks' fins, poking themselves out from amongst the foam formed of the splashing high tide. The water was not cold, however, nor terribly violent, and it was not with any reluctance that the girl slid into the sea and began to swim towards the rocky island.

The sky was losing light, the atmosphere taking on a greyish tinge, so that by the time the girl had reached the island, she could not tell a great deal of difference between the dark of the rocks and the dark of the sea. If it had not been for the luminous white foam, she might have swum passed it, and possibly carried on swimming to the edge of the Earth and beyond. Each time she lifted her head from the waves, she could hear the soft singing clearer; it became more pressing, more tempting, with each stroke. Yet, it did not call her directly to the rocks; it seemed to be everywhere, this voice, to surround her, so that it did not matter if she *had* continued to Earth's end.

When she felt her arm hit cool stone, though, she knew this was what she had come for. She pulled herself up, feeling that her shoes and clothes were a nuisance, and she would have been much better off without them. But as she was about to unbuckle her shoes to throw them into the waves, a hand came down in front of her face, offering assistance. She looked up to see the face belonging to this thin and elegant hand.

Black, black hair; the black of the hard, wet rocks, which seemed to want to reflect the sea and sky, but were not quite smooth enough to replicate anything more than the dull tinge of light's colour. In this sense, however, his hair had more success than the rocks, as the girl distinctly saw both the iron red of the horizon and the atmosphere's grey shine on its dark surface. It was as though the hair was a separate entity, revelling in its superiority over its inanimate brothers, the sea-sprayed rocks. It was proud to reveal the secrets of the day's dying embers in its blind blackness.

She did perceive this figure as male, the hair being *his*, but in her dreamlike state, she was aware that he did seem genderless. In fact, she would not have even described him as androgynous; his whole being seemed too *neutral*, too *lacking* of any human-categorised definition. The girl was acquainted with this sensation. She knew it reminded her of someone else.

The eyes were familiar too. Allowing the figure to lift her to her feet, she could see his face more clearly, no longer obstructed as it had been by shadows. It was beautiful, of course; she had not expected otherwise. There was something of a raven about him. His skin had caught enough sun for its relative paleness not to clash unaesthetically with the hair, and his dark eyebrows were refined and perfectly curved above his grey eyes. Where had she seen those eyes? There was something different about these eyes, something missing. But they were mesmerising, and the eyelashes seemed to take on an air of modesty, as though their coal black lines were made to shade the shining splendour of the eyes beneath.

Ah! Beginning to wake from her dream state, she realised how tediously often this seemed to be happening; she was constantly seeing faces, or feeling something familiar, and trying to recall the original. It was recent, the original to this.

But, though she felt herself emerging from thin layers of her trance, she also felt herself fighting against reaching full-consciousness. That upper layer seemed too much effort to break into. The inertia this imminently and eminently encouraged prevented precise recollection. Come on, girl! Focus! It was the androgyny … that was the stem of this familiarity … androgyny … so. Something not quite *natural*. Not quite human.

Tell me, how do you define a human?

And suddenly, above the possessive and obfuscating lull of soft singing, which somehow vibrated through her every fibre, she heard clear and pronounced words. Words which brought meaning out from their music. She could picture the violinist as he played them along the road. She smiled to herself as she remembered his energetic country style dancing, and slightly impish grin. However much she tried, though, she did not feel fully in control of her senses, and she could not recall his voice. The words and music were there, but they were spoken by an internal version of herself, not the violinist. Picturing his face, she tried to force the words into his voice, but there was an irritating noise preventing her from hearing it.

The noise was awful. It started simply as a slight nagging irritation, like a fly she needed to flick away. But it grew more persistent and gradually felt as though it was eating through the soft confusion of her brain. It was loud and ugly, and there was no soft singing. The soft singing had been drowned to silence by its ugliness. Oh! How its intensity threw her to the edge of madness! She put her hands over her ears and looked at the figure who still stood opposite her. He had dropped his casual smile of cat-like contentedness and was now looking a little perplexed, perhaps even angry.

She did not want to hurt this raven-resembling young man; he had been so perfectly formed that she did not feel it her right to offend him. Nevertheless, though the noise only grew more painful through her hands, she did not feel she could take them from her ears. She dragged her eyes away from the raven to look around the island; she wanted to see where this sickening sound was coming from, this *noise*. It was enough for one to think they were deaf, because its inexorable dominance and volume meant that one could hardly be aware of anything but the *noise*, such that it should have become silence. Just as silence had the potential of becoming maddeningly loud. Sadly, though its power had this terrifying potential, which would have been a relief to the now tortured girl, it did not maintain one pitch, but rather modulated between every foul and jarring note that ever existed. The noise appeared to have been borne of putrefied dissonance. It had not simply come from badness, but from corrupted good. This meant it could not be escaped even through silent madness.

Her eyes felt they were becoming ears too. Every pore of her skin was another ear, and every blood cell served to amplify the entering sound. She could still see and she forced herself to *look* around the island, to focus on its solid rocks … Or what she had thought were rocks. With nightmarish speed she saw that they were not rocks at all. Instead, girls in long white robes stood unmoving in stalagmite-like formations. They had their mouths open in song and seemed hypnotised by some sort of tragic ecstasy, if such a thing were possible. Though their robes seemed to glow in a blurring way, their solidity seemed well and truly real. They were *there*. She dropped her hands from her ears at the horror of it, and as she did so, she saw Elizabeth. Standing naked amongst the robed figures, she was the only one without her mouth open. She stood out prominently against the slightly blurred whiteness of the others, such that Edith could see she was smiling with wet eyes. Hypnotised as she was, to the same all-consuming degree as the rest, Edith could see she was still the most vivid and sentient. The others looked blankly expressionless in their tragic ecstasy. Elizabeth was on the edge of something scarily empty.

The horror! The girl's nakedness was cruel and ugly. It was ready, open, and waiting to be eaten by the pure and evil whiteness of the robes and their mouths' foul song. It was from these softly open mouths that the *noise* resonated. She could not bear the sight of it!

The girl turned away to again meet the cool, depthless grey eyes of the figure. She had not seen before how icy and shallow they were. Even with the *noise* slicing through the deepest parts of her consciousness, trying to find its way to her soul, she began to notice everything. As she looked upon him, the upper of his perfectly shaped lips drew itself upwards, slowly and delicately, into a sinister sneer, revealing a small strip of perfect white teeth. But, though these eyes were hollow, the lips thin, and expression cruel, he remained astonishingly beautiful. The chilling imperfections seemed only to heighten his exquisiteness. It made her feel sick. Sicker now as she knew without a doubt the origin of his familiarity. Miss Thomas … The violinist. His otherworldly aura and carefully sculptured features. Had they been literally sculpted, they would so clearly have been imagined and formed by the same sculptor; each aspect designed for aesthetical perfection, and each successfully pleasing idea used more than once, slightly modified.

She grew confused, her imagination merging with the figure before her, so that she did not know whether it was the violinist before her, or the raven, or a version of one or both of them. She did not know whether both were beautiful or whether the sickly cold perfection of the raven surpassed the violinist in his warmer magnificence. At that instant, closing her eyes at the horror of it all, the raw nightmare of it, she knew that she thought the figure before her the more wonderful. And with despair she felt the *noise* become soft and lovely once more. It should not have been with despair, since the pain which had rung through her body and consciousness was no longer there now that the violent sound was translated. But she knew that she must feel despair rather than relief, as there was otherwise no hope— she could feel the imminence of numb darkness threatening to overcome all that she was and would be. How dare such base corruption disguise itself in such beauty! How dare it abuse the name of sound!

But it was too much—too powerful and too horrible. There was nothing that could be done except escape its presence or drown, drunkenly, into it.

XXII

She tried and tried, pushing to hear the *noise* behind the song. Delicate fingers were caressing her hair, stroking it ever so carefully, but she would not open her eyes. Detached as her mind and body seemed to be, being unable to negotiate with one another, she was physically incapable of moving. The fingers induced a feeling that was at once torturous and delightful, vibrating right through to her feet, so that she must clench to avoid shivering. As the cool fingers moved from her hair to her neck, she felt she would scream but that she was mute.

Her eyes still closed, she felt the raven take her from behind and lower her to a reclined seating position, his arms around her waist. He had folded his right leg and let the other lie straight, crossing over his right ankle, so that they formed a triangle securing their positions. The girl sat in this triangle of his legs, feeling his right calf under her thighs and his left leg beside hers. The rough rock beneath them was unfelt by him, failing to form a single mark on his clean skin. He had her back leaning close against his chest and his chin resting upon her right shoulder. He was rocking her slightly and delicately, whispering softly behind her ear. She could not hear anything he said, but that it sounded like a lake, lapping against the side of a boat at night.

If she just let herself, she could easily have fallen into its beautiful perfection. She only had to accept, and allow herself to appreciate and love the peaceful sensation, to have it forever. She knew it was being offered to her forever. She could remain here, like this, always.

The violinist. The violinist. Remember the violinist. Oh! That he could not be forgotten! He was in front of the consuming song which filled the atmosphere, amongst it, behind it. His face was fighting to take its place in her dissolving heart, his voice was battling with the raven's whispers. Random words, always, inescapable. No meaning, just sounds. Awfully detached, floating. Letters as shapes, pretty and ugly, definition transparent, unattainable. She hated him! She hated the violinist! He would not leave her, but nor would he take her! Not like the raven, who would have her now.

But *the little bird was right to be frantic*.

Quick, quick! Go!

The little bird was right to be frantic.

His words echoed and echoed, and she saw the little bird behind her closed eyes. It flapped in the fountain, water droplet dripping down its black, clumps of wet feathers sticking vertically on its head. *Oh the tragedy, oh the tragedy!* She could hear the little bird too. These fragments of abstract meaning were falling into place, forming a strange mirror at the front of the head. *His smile was so beautiful! So beautiful! Oh it would make cruellest of cats cry!* The mirror was making its way further forwards, pressing against her eyelids.

You see, every life is a song, composed by the Composer and sung by a Songbird.

She smiled. But the sweet, all-consuming song was being re-translated to the torturous *noise*. The mirror was vibrating, ready to shatter.

Extreme anomalies must occasionally occur.

Its vibrating felt hysterically hilarious. *The little bird was right to be frantic.* Finally the mirror forced her eyes open. It made her laugh. Why did she laugh? There was nothing she could understand, hardly feel, let alone laugh. She could still see the mirror; it seemed to contain many eyes, many grey eyes. The image of the flapping bird transformed into the dancing violinist. She laughed again, and this time she heard her laugh, aloud. It acted as an arrow slicing through the air. The pain reintroduced into her numb body by the growing *noise* was unbearable, but funny. The raven had stopped whispering. She wanted to cry. She wanted to scream.

And when there is no one to confirm one's language, one cannot know that they are in fact communicating.

With a sudden jerking movement, she turned to her right. Her nose collided with his with hard force and she knew he was shocked. She twisted herself round in his arms to see his eyes. He was close, very close. She could not even see his lips beneath his nose. Every eyelash could be counted.

"The little bird was right to be frantic." She laughed into his face, her warm breath making him visibly cringe, closing his eyes for the first time. She had said the words aloud. She did not really know what she was saying, but she knew she must say anything, anything the violinist had said.

"What happens to the unfinished song?" The words refused to be spoken, they came out as song. She was singing. Singing into the face of the raven. *"In this lengthy silence, I have learnt to hear everything I want to hear."* No word was her own. No language belonged to her. It was all seemingly random.

"It takes more than the glass."

Did he have the glass? She desperately wanted to ask him, but of course she could not. Did he have the glass that "*makes fools of men*"?

"To intercept the Composer's songs, to destroy the beautiful points of intersection"

She was strong. She would live. The *noise* was threaded with the faltering soft song. The girls were crying; their tears, tears of true feeling, were disrupting the song. The raven opened his eyes and stared horribly at the girl. He was in pain. She was cruel, she was evil, she would laugh at his pain. He bore her warm laugh with a brave flinch and pulled her twisted body close to him, his hand appearing to grow.

"No earthly murder has been committed, yet their song has been stopped. What happens to the person? What happens to the unfinished song?"

Elizabeth had stepped away from the sobbing girls. Her eyes were now dry and pleading. She was no longer content, but she was not entreating Edith; her pleading was for the raven.

But the song's unity was fragmented. It lay in ruins. Tears dissolving it more and more frequently.

The hatred and pain in the boy's eyes was like fire, burning right through to the girl's innermost self. He was contained in the essence of confusion. Never had this happened before; there was something very wrong with the girl. But he could never lose, he liked to fight. He had forgotten—at the height of his power, he had forgotten this; it had been such a long time, such a very long time since he had last had to fight. The last time had been with his mother; she had tried to destroy him, running across that table and clawing at his eyes. His father had appeared. Yes, he remembered. He was being weak. He liked to fight, he liked to win.

"What happens to the unfinished song?"

He was infuriated. He had to silence her, stop those lips from that evil singing. In an instant, he lifted his right hand to the back of her head, and pressed his lips hard against hers.

It disgusted him; he had never tasted another's lips. They were warm, too warm and alive. Yes, the taste of life, a separate life to his own, was disgusting. Like sea salt, that's what he could taste—warm sea.

But he held his lips there, and the warmth of it sent a threat of heat down to the pit of his stomach, making him feel physically sick. How could he *feel* sick? He must not lose! The girl was his! He would make her life his. His life would be hers. They would become one through this kiss, this dark and torturous and victorious kiss. Yes, that was the word—a kiss. Their doors of language had met, so opposing, so complementary. She did not struggle. Why did she not struggle? He wanted her to struggle. He could not bear the warmth much longer, but he must. He must!

He tried to prise her lips open with his. He wanted to eat her language; he wanted to breathe in all her words, all her music. It was rightfully his.

She could not push away or make a noise. He was far too strong. His hand holding her head seemed made of rock. Though his lips were soft and warm, she felt their ice cut her soul.

He would find the unity in their disunity. She felt him searching, struggling. Both their eyes had been open, though they could see nothing, and they shut them now to focus on this battle. Deep down, she knew he would win. He was so close; it was as though they were already sculpted into one person. It was only the ice and fire which refused to cease being separate. They were no longer individuals, only fire and ice battling through opposing doors of language.

Their mouths opened into darkness and she felt him try to breathe her. And somewhere, somehow, she felt her soul move dangerously close to her lips. She did not want it to take that risk. But it did, and it sang. She did not know that a soul could speak words, but it did, right into the opposite being. *What happens to the unfinished song?*

He could taste her soul. Her song was close. He would win, but the words fell deep. At least they were not sung aloud; his song could triumph over the world. Their mouths opened further, he would take the risk. But she was laughing into him. She was abusing the darkness. It was her *own* laughter. He held her closer—she would not get away. She would be silenced.

And a searing bright light blasted behind his eyes. Through her continued laughter, he could suddenly see the

Lines and layers of language that threaded themselves round her soul. He could see her singing Songbird, and a boy. The golden threads seemed to pass through, and emanate from, this boy who knew and understood their very essence. How did he hold them all like that? The light was too bright to see the boy clearly, but the raven knew that he was the girl's. He was at the heart of her soul, tied, but not caged, by the organised chaos of those threads.

He tried to close her mouth again, to stop the laughter. But he would not let her go, and he could not open his eyes. For the first time in his life, he felt that he was falling, that he was not in control. Perhaps he should move away, perhaps this was not such a good idea. If he let her go, he would continue to fall, he knew that. The damage had been done. He had never killed a person—not in the true definition of it, anyway. But what else could be done with this untouchable. She was not even his equal, she was superior. As soon as he released her from his mouth, she would sing again. Oh! Maybe he had lost! He could not, everything would fall apart, everything! He panicked. He was afraid. He felt the fear.

He relaxed his grip slightly, but not enough for her to move. He let his mouth fall so that it only held her lower lip— he could not allow her to sing. He must think what to do. The blaring light would not go away. It was horrible, maddening, blinding! He was crying; he could not stop himself crying. Were they real tears? He had never cried, he did not cry, he could not cry. But he was crying. He felt them imprint themselves on the girl's cheeks and fall upon her mouth. Hot tears. Perhaps she was crying too, he could not tell.

Never, never could she go. She could not go. But he was sobbing and he had to fall from her mouth, or he would drown. The light went, but the beautiful darkness was now contaminated. And when he opened his eyes to escape it, they opened into the same darkness. Eyes open or closed, it was the same. He was blind.

He screamed and pulled the girl against the rock, so that they were both lying upon it. She was silent. She did not sing. He could not stop his crying. Groping in his blindness, he pushed himself up and felt for the girl's shoulders. He had to kill her. Through his screams and sobs, his failure, he heard silence, and it was terrifying. He could not escape the terror. He pulled the girl up and pushed her forward, but they both fell over. He must break her and throw her into the waves.

To the girl, there was not silence. The figures in robes were silent now, though she could no longer see them, but the *noise* continued. And she knew that the raven was the *noise*. She had no strength left. There was only so much a human could bear, and she had had her fill of it. When the raven fell against her upon the sharp rocks, she knew she had won, but that she had also been won over. She was so tired, so thoroughly exhausted, that she could hardly feel the deep cuts over her arms and legs, and the burns the raven's tears had left upon her cheeks. Her own tears had soothed her injuries a little, but she was barely aware of it.

She did see Elizabeth's feet when they arrived beside her face though, and she placed her bloodied hands over them. She felt a complete wreck, but there was no pain, and she remained conscious of the reason she had ever come to this place. Elizabeth needed to be drawn away.

The raven lifted them to their feet again and pushed Elizabeth away. The violinist—why did he not help? If only Elizabeth would speak! So weary. Why could no one just *speak*?

Deep and full, a sound made its way from the cliff. No words, he was not saying anything, but the violinist was playing. She had not been abandoned. The sound was so rich, so wonderful. The girl cried, and laughed, and cried. A mess of emotion.

The raven pushed her further up the island to reach its highest point. The sound from the cliff reached him powerfully in his blind silence, and he screamed again, loud and chilling. It sliced through the atmosphere for miles around, forcing every living thing to shudder, their hearts skipping a beat. Every squirrel and bird ran quickly into their nests, every flower hastily hid itself, and even the people closed their curtains with unreasoned alacrity. The music opposed his quintessence; it broke through his darkness, but did not remove his blindness. He knew where it came from—not physically where, because it was all around and within him, but its source. It was his mirror who played, his brother. He knew too that the boy entangled in the threads of language travelling through the girl's soul was him too. The girl belonged to his brother. His hated brother. His brother who should not have existed, who had not nearly the same power as he had. He had accepted his father's offer, he had accepted his father's love. His brother never had, he had declined the chance of power, he had run from it. It was he who had challenged their mother, who had suffered her, and defeated her. His brother never had. His brother should not have existed. His brother was a parasite living off the girl. His brother should not have existed. Language was his! He could crush Songbirds, he could escape the Composer, he was *noise*. His brother was only *silence*.

And the girl, the girl that belonged to his hated brother, was beginning to mumble. She was beginning to hum with the violinist, so that her voice was united with his. He fell to his knees, and the girl remained standing. He tried to grasp her by the ankles as she walked back towards the other end of the island. Elizabeth was standing staring at the girl as she came closer. It was as though she was facing a debate between her two shoulders, two separate worlds, and she was frozen with indecision.

The boy, crawling behind the girl with his arm outstretched towards her feet, could not reach her, and Edith took Elizabeth by the hand, holding her firmly. Elizabeth would stay back in her world. Now at the other end of the island, Edith felt the spiderlike grip of the raven's fingers twist themselves round her ankles. *She* was not to leave *his* world. Through all his immense pain, he could still *feel* his desire to consume her fire, her song, into the hollow ice of his soul. It shocked him, this feeling—the fact that his *will* was capable of inferiority to *feeling*, to *his* feeling. It made him so hungry, so mad with hunger and this one, all-consuming obsession. Now, he did not even remember the purpose he had been set, the Songbirds he had silenced and frozen to his heart, the white-robed, lost and wandering songs which still filled the island. Everything was this girl. This girl who was also her brother. He would have his brother through her.

He was salivating with his tortured hunger for her.

She felt the burns of his acidic dribble on her ankle. But the power of the violinist's note took control of her whole body, so that she need not use any of her own strength; she could rely on the sound itself to carry her. Freely dictated by the note, whose ends were tied between the source on the cliff and her echoing lips on the island, she knelt beside the drooling raven figure, bringing Elizabeth to kneel too, and whispered in his ear. In doing so, the note between cliff and island was broken, but it did not matter because, before their very eyes, the raven became well and truly tied to his island, frozen forever. All the white-robed figures became rocks too, looking as they had done to the girl before.

She felt Elizabeth go unnaturally cold, like glass, as though she too were meant to join her rock-sisters, but her hand was clasped in the warm grip of Edith's and, naked as she was, her Songbird had not been crushed by the raven. Somewhere, Elizabeth was returning from a day trip to Penzance. Yet, here too Elizabeth was standing.

Both were *her*. The Elizabeth with Mrs Lorton was void, internally cold, though her ivory flesh was warn to the outside world. And, since the vast majority of her world concentrated only on the external, and never notice anything, her suddenly vacuous person made no impression on those around her. As far as they were concerned, this was the Elizabeth that had always been. The other Elizabeth, now standing naked with Edith, was an insubstantial reflection made substantial through the detachment of her bird's song. To explain simply, it would be best to recall the complex nature of mirrors. Standing in front of a mirror, one expects to see their reflection—their three-dimensional self reduced to two dimensions, under the complete command of the beholder. The reflection has no life outside of the mirror, and no freedom inside the mirror. This is how it should be.

It is, after all, essentially mirrors which form the sphere of the Songbirds' world: the layers of language separating and integrating all types of understanding hang from reflective strings of light. The birds walk along these threads of mirror, chirping our lives, and occasionally flying off the threads so that they are *within* a layer of language. It is at these points, when a Songbird sings without the security of the thread below him, when his composed song can be temporarily lost in the folds of language, that his song's essence, his human's soul, is at its most vulnerable. At these points, the soul's rapture can permeate the mind and body of a person, such that the body shivers, and the mind is momentarily free. Of course, time is not drawn to scale in such matters; there are no 'moments'. However, it is at these points, these vulnerable points when the song is, as it were, 'detached' from its Songbird, that the Decomposer can steal and abuse the song. If the song is obtained by this abusive creature, so that the Songbird is silenced and confused in his inability to find the temporarily freed song, it can be brought into the physical sphere of Earth, and then destroyed. Nothing can be destroyed in the sphere of the Songbirds, so a song *must* be brought to Earth to be crushed. On Earth, the isolated song looks like the naked reflection of its human. Once this song is defeated, and no longer an individual song, the naked reflection gets clothed (white-robed) in modesty. Now, if they were to look in the mirror, they would find it empty, as though they did not exist. Inevitably, it is not long before the void, song-less beholder of the blank mirror dies in a heap of mad despair: a person cannot exist purely through the perception of others; they must feel that they exist for, and in, themselves too. Faced with this permanently empty mirror, the mind cannot distinguish light and dark, silence and noise, truth and lies. Then the dead beholder is simply dead. There is nothing but their physical remains, since their soul has already been consumed into the mass of the Decomposer's noise. And so, the individual soul is forever lost, unable to fall blissfully into the depthless layers of the Composer's language.

Standing here, beside Edith, was Elizabeth's naked reflection, currently more substantial than her 'real' void self walking beside Mrs Lorton, or more likely in bed asleep by now. This was how an uncrushed song looked.

The fragmented Elizabeth needed to be made whole; her reflection needed to be united with her person; her song needed to be returned to its Songbird.

Instinctively, Edith held the cold child close, trying to cover as much of her as possible. She had no idea how she was to get the two of them back on the mainland. The sea and sky had embraced each other's darkness to surround them in a thick and inky blackness. No stars, no moon: these two unfathomable entities would not be disentangled until dawn.

XXIII

The violinist was in the water making his way towards the girl. The sharp sound of his splashing contrasted strangely with the stillness of the night, echoing eerily through the darkness.

"Thank goodness for you! Thank goodness you are here," Edith heard herself say as she crouched to reach for his hand.

He took her hand and pulled himself onto the rocks with graceful ease. He glanced quickly at the two huddled girls and then turned to the solid form that had once been his brother. Cautiously putting forward his fingers, he traced the lines of this rock which had made the face of his twin. He wore slightly mournful expression as he did so, as though remembering a previous life and what might have been. Indeed he *was* remembering a previous life, a decision long ago made and never regretted, but always questioned. This questioning, though repetitive and tedious, reminded the violinist of his humanity and made him feel alive. If he had accepted one of his conclusions as the final answer, he would have felt as silent inside as he was to the world outside.

Here, standing beside his frozen brother, streams of emotion surged through him and his mind was filled with flashes of past events and thoughts. If only his brother had been stronger, if only he had been able to break free like him. It was unfair, this life—that he had been created like this, and his brother like that. Well, there was nothing that could be done about it. But then again, that knowledge of one's own helplessness in it all did not serve to stop the questioning of it all.

The violinist sighed. His nostalgia was evident; not because he missed the life he had given up, of course— far from it—but because … because … well—because of many things. He missed the unpremeditated superiority felt through the unexpected joy immediately following his release from this world which had forever surrounded him. Though he had always *hoped* there was another world, other possibilities, he had never been sure. The terror at losing the only world he knew, in exchange for one he merely hoped existed, was a horrifying vulnerability he prayed he would not experience again, though, at the same time, he missed that terror too. With it all gone, it can never fully be remembered. That being the case, one cannot be sure that the distress of that past life has not been exaggerated, and the goodness of the current life not invented, or vice versa. It all hangs upon that moment of transition, the initial release, as to whether the current, conscious conclusions are genuine, if they are as true to oneself as they could be. It is easy to forget to appreciate the change, to remember there ever was a change, once the change has been established.

So, it was the unconscious acceptance and unarticulated appreciation of the experience and transition that the violinist was nostalgic for. Though he felt his present world to be beautiful, he had grown so accustomed to its beauty, and had questioned its beauty and his relationship to it so much that he had forgotten how beautiful it had been at first. He even frequently lost faith as to whether this extreme initial awe had either been forced, and had therefore not been unpremeditated, or whether it had been invented later, for some reason or other.

But—it is true to say that the violinist was not like other people. His silence served as a constant reminder of his blessed escape from darkness. He was pretty much safe too in his humanlike questioning, because the only living things he was able to seek reassurance from through interaction were the woodland animals and plants, who always told the truth, whether they wanted to or not. It was difficult for him, then, to get confused, or create a fiction of himself and his position.

He felt the repulsing magnet of darkness emanating from the core of his frozen twin. He controlled his urge to shudder, and shook himself back to the reality of the present. They needed to get back to shore; Elizabeth preferably needed to be reunited with herself before dawn, and he and Edith needed a long sleep before returning home. For the first time in a long time, he felt a weight upon him. He felt the burden of a thousand things he needed to do, and would probably never be able to do. He felt the burden of expectation. Whose expectation? The Composer, Edith, the creatures?

More likely the unknown expectations he had invented for himself, expectations which could never be fulfilled. But he had always known that it was this unattainable ideal of oneself which enabled one to continue with the ultimate search for life. So why this sudden weight? And suddenly he knew that this was it; this was the beginning of the end for him as he knew himself, but it was also the end of the beginning as the Composer knew him, or as he knew himself and the Composer through the Composer.

He was sorry for his brother. And he felt the weight of his brother's end. He leant forwards with both his hands on his rock brother and kissed the top it, holding his lip there a moment too long. Either the cold of the rock would freeze his lips to it, or the warmth of his mouth would radiate through his as yet unloved brother. Well, he did love him. He felt that now. He loved him quite aside from the hateful blood connection and the shared misfortune of their creation. Pity.

Now to the matter in hand—he turned and saw Edith's slightly aghast face and nodded at her. (She vaguely understood why he kissed the rock, but she did not like it). She acknowledged his nod with a slight movement of the lips, and then, between them, they lowered themselves and the inanimate Elizabeth into the sea.

Somehow—and the girl never remembered how—they carried Elizabeth to shore. What Edith never forgot, though, was getting her feet splintered with the remains of the violinist's shattered violin. In the iced, numb agony surrounding him as he forced himself to play from the cliff, he had become utterly disorientated to anything other than the girl on the island. In this state, he had been oblivious to the heart-rending smash of the instrument as it fell upon the rocks at the bottom of the cliff, its strings snapping pitifully, the echoes of its discordant cry muffled immediately by the sea's spray.

It was not the discomfort of the walking upon feet punctured with bits of wood that made the girl cry, but the sharp pain that grasped her heart as she felt the boy's inescapable silence surrounding him. As is often the case when one is desperately tired (an understatement in this case), the girl did not see any possible solution; the world seemed void of meaning; there was no hope. Give up.

Sleep *is* the only solution at such a time, and this was soon delivered to the girl. The violinist had led the two girls to a cave inhabited by large seagulls. Usually an inhospitable breed, the great black-backed gulls realised the urgency of the situation and stood at the entrance of their home, swaying from foot to foot as they squawked quietly to guide the boy. They gently helped the three humans up into the cool space, and it was they who knew instinctively what was to be done with this strange version of Elizabeth, and carried her away to be reunited with her other self, never missed, never witnessed. To Elizabeth, it would always remain a most peculiar dream, over which she would spend a long time trying to remember the just-out-of-reach details, never quite grasping them. It was better that way. For humans, it is always better that way.

The seagulls proudly gave up their soft, feather-filled nests for the violinist and girl to sleep upon. They did not speak to the humans but practically carried out all that was necessary. With Elizabeth returned and the boy and girl deeply asleep under an added layer of cliff-moss and feathers, the big sea birds congregated in a far corner to finish off their evening chat (incomprehensibly, all their meetings were held every new moon, in utter darkness) and discuss the newly arrived issue.

"Let us quickly finish where we left off, before going on," the lead bird said quietly. "You were speaking of a solution to the Rotterdale Rock issue," he motioned a seagull opposite.

"Ah yes, yes. The Rotterdale Rock. What was I saying? Yes. Well, as we all know, our gentle neighbours, the 'kittiwakes', have sent in a formal complaint *again* to put their distress on record. Dear friends, their distress is caused by our 'snatching' food from their mouths, which they claim is 'unfair'. [Here there was a quiet amused murmur]. Quite unaware of the necessity of our presence in offering protection of the *whole* area, they have asked that we stop 'stealing' and catch our own fish, leaving the 'small' area of Rotterdale Rock *entirely* at their disposal. Personally, I feel this is uncalled for; they pay for protection with food. They should be grateful we don't ask them to *come* to us *here* and *give* us the food. How are we to safeguard the coast if we are to spend our time sourcing food?"

There was a quite murmur of agreement.

"I am sure I completely understand your feelings on the matter, Comrades, but I must insist you try to keep your flat feet level, wings back, and see the situation a little more objectively," their leader spoke.

"You think they should have Rotterdale Rock?" a young one piped in.

"I think it is no loss to us if we keep away from Rotterdale Rock—we all need some privacy. Put yourself in their wings (I think they say 'shoes'?) for a moment. You must see that we are intimidating. In any case, I am quite sure it will not take them very long to ask us to return to our post at The Rotterdale, once they see the threatening shadows of *real* predators overhead. Autonomy in small doses will always enable greater command. You must learn that, Comrades: convince your inferiors that they are free, and you will have unquestioned supremacy. Be kind to them, try not to take fish from the same kittiwake twice, tell them how vital they are. You might feel a small loss of pride initially, but I tell you: your pride will have multiplied tenfold before you can think ('wink' or it could be 'blink'?)!" the leader's brother spoke.

"I agree, Comrade," the leader said. "Let them have Rotterdale Rock, and let us be polite to our little friends— we shall lose nothing by it."

"But, don't you think—" a gull with a black patch around his eye (he was known as John by his friends, after the famous pirate), who opposed anything for the sake of arguing, was cut off.

"Enough. Enough on the subject. We must now speak of those two. Thank you."

"But what really is there to say?" 'John' could not help but respond. "We all know who *he* is, I'm sure. And most of us realise who *she* is too. We did not even have to debate whether we should take them in or not; none of us have any authority in such matters. And, tomorrow, we should get them on their way—of course, we should *help* them on their way. I, for one, don't mind flying them back North. They certainly look exhausted."

A couple of his fellow gulls laughed nervously, seeing as John's display of sympathy was somewhat unexpected.

The leader hushed them at once. "Yes, Comrade, I think that is a good suggestion. Tomorrow we shall fly them back."

"Erm … excuse me …" a young, slightly over-fed gull's cheeks at once took on a definite pink tinge as all eyes turned on him. "I … er … don't think I know … er … who *that* is …?"

The gulls loved the opportunity to feel that they contained more knowledge than another, so they laughed again at the embarrassed young gull and delayed answering him for as long as possible. Finally, as always, their leader interrupted their jeering.

"Alright, that is enough, Comrades," he turned to the embarrassed gull. "In short, he is free of the restraints of language; for him, there are no barriers. He was a twin, born of a human woman and the Decomposer."

The leader's brother did not think this was enough. "Yes. Do you remember the *noise* on the rocks? Remember that, until recently, we believed he, *it* was of the common siren breed but we realised he was the source of that awful silence and heavy pressure we were all feeling, the abusing of the Line intersections. He, *it* was this boy's twin, the Decomposer's son."

"Can you not feel the change in atmosphere? We were speaking of it only a little while ago. All the creatures around felt the *noise*'s destruction; we all felt the torture of the process and the relief at its end. Perhaps you felt it but did not understand it, little one," the leader's mother said.

John thought it might be a good idea to show that he too knew the details. "The Decomposer had intended that his sons be his advocates on Earth, entirely under his command as a direct mouth-piece to our world. And so, his work could be done without him even having to move from his allotted time and space … I am sure you know what his work is—it's in the name after all! He wishes to suck the power contained at each intersection of the Lines; ultimately, he wants to dissolve all Lines and instead inject every layer of language with the *noise*—"

"But how? How could he?" The slightly overweight young gull interrupted. His cheeks had now lost their embarrassed pink tinge but were instead flushed red with the excitement of his curiosity.

"Look, fledgling, now's not the time to go into the intricacies of the Lines, and how it structures our lives. Save that for another day—for another *few* days. But this is how it is—we share this world with humans, right? It hasn't always been that way, but we appreciate their presence now. In fact, fledgling, if anyone ever tries to tell you times were better before we were shoved to the side to make room for these 'greater species', ignore them—they *are wrong*. Truth is, in the great 'Before', we did not really exist because there were no Lines, there was no language. Sure, we ate, slept, bore offspring—but there goes language-less life. Such banalities can be achieved without the Lines.

"However, now, we live within a layer of the Composer's Language. My life, your life, our lives, are conducted by the Composer from the Line from which our layer hangs. We do not have Songbirds like humans do—this is what makes them so special, so powerful, containers of so much potential—but we still have our Line. See, humans have the potential of crossing many layers of language, because their Songbirds are free to fly under Lines, while they go about their daily lives, walking the streets of Here. There are lots of humans who do not grasp this beautiful potential they contain, though—throughout their lives they remain closed to the suggestion of such wonderful communication.

"Of course, humans do not know about the Lines, or the Composer. They do not know the Truth. This is part of their specialness. You see, they go about their whole lives running from death, terrified of it. Some convince themselves they are not afraid, or that there is no point questioning it, since it is inevitable. Nevertheless, there *always* remains a doubt—however deep, it is there in every single one of them. Take the central figure of this country's religion, for example—even he, as he died upon the cross, uttered words of despair.

"Now, though we are terrified at the idea of being killed, and we will scream if a gun is pointed at us, when we know it is our time to die, we accept it, just like dogs who curl up in the corner, having never questioned the Truth they are born with. Don't get me wrong—humans are born with this Truth too, only they are given the gift and curse of the freedom to question. But see—I am running away with myself, what was I saying?"

The flushed young gull reminded him.

"Yes. How does the Decomposer propose to go about dissolving these Lines? Yes. Well, if he is able to intercept the Lines, and corrupt the points of intersection, the True music as composed and conducted by the Composer will not be heard. The Decomposer cannot abuse the Lines through us, since we have no partially-separate-entities, no alternate self inhabiting another realm, like humans have their Songbirds. And so, the Decomposer seeks to steal the songs from the beaks of the Songbirds, and thereby draining a human of what some call the soul. Having detached the song from the bird and the multiple selves of the human, the Decomposer can crush the song, can speedily go about his dark decomposition of it, infecting it with corruption— with the *noise*. Still, I hear you ask—how?

"At times, as the Songbird flies in the spaces between and under the lines, the song is momentarily lost, as though the Bird is hiccupping. This is when a human soul is without protection—usually, at such a point, the human experiences a rare and timeless instant of indefinable ecstasy. Sometimes, though, if the Decomposer has timed it just right, it is now that the song can be seized for decomposition."

"I never thought you knew all that Comrade 'John'— this really is the night of revelations, isn't it? First we discover you are capable of sympathy and kindness, and now that you're a secret thinker!" said a rather spiteful cousin.

"I think our revelations this New Moon go a little beyond any idiosyncrasies of John's nature, Comrade," retorted another of the company, speaking up for his friend.

"Please, Comrades, please. And do not call our brother here '*John*' again in my presence!" The leader shook his head and raised his wings to get their attention. "Now, let me just add to the lengthy explanation already given for the benefit of any who do not know: our friend lying here was supposed to be like his siren brother, carrying out the decomposition commanded by his father. Something strange and inexplicable happened for which we must all be grateful, such that this boy rejected his father and called upon the Composer, whose work and words he now performs. It is all rather difficult and tragic because, though his mother was human, he was created by the Decomposer and so inevitably he had no Songbird. Not being able to recreate the boy, the Composer could only compose some sort of song for him by weaving a few phrases into other peoples' songs. Also, because his voice was only designed for potential *noise*, having opposed his father, he was cursed with *silence*—the Composer could not remove this, but again had to compromise, giving him a part of his own universal language which includes all but the superficial, upper level of human tongue. This is why, to the physical human ear, he is a 'mute'. The girl lying beside him, as the only human able to understand *and translate* his voice, is the sole secure connection between her world and the 'hidden' world—the 'hidden' world of us, our fellow birds, mammals, trees, skies, etc., as well as that of young human children and the Composer. This 'hidden' world only exists through its language, its sound, its voice—Comrades, we are united under one voice! Let us never forget: we live in the voice, the voice lives in us; we speak the voice, we hear the voice; we *are* the voice, forever equal and united!"

Here their leader broke off, flushed and out of breath. Had he been a leader of the traditional sort, in the traditional world, he would have been offended at the silence which met his exclamation—he would have expected cheers; cheers not reacting to the *words* spoken, but to the *way* in which they were spoken. And he had spoken them *in that way*.

Instead, as was expected in what they called the 'hidden' world, they covered themselves in reverent stillness, bowing their heads as though listening for the one voice, each of them very much aware of the threads emanating from every life around them.

XXIV

When the two guests woke, they found breakfast waiting for them. Rubbing the sleep from their eyes and blinking a few times, they looked around them, appreciating for the first time the softness of their bed. The girl thought that it was the most comfortable thing she had ever slept on, and made a quick mental note to have her mattress covered in moss and filled with gulls' small feathers when she had her own home. Ah, yes, she would be married to Gabriel then!

The gulls had conscientiously taken into account human tastes, and realised that the insides of raw fish might not be to their liking. So they had eaten the insides themselves, and then flown over the coastguard's cottage to smoke the rest of the fish over the chimney. Holding it there for as long as they could, they chattered amusedly about the human diet, and wondered how a creature could possibly prefer warm—hot—meat. They pecked at the wild, cliff-top flowers too and took them to the cave, and called upon the woodland birds to bring a supply of fruit.

As already known, gulls are not in the habit of casually allowing the coming and going of various creatures through their territory. But since they had extended their hospitality to *humans*—however special or strange these particular ones were—they saw no harm, on this occasion, in letting every passing creature come and satisfy their curiosity. In fact, they enjoyed the attention and respect they had gained from accommodating such important guests. Perhaps this would become a place of pilgrimage.

The girl jumped slightly when she heard a hideous squawk close to her ear, and she turned to see a beady black eye watching her steadily and a huge yellow beak. She could even see the creases round the eye and small dents on the beak. She concentrated on breaking the layer of non-comprehension one sometimes almost physically feels when going between two languages.

"Good morning, good morning," the gull repeated several times. "Breakfast?"

"Erm yes, that would be nice, thank you," the girl turned to the violinist who smiled and nodded too. She was surprised to see how pale he looked, with small patches of dark blue under the corners of his eyes. Still, she probably did not look in the best of health herself after the strain of the day before. (Had it really happened?) They went forward on their knees a few paces to where their food was laid out. The gull followed proudly beside them. She heard her stomach rumble as she smelt the freshly cooked fish, and she lifted it with graceful speed to her mouth, not able to remember the last time she had eaten. (Had it all been for Elizabeth? It seemed so distant, and Elizabeth seemed such a minor, dream-like figure in it all.) The fish was delicious.

"It's wonderful, thank you," she said to the gull beside her. She became aware of the other creatures at the cave's opening, and smiled at them. They blinked a few times, embarrassed that they had been caught staring so blatantly, but they did not look away. A couple of the younger creatures waved. Today was the start of a new era—they all felt it. The heaviness had lifted; the atmosphere was lighter than they had ever known it, the air filled with a fresh and delicately sweet fragrance. Everything was going to be good! Their music would fly with the breeze without obstruction, and all the songs and sounds of the land and sea would be heard as a harmonious and beautiful composition.

"Alright, quickly now! We've got to get a move on— with the crowds you attract, you won't be able to get away if you hang around much longer!"

"You're going to come with us?"

"We're going to take you, of course! How else do you propose to get home?"

"Oh! Well we did walk here—"

"Alright—suit yourself! You can walk if you want to! But *he* is *not* walking: look at him—that would be so impolite!"

"No, no! It is very kind of you to take us back—of course I'll take you up on your offer. How will *you* get us back though?"

"We have wings, don't we? See here?" he said flapping his wings a couple of times as though to show this simpleton how they worked.

"Yes, I see that. But we don't have wings and you won't be able to carry me."

The gull laughed. "Ah, I do like you! You are very funny, and I think a little tired. Look, I said we'd fly you back quickly, and we will—you'll see! Now eat up!"

A set of gulls at the front of the cave were proudly telling the wide-eyed audience that they needed to make way, as the special guests' transportation needed the space. The violinist and girl finished their breakfast within a couple of minutes, and a couple of young gulls were told to collect part of the remaining food to give to the guests for the journey.

The girl turned to the violinist to smile as she saw the gulls preparing their transport. They were so organised and sincere. She even noticed for the first time the diagram drawn into the soft ground of the cave, working out exactly how many gulls were needed.

A hundred gulls had formed an orderly square at the cave's opening. They were standing with their wings spread as two more lines of gulls pulled an old, circular fishing net on top of them. Others carried massive sections of the nests to put into the net so that a solid base was formed. During the night, they had pecked away at the net so that there were many long strings coming extending from the left and right of the net, like wings, each end held by two gulls. A circle of forty five stood with the top circumference of the net in their beaks.

"What will people say when they see us in the sky?" the girl suddenly asked.

"Oh I wouldn't worry about that," said the leader stepping towards her. "They are sure to invent some sort of story to make sense of it. And they won't know it's you."

"Come on, get in," their breakfast companion said. "Lie flat in the middle until we're safely in the air. Come on, don't worry about stepping on our Comrades at the base; there's enough nest between you and them."

The violinist smiled faintly, taking the girl by the hand as he stepped daintily over the circle of gulls. They did as the gull told them, and lay flat. The gull came and sat comfortably beside them. He called to say they were ready.

The leader stood at the back of the cave with others posted strategically to ensure a safe departure. He shouted commands.

"Alright—Wings: fly forward!" And the birds holding the strings of the net flew out of the cave and hovered.

"Good—Circle: fly upwards!" And the birds round the top circumference of the net flew as high as they could to the cave's roof.

"Now—Base: fly forward! Circle: follow their movement!" The base, slightly clumsy, made a step forward and began making small flaps of the wings until they were outside. The net hovered in the air in front of the cave a moment. The leader came forward.

"Remember: keep the rhythm—One, Two; One, Two … Bon voyage!" And the birds flew off, flowing into the rhythm with much more grace.

They moved with unexpected speed once they had reached their maximum height, and there was a favourable wind. A team of all sorts of birds flew around them in case they were needed, with tired gulls replaced whenever necessary. When darkness fell, the girl and violinist lay back down on their stomachs and looked through the small gaps in the bottom. Occasionally, they could see the blinking lights of small towns, and the greater, glowing smoky blurs of the cities. There were flashes of flat and rippled silver as they flew past lakes and rivers, and the light coming down from the fingernail moon and up from the land met at the few floaty clouds just below them, giving them a pale gold lining. The only sound was swish-swashing of the birds' wings and the faint whistling of the wind.

The net was just over a metre deep, so if the travellers had stood, they could have observed the landscape of England without obstruction, and watched the graceful movement of the gulls holding the strings of the 'wings'. The girl was worried about the violinist though, whose stillness was almost disturbing. She had never thought he could be so exhausted, and surrounded by such stagnant silence. He dismissed her questions of concern each time with a smile and wave of the hand, but she still felt unsettled. He motioned for her to look upwards and they turned on their backs to watch the stars pass over them. And although they knew that they were relatively no nearer to those distant suns than they would have been laying on some hill somewhere, the coolness of the velvet atmosphere all about them made them feel the close and distant presence of their eerie sphere much more prominently. They were encompassed by its unobstructed entirety and timelessness.

It had not been dark very long when the violinist nudged the girl who turned to see that she recognised the landscape. Soon after, the gulls began to make their descent and within a few minutes, the girl saw the glimmer of a familiar lake.

It was here that the seagulls landed; they hovered a metre or so above the lake so that the Base could fly away, then it was lowered, and the rest of the gulls released their hold with relief.

The nest and net holding the violinist, girl, and their breakfast floated in the middle of the lake. Familiar faces could be made out from the dark green shadows; all the creatures knew of their arrival and had come to welcome them. Today was a great day! No creature, not even the Great Owl (who, incidentally, had grown to such a state of exasperation at the constant flow of visitors and impossible questions, that she had handed in her notice as of tomorrow to go on retreat), knew the precise series of events which had led to this Great Day. None of them knew exactly what it meant: that the Decomposer's mouthpiece had been destroyed, the Lines protected, the atmosphere lightened. There would be no more cruel and corrosive Line interceptions, no more abuse of the intersections. But was that all? Some were satisfied with the joy they felt, though they had no clear explanation for it; others, of a more sceptical nature, were more critical. These latter ones, though they could not avoid the contentment the change in atmosphere had 'forced' upon them, could not help whispering to each other, loud enough for the others to hear.

"But he hasn't *actually* destroyed the *Decomposer*, has he?"

"No, he destroyed that siren brother of his."

"So what does that mean?"

"Did you ever see that smile? That smile that made the cruellest of cats cry?"

"No, I didn't, but—"

"I don't mean to be rude but, if you never saw the 'siren brother', you can't go about belittling the significance of his downfall. You cannot lie to yourself, and say you did not feel the pull of his death."

"Look, all I'm asking is what exactly has been achieved. I'm not belittling anything. I think it's great that such a vile creature has been destroyed—but what does it mean for us? Life goes on, you know, and the Decomposer still exists."

"While there *is* Life, the Decomposer will remain. Anyone in their right mind will realise that: while there is Life, there is no Perfection in any permanent sense, and therefore the Decomposer can always find the resources to survive. Even the search for Perfection, in Life, invites the Decomposer's corrosive hand; in fact, the dedication to Perfection in Life brings more corruption than the acceptance of Life as Imperfection, with Perfection heard only as a distant promise. Simply: how can you expect complete harmony when, from the sheer multiplicity of the Composer's compositions, one can see that there will always be dissonance? This low-level dissonance is what defines our relationships with each other, while the notes just guide the course of our lives."

"And the siren?"

"Yes, what was the siren doing?"

"He was the Decomposer's mouthpiece on Earth. Through him, he had a direct channel to crush humans' songs, with each song adding the greater volume to the *noise*. Without such intimate access to the physical world, the Decomposer will have great difficulty in crushing any songs. Without that son of his, interception of the Lines will only be achieved by chance."

"So the Lines *will* still be abused!"

"I just said! Look: I will put it very simply: the Decomposer always existed, and always will. Therefore the Lines will always be abused. However, with no map of the Lines, with no knowledge of the intersections' locations, with no direct access to the inner human, the Decomposer's *noise* cannot grow!"

"And our friend the violinist?"

"Can we stop talking about this now, please? No one knows any more than anyone else, really!"

"I think we must not forget how very dangerous the Decomposer's abuse of the intersections was getting; it is all too easy, once safe, to laugh at a bygone fear. We must appreciate the present as it had become, as it is now."

"Yes, we can sing without heaviness now, and walk wherever we please. The Songbirds of the humans can skip along the Lines of Language, and fly within their layers in complete and ecstatic freedom!"

"Oh, that does paint a pretty picture!"

"Stop it! Stop being so cynical! Can't you simply accept the fact that you can never know everything, that it is a mystery for a reason? Can you not simply be excited by the very *beauty* of such a mystery?"

"Ah, but that is just what they all say! What an evasion!"

The violinist was making signs to the girl and seagull. He drew letters in the air but this did not work. The paleness of his face, and her inability to understand him as he tried and tried to communicate, brought tears to her eyes. It was as though he was caged in a glass box, able to look out and be looked at, but remaining completely isolated. Eventually he sighed and pointed at the girl's ring finger, and made the shape of a 'G' with his fingers.

"Gabriel?"

He nodded.

"What of him?"

He pointed at the seagull, then off into the distance, and then made a beckoning motion with his hand.

"You want him to come here?"

He nodded again.

"Why?"

He shrugged with one shoulder.

"Alright …?"

The accompanying seagull spoke. "They've gone to get him already: he'll be here very soon I'm sure."

"How did you know …? I'm sorry, I'm very confused!" said the girl, frowning.

"You don't think we birds are stupid, do you? Of course we knew the violinist would want 'Gabriel' to come here. We know everything! Well—almost everything! Yes, Gabriel, that is his name, isn't it? He kept your absence here unquestioned, didn't he? Ah! I'm scaring you! You don't think I should know so much about you! He, he, he," the seagull chuckled, clearly enjoying himself. "You realise, of course, that we have a keen interest in the violinist and yourself … surely you won't be too surprised if I say that we also have deep concern for him, Gabriel, too? He is, you should know, the only one around here who is very much—how shall I say—'open'? Oh, actually, your butler George has quite an ear too."

"George? I'm not sure I understand what you are telling me. No, I don't understand *why* you are telling me this? Gabriel is Gabriel—he always has been and always will be. Yes, Gabriel is Gabriel and he is decent but dull."

"Oh! I see! You are harsh, sharp! What is wrong? You are planning to live with him and love him, no? 'Marry' him? (Yes, that's what you call it!)"

"What …?"

"He, he, he," the seagull chuckled again.

"I don't know what you're finding so amusing?"

"Irritating you is actually rather fun, I must admit, though the leader would probably tell me off for doing so—however, I think you're in need of it. Anyhow, it's dark, and you'll probably forget everything I've said when you wake up tomorrow! Yes, you see, we know all about the struggles you've had all your life; we know how difficult you've found the whole 'marriage' prospect thing. But we also know that you have assessed him, and told yourself that assessment is final; in this way, you have failed to notice how purely devoted he is to you, and in this pure devotion his ears have been opened. That is not infatuation! That is something much more special, something that gives you power; power that, if used properly, will allow you to unblock many other people's ears. This is what we expect of you!

"I'll tell you what *I* don't understand: I don't understand what you're so afraid of? And don't deny it—it's written over all your actions! You have the unique gift of free travel between languages; there is no communication closed to you. Yet you won't *communicate* to your first 'convert'. Look deeper: accept that *you* are special, but also understand that he too, that *Gabriel* is, special.

"It is the biggest mistake anyone can ever make to deny possibility, to close an open door. Just because of your own fear of the depths it might lead you into. Yes! That's it! That's what you are afraid of—you are running from the potentiality of the 'fall': the subconscious fear that, once you've leapt from solidity, you will fall alone in darkness. Ah! But the beauty of the risk alone brings light to your fall, so that it becomes a flight, not a fall at all! And don't you see, can't you hear, that you will never fall, never fly alone? The selflessness of the leap, the self-sacrifice it necessitates, proves you are flying for someone else. Therefore, even if an individual fails to hear you, the language, the double metaphor, the Composer, they are always with you! The only thing you should *actually* be afraid of is not loneliness, but the fact you can never escape *to be alone*! And there is no end to affection: if you show concern for one person, it does not lessen your care for another."

The seagull stopped, looking proud of himself. But the girl did not have enough time to process the hurt caused by some of his words before Gabriel came running through the trees, grabbed hold of the floating ropes, pulled the net and nest onto the bank, threw his arms around Edith and kissed her on the mouth. In her shock she turned her eyes towards the violinist whose eyes had suddenly lit up as he gave her a brief but mischievous grin. This impish smile forced her lips to curve upwards too and then laugh lightly.

"Oh!" exclaimed Gabriel, stepping back a pace. "I'm very sorry Edith; I didn't know what I was doing … I'm … I'm so relieved, so astoundingly happy, that you're here!"

The girl took his hand in hers. "I'm very pleased to be back, and to see you here, Gabriel!"

He looked at her then, directly in the eyes, with such a searching and grateful gaze that her heart skipped a beat, as though she was guilty of some unknown crime.

XXV

"Are you sure we should leave him? You saw how exhausted he looked: I'm beginning to think he might be ill," the girl asked Gabriel as they walked away from the lake towards her house.

"He was adamant in wanting to stay."

"I know, but I don't think he's well enough to be on his own."

"But he's not on his own is he?"

"What do you mean?"

"Well, it was the seagulls who came and brought me. I'm sure they, and all those other animals, will make sure he's alright."

"You saw all the other animals?"

"Look, I'm not quite that pathetic: I do actually notice things!"

"Did the seagulls speak to you?"

"No, they didn't." And, after a moments silence, Gabriel asked, "Have they spoken to you?"

"You think I'm crazy."

"No, I don't. I told you I am not *that pathetic*." He was met with another moment's silence. "So, have they spoken to you?" he asked again.

"Yes, they have."

He wanted her to say more. "Are they the only ones you have spoken to?"

"Are you serious?"

"Yes."

"I've spoken to many others, too: I've spoken with birds, squirrels, deer …" her voice faltered and she broke off.

"I don't understand: why are you crying?"

"Because *I* sound pathetic! And not just because I sound *pathetic*, but because I sound pathetic *to myself*: I don't even believe in my own ears, eyes and mind, let alone ask anyone else to believe in what I say! I am so confused—that's the only way I can describe it!"

"You're tired! That's all it is! Everything seems lost and confused when you're tired—you mustn't try to clarify and justify anything when you're exhausted: I know from personal experience it's entirely counter-productive!"

"But I'm not tired!"

"Yes you are! You look as though you've been traumatised! Come, let us sit here a while: it is a dry night, and no one is expecting us."

They had got to the wall enclosing Edith's land and he guided her to sit beside him, with their backs against the wall, facing the darkness of the forest.

"I have to say, though," he added as she fell asleep on his shoulder. "I don't understand why you're so concerned about speaking with the birds. It would have been very useful for me to have been able to understand in all clarity what the seagulls were telling me. I mean, it wasn't too difficult for me to work it out, since they didn't really give me much choice but to follow them. Still, how exciting to be included in that secret garden of language! I suppose the violinist belongs more to that garden than this one. I would be jealous, if I didn't feel so very close to you, so close to you that I can understand all *that*! Oh, it is *so* exciting! I think I would be happy to go on talking and talking about it forever, and hear you talk about it, and discuss it—oh, we could discuss it together forever!"

The girl muttered something indiscernible into the folds of his coat. He thought she was laughing at him.

"Oh, *I* must sound pathetic now. I'm sure you think me very naïve!"

"No, no," she shook her head sleepily, and then raised it, looking at him with heavy eyelids. He could barely see her by the light of the fingernail moon, but he saw the thickness of her eyelashes, and the elegant curve they formed over the curves of her eyes, and below the curves of her eyelids which were drooped so low that she had to put her face almost perpendicular to his, her nose horizontally parallel with her forehead, in order to look at him.

"Naivety is an invention borne of jealousy, jealously of youthful candour and vivacity and its appetite for truth. While we are young, we can't be naïve, only young. It is through no fault of our own that we are not older, that we do not have the experience that comes spontaneously with age. And it is through no personal achievement that one does become older as time goes by, that one is able to become more diplomatic, artful, and obsequious to a certain form, as one becomes more experienced." She slurred her words as though she was drunk. "No, Gabriel, you are not naïve. You are young like me, and yearn for truth—aware of the limitations of a misguided ideal of truth, you want to be true to yourself, and extend this truth to others. This search for truth might come out sounding simple or vague, but I am sure (in my youthful state) that there is no less value in it, if not more value, than that to be found in the words of some person endowed with twice our years." She let her head drop back onto his shoulder. "You understand it all, more clearly than me, I think. I am very grateful." And hearing her breathing become regular and peaceful, he knew that she was now properly asleep.

He could not remember a time when he had felt so complete, so content and proud. He vowed then to the sleeping girl and whatever greater being that might be listening, that he would never leave her. Suddenly everything seemed so very bright and clear to him, such that he was almost afraid of his own happiness, as though being this happy encouraged an imminent tragedy. He told himself there must be a fault in the perfection he felt himself consumed by—something must be wrong somewhere in it all. Then he found something and grasped onto it: the girl was upset, deeply concerned about the violinist who seemed changed, ill. Having grasped this idea, he held it fast, concentrating on it, as the one thing that fastened him to reality. This small imperfection made the greater perfection of the moment, and the promise of perfection to come, all the more real, because it somehow perversely justified his happiness.

Having justified his contentment in this way, it opened himself up even further into appreciating this moment, and continued with his vow. Whatever happened to either of them or the world around them, he would stay with her. She would never be alone. Simply the weight of her head on his shoulder, leaning there for support, seemed to give his life a purpose. For what else had he been born, than to have the experience of this pure and powerful love that burned all about and within him, ignited by the beauty that emanated from every fibre of her being? What magnet was it in her that pulled the light from him? As he could feel his own beauty, till now unbeknown to him, radiating from his pores too.

Devotion to her would mean a lifelong pursuit of translation. He could see that. And he could see too that he would often feel excluded from her secret garden of language. She could teach him, but he would never be entirely fluent, he would never feel a legitimate part of that world, other than as a part of her. But that thought did not extinguish his thirst for understanding—he wanted to be able to hear and comprehend enough to show other people the beauty of listening. To give to others the joy he had received so recently at the discovery of this whole depth of thought, emotion and meaning. The intricacies of everything about him; the wonders of sound and how it was in his power to shape it however he pleased into communication. Though he actually enjoyed not *understanding it*, and would not have been adverse to the idea of remaining in the mystery of it all, he knew he had comprehend to some extent so that he might be able to articulate it to others. With this in mind, he felt his vocation answered and he fell asleep.

Gabriel woke at dawn with the girl still asleep on his shoulder. They were covered in dew, and the air was cool. He wanted to stay and watch her, but that felt almost wrong, like listening to a conversation through the keyhole, and he knew they should be getting home.

"Edith," he said softly in her ear, brushing the hair from her face. He noticed that it had dried dark and hard with salt water. He wondered why she had swum in the sea.

She took a deep breath through her nose before blinking a few times, squinting as her sleepy eyes battled with the early light to see where she was.

"Hello," she said.

"Hello," he replied. "I think we should get back."

"I fell asleep?"

"You did."

"What time is it?"

"I'm not sure, it's only just dawn."

"The violinist! We should go back and check if he's alright."

"We only left him a few hours ago. He'll be fine. Let's get back home first and we'll go and see him later."

"Alright, I suppose you're right," she shivered slightly as she got up. "It's a bit chilly isn't it?"

"Here—have my coat. It's a bit damp but it's better than nothing."

"Thank you," she let him wrap the coat around her,

watching him peacefully. "You're very kind, Gabriel, have I ever told you that?"

He smiled. "Perhaps when we were little."

She was still shivering, and he felt like shivering too, but he forced himself not to. He put his arm firmly around her shoulders to pass some warmth onto her. He was worried about her; she really did look like she had experienced some trauma that had had serious repercussions on her physically. He felt her fragility against his body, and he had known her long enough to know she was not generally a fragile sought. Her face looked slightly bruised, and her eyes too large. He remembered with a slight spasm the last time she had looked a little like this. It was when her parents had tried to force their marriage. What a distant world that seemed! They were different people now! It would all be alright now, as soon as she got a little more rest: her eyes' expression, after all, did not look lost. It would all be alright as long as he stayed with her—no one could harm her again.

He did not try to start conversation since he thought she probably was not in the right frame of mind for it. However, after a couple of minutes, the house now in sight, she began speaking.

"Don't you want to know what happened? Why we went? All of that?"

"I think I know most of it. Don't ask me how I know, but I feel as though I do. There's plenty of time for you to tell me absolutely everything. You don't need to now. Just be at rest, don't worry about anything, alright?"

She nodded, looking relieved and a little confused.

"Oh yes! I completely forgot! Will you be alright going?

No, you won't need to go. Oh dear, that is annoying!" Gabriel said.

"What?"

"My parents have booked for six of us to go to 'Don Giovanni' tonight. A school friend of my mother's, Susanna Cherubini, is playing Donna Elvira. Obviously you shouldn't go."

"Why not? Have you forgotten? I've never been to the opera, and I've wanted to for years! You used to get annoyed with me for asking about it!"

"Yes, I do remember. That is why I made sure they got you a seat too. But I don't think you should go, really. You're very tired."

"Oh don't worry about me! I'm fine! Ah, this is very exciting! How did you know I would be back in time to be there tonight?"

"I didn't—it's lucky I guessed right though, isn't it?"

"Yes, I don't believe you can have guessed: I think you have some secret knowledge you're hiding from me! You could not have guessed the very day I'd be here!"

"Alright, I did sort of know! You're going to think I'm so strange!"

"Who am *I* to judge!?"

"That's true."

"Well! You're not supposed to agree!"

"Oh, I'm sorry, of course, you're not at all odd!"

"No, I like you when you speak the truth."

"So you don't like me at other times?"

"Come, come! You know I've loved you since I was born, and liked you from a short while after! Only, you can understand it gets irritating when you agree with everything I say, and do everything to please me! On such occasions, our conversations seemed as though I was talking to myself!"

"Alright, I see how it is—truly, I do! I promise I won't hide my true thoughts from you ever again—will that please you?"

"Yes—but don't do it just *to please me*, alright? Be an individual in your own right, for goodness sake!"

"Say! Where did all this 'let's get at Gabriel' come from?"

"I'm sorry, I'm becoming too familiar."

"No, no, not at all," he said laughing. "But I think you need to realise that we can't all be individuals without the company of others; you can't ignore the presence of others, and you can't deny that it isn't others who help shape you as an individual. If people are to live intimately, or even just closely, they must respect individuality and personal space, of course, but their interaction and influence cannot be dismissed. Perhaps pleasing you pleases me *as an individual* too! And—and, there is no one I want to be more familiar with than you!"

He laughed again, this time as though he were laughing at himself. She marvelled at how he had grown so confident so quickly. His person felt so much more real and comfortable to her now. He continued speaking. "What were we talking about? Oh yes, the Opera! Well, in all honesty, they only booked it yesterday, because Susanna Cherubini called by for tea and offered us her special tickets which she still hadn't given away. She said she would be able to reserve up to eight seats and asked how many we'd take. My parents said they'd be very pleased to take five, with three for us and two for your parents, of course.

"And I suddenly remembered how much you used to speak about going to the Opera and particularly about Mozart's. I was about to say something, then realised you weren't there, and I did not know when you'd be back. But just as I stopped myself (you won't believe me), a *sparrow* came and landed on the windowsill, hopping to the far side as five others came and joined it. Then they all stood there in a row, with all six pairs of eyes staring straight at me and waiting. Almost without thinking, I said that we would need six seats, since you were expected back the next day. Once this was said, the first sparrow began to chirp, and then they all flew off. I'm pretty sure they were accompanying you on your journey here—you were brought by the seagulls weren't you?"

"Yes, we were!" They stopped as they reached the side of the house. "Wait, are you staying here?"

"Yes, we are all staying at your house again … before we go in: they'll all be asleep, but do you want to know what I've said about you?"

"Yes, how did you explain my absence?"

"It was a little risky: I tried the double bluff. I think your violinist friend gave me the idea, somehow, before you went. Having told 'the parents' I would vouch for your sanity always, and that you had agreed to marry me, I wrote Dr Tarten a letter signed by both your parents. I took it to him after I'd seen you and, since it was before breakfast, they never discovered you had left. He made a bit of a fuss at the unexpectedness of it, and the fact it was me standing in front of him. I told him your parents had not wanted to come in person, as they wanted the whole thing to be made as discreet as possible, and that I had come in my capacity as your official fiancé. Once he read that there would be a generous donation, he agreed wholeheartedly with the request for discretion and said I could take you away from there at that moment, without having to go to him for your official dismissal. I then told 'the parents' you would be staying there a few more days to have things sorted out. They were very angry, and threatened to march straight there, but I convinced them that it was by our own volition that you were staying and that, in any case, it gave them time to get ready for your return and the prospect of the wedding. So Dr Tarten thought you were here with family, and they thought you were there with him. Then I only had to make sure I went out to 'visit you' so that they never did."

"I'm impressed it worked! I don't know what I would have said in that situation."

"It was quite fun actually, the sense of danger it gave! But yes, are you sure you're up for going out tonight?"

"Yes, of course!"

"Alright, as long as you sleep enough now. Come on, let's go inside—I left this door open. I'm going to wake George and tell him to inform your parents of your arrival, and not to disturb you however late you sleep."

The girl laughed. "Alright, thank you. I'll say good night then." She gave him back his coat and went up those familiar stairs to her room. She did not think she would be able to sleep at all, now that it was morning and she felt fully awake, but as soon as her head touched the pillow, she was asleep.

She slept until past midday and woke feeling healthy and satisfied. She washed all the sea water from her hair and called for Mari to make her a bath with rose petals. When she went downstairs, they were impressed by how well she looked, her mother immediately satisfied that she would not look pale and undeveloped in a wedding dress (this had been her main concern). Her hair was light and silky, her skin smooth and well-coloured, and she was wearing a dress that was complementary of her elegant curves. Gabriel was astonished at the transformation and was reassured that he had been right in thinking sleep was all she needed.

"Good morning Edith," said her father. "I don't know if you've been informed that we're going out tonight to celebrate your return."

"Oh yes, Gabriel has told me, thank you." She looked at Gabriel who smiled quickly to hide his look of deep embarrassment at the openness of her father's lie.

"We'll have tea at the red seats at three o'clock. Then we'll get ready to go," her mother said. "You know that it's Susanna Cherubini who's playing Donna Elvira? Harriet's school friend?"

This was about as far as their conversation went. They had all just come out from lunch, and they continued on to their various rooms as was part of their daily habit. Gabriel stayed with the girl and went back into the dining room.

"We'd better be quick."

"What?"

"We've got less than two hours if we're going to see the violinist and get back for tea."

"Oh yes, I suppose we'd better go before tea. Are you coming with me then?"

"Yes—that is, unless you'd rather I didn't."

"No, no, that's nice, thank you."

"We being engaged and everything, I'm sure they'd be willing to let us go on a walk together."

"Ah, of course," she was confused as to why she did not feel any apprehension over this change in relationship with her friend. She supposed it must have been that, with the idea put around her from such a young age, it had become inevitable. Still, she had never expected her inner contentment to remain unruffled. "Shall we go now?"

"Yes, if you're ready?" he was worried that she had only eaten a corner of her ham and a leaf.

Gabriel found his father and informed him they would be gone for an hour. Lord Albert muttered something under his breath about the lack of restraint among young people these days, before giving his son a permissive nod accompanied by a disturbing, and apparently knowing, smile. Gabriel shuddered slightly, and then took the girl by the arm and led her outside into the sunshine. Outside, he was suddenly caught unawares by a surge of joy that leapt through his chest and brought water to his eyes. He felt like throwing back his head and laughing at the sky, running and shouting, 'Here I am! Look at me! Look at me!'

He looked down to see Edith looking up at him, about to ask what brought such a smile to his face, but as their eyes met her unasked question was answered, and some of his joy passed onto her. So pure was the hot white light of day reflecting off their skin, that their faces seemed to be giving off their own glow. Any passer-by could not help but grin themselves as they saw these young, radiant faces. Such happiness is contagious.

When they reached the lake, however, they were met with a hideous sight. Not that it was hideous from the outset; it was beautiful. But the tension in the air was unavoidable, and the flowers and pretty leaning branches were disguising something dreadful. There were many rodents and birds all around the lake, standing or sitting in a strange and hushed stillness. It was as if they had only just stopped a frantic rush about to get things ready; the dust risen from the quick scurrying of little feet and flapping of wings had not yet settled. They were waiting—that was clear.

The two people entering the scene were confused; they had left it only half a day before. Why all this change?

They approached the foot of the lake where many flowers had been piled to form a cyclical wall. Branches had bent down to meet the flowers, and the animals had weaved more flowers in amongst the leaves of these trees. It was like a cradle with sides curving elegantly outwards to introduce an infant's eyes to the heavens above. With the dappled sunlight, the flowers were stained glass joined by the stone arches of a cathedral.

There was a small, disguised opening close to softly lapping water. The girl and boy removed their shoes and stepped into the water, edging their way sideways into the flower wall. Upon a familiar bed of moss, feathers and dry leaves, the violinist lay like Endymion. He was not asleep, but his face was so awfully grey—like an effigy on a tomb. His perfectly carved lips were dry and lilac, and the grey patches at the corners of his eyes had darkened and spread. He was still the most beautiful being the girl had ever seen.

"What's happened to you?" she cried, running forwards. "Why's it so quick? What's happened?" Inevitably, she got no reply. "Oh speak! Please speak to me!" There were tears in her voice but none on her face, and her voice was surprisingly untroubled overall. The truth was she knew that nothing could possibly happen to violinist, simply because *he was the violinist*. Gabriel was comforted by her apparent lack of concern, remembering that the tears in her voice were only the natural result of femininity and nothing too serious. He knew, though, that the figure on the bed was far from alright, and needed medical attention.

"Edith, I think he should see a doctor." As the words came from his mouth, he felt he was committing a sacrilege in bringing some aspect of the outside world into this space. He could almost see his words hovering, foreign, in the air above the violinist. The girl looked at him, confused.

"He needs a doctor?"

"Yes; I think he does."

"Oh, yes, of course," she said, looking down at him. The violinist shook his head and brought colour to his lips by pulling his teeth over them. He shook his head again and smiled to reveal the glorious white of his teeth.

"Why not?" the girl asked. "We could bring a doctor here."

He shook his head again. He looked up at the sky, as though there was someone there, understanding him in his silence. For the first time in his presence the girl felt she was unnecessary—superfluous.

There were a couple of birds near the violinist's head, but they did not speak to the girl. It was awkward—Gabriel and Edith could have stayed, standing over the violinist, or sitting on the sand but, standing, they felt helpless and, sitting, they could not see him. So, after about half an hour, they left.

"Are you alright? Are you sure you're alright?" was all the girl could ask. And, yet again, the violinist nodded and smiled, surrounded by a strong and powerful silence.

XXVI

The opera passed like a dream. There were moments when she wanted to fly with the music, laugh or cry, but, throughout the girl's life, she always looked back at this event as a dream. It was always 'before', that 'before' which is forever remembered after a subsequent major and most devastating incident; the time that one holds in their memory as the last notable occasion when they did not know what was to follow. Thinking awhile on this 'before', with occasional details somehow more vivid than those of the present (just as might happen with a dream), one begins to disbelieve the idea that they were not aware of what was to follow. Instead they can become absolutely convinced that they knew what was to follow as clearly as they know now in hindsight. That is the unchronological nature of true time; the mind wants to give order to the confused signals it gets from the heart. And so nothing is ever remembered without some hopeful alteration of the unconsciously creative mind. Past and Future become indistinguishable as two unattainable concepts, and the peculiar intangibility of Present encourages the questioning of the world outside the self.

She loved the way the opera seemed to involve all forms of expression, and thought that this must be very hard to achieve, both for composers and performers. The words did not matter so much, she thought, since few in the audience would have understood them; they were an extension of the sound, a further overlay and contrast. It was the power of the sound that shook her when Don Giovanni was given his chance to repent. The words had not mattered. Her mind was pleased to have a translation in her hand, but they did not actually matter at all.

For some reason, she felt strangely akin to Leporello throughout the performance and most particularly when he hid under the table at the sight of the statue singing with the dead Commendatore's deep, sonorous voice. She did not find out until several years later that Gabriel had felt the same.

Gabriel would not have likened Don Giovanni to the violinist's brother, however. The singer even shared similar facial features and gestures with the raven. From the start, the mere sight of this performer made the girl shudder, and she felt a reminiscent relief when he was pulled into the flames close to the end. That was the end as far as the girl was concerned, and this was the point as which, thinking in this way, she began to wonder if anything else had ended with the raven's end.

She remembered the annoyance she felt at the conversations afterwards. Most of them concerned the statue scene, suggesting that they wanted to criticise this most powerful scene to ease the fear it had provoked in them, to disguise the emotion it had evoked.

"I thought he really over did it—all those long, drawn out notes. Much too slow," one woman said.

"Oh yes, I quite agree—seriously exaggerated. Quite absurd. Did I ever tell you the time I was in Vienna, at the …" another one went on.

And in another group:

"Ah, the *staccato* was much too emphasised! It became rather piercing …"

"Yes—contrasted ridiculously with the others' *legato*."

"Oh, I don't think so. I thought it was sloppy—the contrast was not brought out enough …"

And a third group:

"Oh darling, but at least the costumes were well done!"

There were others she heard passing by who did not criticise it negatively, but took the opportunity to show what experts they were in explaining the science behind the music's power, or the reason for its structure, or the genius and personality of Mozart.

"The exploration of tonality in that scene is quite extraordinary; it is unheard of in any of his other operas. One comes to understand the secret feelings of the characters through it! You would not think Don Giovanni was actually nervous, would you, for example?"

"But it isn't just that, is it? There are the keys attributed to the peasant characters, and ones dedicated to their various emotions, but there's also the clever little additions ensuring the whole story is pulled together for the audience: didn't you notice the familiarity of that scene with the Commendatore's death? I'm sure it is the same chord used as he dies, as when his statue rises!"

"Oh, that *is* clever! Yes, I see that now! That is why we are left feeling so satisfied—some aspects are sustained throughout and others complement this consistency: it is all neatly fitted together, reflected and resolved …"

"Ah, now have you heard the stories of Mozart's recreational activities? His … how should I say … scatological preoccupations?"

Her own family ignored comments on the technicalities of the performance, thinking this a lower-class activity. Instead they talked on their connection to Susanna Cherubini.

"What was she like as a child? Did she always sing?" Lady Norton asked Gabriel's mother.

"Well she was always a rather quiet child, I have to say. I would never have thought of her becoming the lady she is now. I mean, I was told I could have been a concert pianist, and that seemed much more likely at the time …"

"I did not know you played the piano?" Mr Norton said.

"No? Well, I don't suppose you would. I haven't played in years, and never in front of anyone but myself …"

"I remember you used to play to me when I was a little boy," said Gabriel, smiling. "It was beautiful."

His mother laughed. "The nurse always had such difficulty in getting you to sleep, Gabriel. It was the only thing that did it! It is good you are marrying someone who plays …"

They all suddenly became a little embarrassed at this display of family intimacy and the conversation slowed.

When they got home, the girl went straight to bed, though she did not sleep until dawn. This was not surprising since she had slept so late that day, and she always found it difficult sleeping after an evening outing but, on this occasion, the real reason for her restlessness was because she could not stop thinking. There was a constant sense of indecision as to whether she should go out or not; she felt she had to go and see the violinist, and that that would ease her anxiety, then she thought this would in fact achieve nothing.

So many half-formed questions flew across her mind. They were so fleeting that she had not the time to catch them and comprehend them before they had dissolved. She knew that something was going to happen, something was waiting to happen, and she would not stop feeling this strange and sudden apprehension until it had happened. Hadn't she been fine and content only a little before? No, this restlessness had been growing, niggling its way forwards, an embryonic sensation conceived that evening in Cornwall.

Then, as the first shadowy rays of grey light filtered their way through her curtains, she heard footsteps outside her door. Having known him for so long, she was not at all disturbed, recognising the tread immediately as that of Gabriel. She opened her door.

"I thought perhaps you wouldn't be able to sleep and I heard you walking about your room several times."

"You can't sleep either?"

"No—well I did for a couple of hours, and then I couldn't go back to sleep. I was thinking of the violinist."

"Yes, so was I."

"I was thinking … he was fine when you left last week?"

"Yes—yes, he was absolutely fine until we were on our way back."

"What happened to his violin?"

"He dropped it off a cliff in Cornwall."

"Was that just before you came back?"

"Yes?"

"Don't you think there might be a connection?"

"Well, yes, it did cross my mind. But what are you saying?"

"Perhaps he's ill when he's without his violin. It sounds a little extreme, especially considering the way he looks, but since, as you say, it is his voice … That is, I don't think I'd be feeling too well if someone tied up my mouth even for a few hours. Perhaps if we get him a violin, he'll be alright."

"Oh, you are delightful! I love you! I thank God—I don't understand how you are able to be so sensitive and naturally understanding. No questions—oh, it is wonderful! Perhaps you are right …"

"I'll go into town and get one tomorrow first thing—or today, rather! You'll probably be looking at dress designs or something, and then we can go together. I'm sure it will be fine."

"Oh, I hope so!"

"Alright, well, good night."

"See you in a few hours!" And she shut the door. With her restlessness now eased, she slept.

Meanwhile Gabriel went back to his room humming merrily to himself. It was the first time Edith had told him she loved him, and as he pulled his blanket over himself, he was convinced that there had never been a happier person to hear those common words than he, and fell asleep smiling.

Gabriel was right: the girl was bombarded with dress designs as soon as she had finished breakfast. Her mother was in her element, a different person entirely, and there were two ladies who had come up from 'the best place in London' to talk them through it. Edith was oblivious to almost everything they said, and had great difficulty maintaining an air of alert interest.

Then, after lunch, Elizabeth got back. She happened to arrive at the front door exactly as Gabriel's cab brought him back from town. Edith was gripped with a wave of nauseous panic at the sight of her friend through the window and could not cope at all with the idea of speaking to her. Making some feeble excuse, she was able to escape to her room. She walked around her room impatiently for two hours (time had never gone more slowly), before Gabriel finally knocked on her door and came in breathing a huge sigh of relief. She echoed his sigh in frustration.

"I've got the violin—let's go."

And on the way to the lake, the girl told him everything. She told him all she knew about the violinist, his mother and brother; she told him about the Composer, Decomposer and Lines; she spoke of Songbirds and intersections. She told him about Elizabeth. She revealed to him all the things she had felt over the past months, all the emotions and thoughts that had accompanied the momentous changes and discoveries she had experienced. She opened up her heart to him, sharing with him all that she understood and did not understand, all that she would understand and all that she would never understand.

The boy listened and accepted, gesturing or commenting occasionally when he thought it necessary. When they arrived at the lake, he let her go alone to the flowery bed with the violin.

The weather was very peculiar. It heightened all his senses in a way he never forgot. As the girl took off her shoes to get to the violinist, he looked up at the sky, thinking of all those Lines of Language up there somewhere. He wondered what his Songbird looked like, and how it sounded. He kind of knew already, but that did not stop his mind from wondering. The sky above was a hazy blue strewn with clouds reminiscent of Piero della Francesca's. In the west, dramatic dark and rich clouds were gathering, warning Gabriel of the severe storm coming. These far-off shadows, falling and stretching across that corner of the sky, played teasingly with the golden light of late afternoon, throwing and weaving it about them. The effect was such that shafts of distant rain reflected purple and silver, and a fiery orange warmed the edges of the clouds, setting them alight from behind.

At that moment, the lake reflected the grey blue of the sky above, fragmented with the black brushstrokes of overhanging branches. But, as the sun sunk a little lower, and the clouds came closer, the water's surface became an uninterrupted pinkish gold. A short while later, the stillness of the air gave way to a gentle breeze which gradually gathered strength, creating, encouraging, and then increasing the ripples which ran across the lake. These little waves were emphasised by the darker pink and purple of their troughs, while their crests maintained the same gentle and tinted gold of before.

It was this strange throwing-about of light and colour which added to the peculiar atmosphere and made Gabriel uncertain whether to feel spooked or dazed, shudder or laugh. He was inclined to shudder, and told himself the whole thing was ethereal and ghostly.

The girl put the violin on the violinist's chest and, when he did not move, put his hands upon it. The woodland creatures had built up his pillow so that his head rested a little higher and he looked now at the violin in his hands and nodded. The girl was horrified by his appearance; he was as grey as any graveyard statue, like the Commendatore in the performance last night. His cheekbones protruded awfully and looked bruised, adding to the shadows which had somehow formed across his whole face.

There was no light left in his eyes. Even the day before there had been light and expression; now they were wide and dim. Their unfathomable darkness terrified her. His eyes, their depths, had always been unfathomable to her, and she had delighted in the marvellous mystery of it. But this was not like that—these were the depths of dark despair. How did this happen so quickly? Why? She remembered vividly the power and draw of his eyes and aurora when he had rescued her from the lake. She still felt the unknown now as she had then. He had been like a god. Oh! In all his fading, for all his faults, he was still a god! Did he have any faults? She seemed to remember discovering that she had been wrong in supposing him perfection itself, but now she could not place the occasion, and could not think of any of these faults.

She felt tears come to her eyes.

"Why are you nodding? Why don't you play? Why don't you speak?"

He stopped nodding and drew his gaze from the violin to her. The instantaneous look of no recognition forced a sob to escape her lips. It was transitory, but it had been there, and she had never before experienced it in the one being she realised she cared for more than life itself. The sob triggered an unstoppable rush of tears. He raised his hand towards her and she fell on her knees beside his bed, grasping his hand and soaking with her tears.

"What's wrong? What have I done?" she cried hysterically. "I know it's me, it's me that's done it! Tell me what I must do! Oh speak, please, please, speak to me!"

Gradually her tears subsided and she gave way to stroking his hand and speaking more softly.

"I can't live in your silence," she said quietly. "It's awful, like a dead weight. But—but what's it like for you, drowned in it? You haven't always felt isolated like this, have you? You were never without a voice! So why must you be eaten by the silence now? Why is it only now you seem lost to me, obscured by the deep silence existing in you that I always ignored? You were never silent to me! Never this heavy, deadening silence! Was it like this for everyone else?"

The violinist heard her words and felt her hopeless isolation. It was she that was lost in his silence. She would understand one day that this silence was not actually his, and, just like his voice, it had never belonged to him. Tears rolled down his cheeks, unnoticed by the girl who was rocking back and forth on the ground beneath him, holding his hand still and caressing it, as though it were a baby. What would happen to her? It was the first time he had experienced the slightest wavering of confidence. It was the first time he felt a throb of uncertainty, and it terrified him. He looked up at the sky, his vision blurred, his ears pounding with the agony of the silence he had not noticed till now. See—he only felt and thought through her; it was only in her silence he heard his own; it was only in her pain he felt his own. It was only in her love, her imminent despair, that he discovered his own.

And, for the first time in his life, he cursed the Composer who did not care. He had never questioned any of it, never, but now he bared his teeth in hot, fervent anger towards the sky. The Composer had only used him, had abused him, had abused the girl, had abused them all! *He* did not care, and *he* only showed him the truth, the whole truth of his insignificance, his pointlessness, in these last moments. Because—he knew this was the end.

"Please speak, please," the girl was whispering into his hand. He felt the warmth of her breath, her life, and her lips as they brushed against his cold skin. He felt sick with nostalgia, so evocative was it of the warmth of the neck of his violin after his fingers had been running up and down it awhile. "Oh I wish you would speak! I've never wished it before!" She sat up over him, still kneeling, as though she were about to pray. "Just a word—I'd be happy with a word. One word."

He shared her wish, so desperate was he to tell her. It had never crossed his mind before—to speak her language, his own mother's language. He had accepted it would never be possible. He had accepted that he was not really real—not in the same way his mother had been, or the girl kneeling here, or Gabriel there. But he was feeling now, and if he felt, he must exist! Surely?

"You haven't said enough. We haven't—we haven't spoken enough. I never tried—I don't think I ever tried," the girl said, a catch in her voice as she realised the truth. The dark and bulging clouds Gabriel had seen approaching were now overhead, so that the violinist and girl were hidden under their shadow. And looking into the vague greyish outlines of the violinist's face, tears once again streaming down her face, she whispered, "I don't know you."

The pain in his ears, the hot tears in his eyes, and the bitterness of the air around him, were becoming unbearable. He continued to grit his teeth, shaking all over with the vehemence of emotion, and shivering at the cold blatancy of his own pointlessness. His brother was gone.

It was then, as the rain began to fall and a narrow shaft of light escaped the darkness, throwing itself at once sympathetically and cruelly upon the violinist's face, that the girl saw the blood dripping from his ears, and the delicate silver trail of tears running down his cheeks.

She yelped, letting go of his hand and bringing her own to her mouth in horror. Little pools of blood were forming on the grass underneath his ears. It seemed impossible that there could be so much of it. She hurriedly and unthinkingly put the violin on the ground and covered both his ears with her hand, wiping the tears from his cheeks with her thumbs, all the while soaking them with her own now-silent tears. "Don't leave! I beg you—please!" She kept trying to say, mouthing the words again and again, but no sound escaped her trembling lips. There were so many things she wanted to say. So many things she would never be able to articulate in her own feeble language.

The blood slowed in his right ear, but it continued to seep through her fingers from his left, trickling onto the grass. Her own tears ceased once more, and she looked down on him with a face tight with the agony of grief. Her lips gave up trying to make sound on their own accord, knowing too well that no words were good enough for him. As never before, she felt the insurmountable language barrier between them.

His own tears did not stop. They fell all the more quickly and heavily as he looked up into the blurred face of the girl. They began to fall across his ears, as though trying to sooth their pain, mingling as they did so with the blood, and broadening the pool at his left side.

And suddenly, as the shaft of light shifted momentarily before disappearing into darkness upon that pool of blood and tears, the girl saw the patterns forming. The rain was getting heavier, and it was difficult to distinguish the salt water of tears with the water falling from the dark masses above. Nevertheless, the patterns the tears were making in the blood, somehow immiscible, were unmistakable. They curved and cut through the rich red, parting and playing with it, leaving transparent lines in their trail.

It was hideous, magnificent. She could not stop staring at it, hypnotised, her situation temporarily forgotten. The liquid seemed to be solidifying, becoming more reflective and confident of its course—if a liquid can become confident.

Beyond, behind, the pitter patter of the falling rain and softly whistling wind, she became aware of a low and gentle hum. This sound, as one might imagine hearing from within the mother's womb, emanated from the dancing tears as they settled down to rest in the solidifying liquid.

"Oh!" she cried, her voice sounding pathetic in her ears as she suddenly realised what was happening. She let her hands drop. She realised what was forming in the grass before her, born of the violinist's silence, his blood and tears, his pain and grief. His brother, a vessel, gone. Hadn't she always known it? Hadn't they all known it? All this—this search, these stories and theories, and it was here, here all along.

The lines were as she had imagined—these lines that mapped the greater Lines of Language above, revealing their intersections, revelling in their extraordinary beauty. With this glass, the crystal glass, one had divine power; one could hear and sound the Truth, even as the Composer weaved a strain of it in every soul's song, for each individual Songbird to sing. With it, the intersections could forever be protected from calculated abuse.

"Look!" she cried, smiling. "Oh, look! It's you! It's you! It never existed outside you! You're the crystal glass! You've formed the glass! The crystal glass!"

She looked back at the violinist, fully expecting him to say something. Then she remembered. His ears had stopped bleeding, his tears had stopped. The rain had stopped too, leaving his face a ghostly silver. He was shivering silently, and he had closed his eyes. He opened them suddenly and looked deep into her eyes, seeing her joy and wondering confusedly at the reason for it. She was beautiful. At this sight, he unclenched his teeth, his features relaxed and he no longer felt any pain. The world was becoming brighter, and he needed to close his eyes again, but he did not want to stop looking at her face. His head turned to his left and then his eyes refused to obey him and shut, just as he heard a most wonderful, sonorous and beckoning hum and the life left his body. He was dead.

She began to shake violently all over and such a dreadful scream escaped her mouth that Gabriel came running into the little enclosure. He did not go up to her, the sight of her suffering making tears fall abundantly down his own cheeks. It would have hurt him less if she had continued to cry loudly, but she did not. She kissed his frozen lips over and over again, trying to force life back into them, stroking his face and holding his hands in her own. And she sobbed and screamed without a sound. She was in a world quite beyond Gabriel.

She fell back on her knees in utter despair, leaning her forehead on his pillow and pressing his lifeless hands to her lips. She wished with every fibre of her being that she could breathe life into him, even if it left none for her. This could not be it, this could not be it. This was not the end. It had not happened. She would wake up.

Her face was wrecked, torn with sorrow and wretchedness. She looked again into the dead face of the violinist and realised there was nothing. She was overcome with such great darkness, that Gabriel felt consumed by it too. That raw impenetrable darkness where there is no ground or sky, no time or space. Where one can close one's eyes or leave them open, and it is the same.

There was nothing. Had he even seen the glass formed of his body? Oh, cruel world! Why had this happened?

She curled herself up and lay beside him, shivering, but no longer crying. She clung desperately to his neck, as though she would fall into that mouth of darkness if she let go. She would never let go. She could not let go.

It was only once darkness had fallen and the moon had risen that Gabriel came round to his senses and saw the little animals that had gathered round. They were impatient to get on with their task. Gabriel could see that, and understood that they knew what to do.

He went quietly up to the still shivering girl and kissed her lightly on her exposed earlobe. She did not react. Neither did she make any attempt at resistance when he gently unclasped her hands and took them from around the violinist's neck, and lifted her from his bed, carrying her out of the flowery enclosure and onto the bank. He seated her on the grass facing the length of the lake and sat beside her, holding her close.

Together they watched as two rows of beavers carried the violinist out of his enclosure and swam him into the middle of the lake before letting him float without support, returning to the other gathered animals. Gabriel thought it was the most beautiful thing he had ever seen; the boy soaked in moonlight, the lake respectfully staying a rich midnight blue so that the floating figure could have all the reflected light to itself, glowing like a silver star in the very centre of Space.

He felt the girl inhale deeply and exhale with one final, violent shudder before becoming absolutely still. She breathed calmly, and her heart beat steadily.

The trees around the lake bent inwards, bowing to this centre star, and many small, blinking eyes could be made out from the darkness, encircling the scene. And, as the trees finished their bow and gracefully made their way upwards to express their thanks to the skies above, they saw the violinist become part of the water, melting to become its faultless and incessant reflection.

"Music begins where the possibilities of language end."
Jean Sibelius

 Matador

For exclusive discounts on Matador titles,
sign up to our occasional newsletter at
troubador.co.uk/bookshop